TINKER'S PRIDE

Other B&W titles by Nigel Tranter

THE STONE
THE QUEEN'S GRACE
BALEFIRE
BRIDAL PATH
THE GILDED FLEECE
ISLAND TWILIGHT
FAST AND LOOSE
FOOTBRIDGE TO ENCHANTMENT
NESTOR THE MONSTER

TINKER'S PRIDE

NIGEL TRANTER

EDINBURGH
B&W PUBLISHING
1994

Copyright © Nigel Tranter
First published 1945
This edition published 1994
by B&W Publishing
Edinburgh
ISBN 1 873631 30 8

British Library Cataloguing in Publication Data:
A catalogue record for this book is available from
the British Library

Cover illustration:
detail from *O'er Moor and Moss*
by Peter Graham (1836-1921)
By kind permission of
The National Galleries of Scotland

Printed by Werner Söderström

I

ARCHIE McKILLOP set down his glass, shook his head, and broke the silence that followed the policeman's departure. "Aye, it's a brave man, him," he commented. "There's times I'm thankful to God I'm not in the polis, at all."

"Aye, man. Aye." That was accepted.

"Like enough he'll no' be after getting hurt, at all," the heavy man behind the bar suggested, but without conviction. "Alastair Dubh could be that way feeling."

The four men sitting in Simon Campbell's bar-parlour did not deny it. After a brief pause, "He could that, even," one of them conceded heartily, and the others nodded. They were mannerly men, all of them—and after all, it was Alastair Dubh they were talking about, and not his brother Ewan.

Big Simon gave his counter a wipe with a cloth handy. "Yes, then," he said suitably, and, feeling for his pipe, slipped light-footed in the way he had, through the door at his back and into his Post Office, that was another of the responsibilities of a busy man.

The others, sitting around the small table in the corner, sucked at their pipes and watched, through half-closed eyes, the lazy plumes of smoke coil to the blackened ceiling, thoughtfully.

Their decent silence was interrupted by a heavy tread, the noisy agitation of the swing-doors, and the arrival of another customer. Striding in, to halt suddenly at the comparative gloom of the place after the level brilliance of the westering sun, the newcomer peered around him, and behind him his golden labrador slipped in at the second swing of the doors, with an adroitness notable in a dog of its size. A mild tentative growl from a black-and-white sheep-collie curled beneath the table brought forth an answering rumble, deep-toned, and his master spoke sharply. "Quiet, Nick." He was a solid youngish man, this, breeched and booted, and no Highlandman at all, as his

1

voice proclaimed. "Evenin' all," he greeted. "Fine night."

"Indeed, yes. It is a very fine night, whatever," he was allowed. "Warm, it is."

He nodded, and stepped over to the bar, to turn and face them, his elbows supporting his back against the counter, and he jerked his head in a vaguely southerly direction. "That was a policeman away down the road—came out o' here, didn't he? First copper I've seen since I come here. Looked like on business, too . . . ?"

Archie McKillop nodded. "Aye, that is so. He was, too." A thing any keeper should know about, this. Bert Clarke was the new underkeeper on Inveralish, and should be informed, duly and properly. "John Grant, that was, out of Corriemore. He is just away down to be having a bit talk with Alastair Dubh MacIver Ross."

The manner in which that was said had the effect desired.

"An' who the devil's he?" Clarke demanded.

The Highland man took a sip from his glass appreciatively, and his companions settled themselves back in their seats. "Alastair Dubh MacIver Ross is a tink . . . a gipsy, as you might be saying."

"The hell of a name for a gipsy?"

"And him the hell of a gipsy, whatever," he was assured.

"Well?"

"Alastair Dubh is not the sort of man for a polisman to be after saying things to." McKillop informed judiciously. "He is not a bad man at all, see you, but wild a wee thing—moody, as you might say. Without the temper he has on him, he is a quiet man, indeed. Moody he is, that's all. And he is long in the arm, with a pair of fists on him that is wicked, just wicked."

"A tough guy, eh—a gippo tough? I reckon I know his kind . . . and how to deal with them, too." Bert Clarke hunched his wide shoulders a little and pushed his feet out a bit farther from the counter. "They ask for trouble and they get it, by God."

"They do so—but Alastair Dubh is not just that way, see you," the other suggested mildly. "A peaceable man he is, by and large—he will tell you so his own self. A pleasanter-spoken

2

lad would be hard finding, six days out of seven."

"I know—smile in your face and stick a knife in your back—they're all the same, these gippos. I've met plenty o' them in my day—not here," and he jerked his head in a comprehensive if uncomplimentary gesture, "but down south—a lying, thieving, fornicating crew." The keeper turned, and beat his open palm on the counter. "Hey, Campbell—what about a drink?" he shouted.

A downright statement of that sort was not meant to be contradicted, and the little group at the table—two fishermen, a crofter, and a shepherd—held their peace. Glasses were quietly emptied.

Clarke, with southern impatience, waited a bare minute before shouting again, a powerful effort. "Where the hell's he hiding himself?" he demanded. "What a place!"

Big Simon, after a suitable pause, inserted himself through his door, wiping his hands with some display on a near-white apron, and met the demand for a nip of Scotch and a pint with dignity. "Anything else, at all?" he enquired.

"No." The other eyed his whisky for a moment, muttered something, and drank it down smoothly. Then he picked up his ale, and returned to his original stance, with his back to the counter. "What's he been up to, then, this gip—Ross, or whatever you call him?"

"Alastair Dubh MacIver Ross," Archie McKillop said that as though he liked saying it. But it was all that he said.

"Well—what's he been doing, that the police is after him?"

Archie picked up his glass, looked at the outside of it and at the inside of it, and shook his head, apparently surprised to find it empty. "A long story it is," he said, and sighed. He did not put his tumbler down.

Clarke grunted, and shrugged. "Have a drink, then," he acquiesced, and four glasses were pushed forward in polite acceptance. Gamekeepers are men of substance in that country.

McKillop, his tumbler replenished, took a sip, and spoke. "Here's the way of it. Major Telfer, Farinish, does not be liking the lad at all, nor any of the tinkers. Last season, with him camping down-bye in the haugh under Balnacraig, the Major, new taken the place, accuses him of poaching and worse, and it was near enough blows they were at, then—for Alastair's proud, proud. There was trouble right till the day the Major went South, and him warning them off the place. He said, the Major, that if ever they were after coming back on his land, he'd have the polis on them." The crofter took a long drink. "And now, see you, Alastair Dubh's back in the haugh under Balnacraig!"

The keeper snorted. "Just like I said—looking for trouble."

"It is not just that, maybe. Always the tinks have camped there. They cut the hazel and willow wands for their baskets that they make, from the shaws there. All my days I've seen them there at the start of summer. That is right, Donald?"

Donald Forbes, fisherman and man of parts, nodded. "That is so," he confirmed, with the authority of his sixty years.

"Himself, Alastair Dubh, would not always be stopping there, for sure—he has a small bit camping place of his own, the lad, over by Lagganlia," and McKillop's glance flickered round his companions significantly, "but he is after being about the place plenty, and him it was the Major made the dead set at. And it's back there he's come with his bit tent, not to Lagganlia, see you. His pride it is that would be forcing him into that, of course."

"Pride!" Clarke exploded. "What in God's name's the fellow got to be proud about? A broken-down cart, a knock-kneed nag, a couple o' mongrel dogs, and a crew o' dirty brats—what's a gip to be proud about?"

Archie McKillop drew strongly at his pipe. " 'Tis not his gear, to be sure," he agreed, "but Alastair is a proud man, just the same, like his dad before him." The crofter turned to the others. "D'you mind of Colin Bán? The pride of him, and him with a drink inside him! God, I've heard him naming twenty genera-tions of the Ross MacIvers before him, and challenging any man to say that there was better blood in all the breadth of Scotland. He was the lad for a fight, was Colin Bán. Beside him Black Alastair's quiet, quiet—but not a man to be crossing, just the same. It's the blood of them that they're proud of, the black MacIver blood, that they do say is the best of all the MacIvers that's in it, the chiefest of the clan. The blood, it is."

"Gipsies! Cripes, what next?" the keeper hooted. "Don't tell me you believe yarns the likes o' that! I've heard tell o' them claiming to be kings an' princes an' Lord knows what. They're the biggest liars on God's earth. I know the breed."

Big Simon Campbell spoke up. "Just the same, see you, there could be truth in it, whatever. They do be saying there's good blood amongst the tinkers. After Charlie Stuart was beat at yon Culloden and the man Cumberland was making an end of the clans, there was many a chief took to the heather, and stayed there. 'Tis them some of the tinks say they are born out of, and like enough too, maybe. This was aye MacIver country, Glenmoraig and Strathalish. Like enough, it could be."

"Even so—what about it?" The younger man was forceful. "What the hell difference does it make? A gip's a gip, ain't he, no matter where he sprung from hundreds o' years back?" He finished off his beer in a gulp, and wiped his mouth with the back of a large hand. "Where d'you say this fellow's hanging out—where the copper's gone?"

"Balnacraig," he was informed. "Down in the haugh, near where the river joins the loch. Easy you'll find it."

The keeper frowned for a moment, at the ready assumption that he was sufficiently interested to go seeking the fellow. Then he shrugged. "Well, maybe I'll have a look down—there's precious little better to do about this place. I could give the copper a hand, if he needs it. I could do with a bit o' fun, strike me. Here, Nick—heel dog." At the doorway he paused for a moment, and looked around at them, consideringly. "Well . . . s'long," he said, and the doors swung-to behind him.

The others sipped their drinks slowly, appreciatively, in no hurry at all, and, after an initial exchange of glances, their expressions were quietly reflective. It would be five or ten minutes before Archie McKillop got to his feet, reached for his cap, and nodded to the big man alean behind the counter. "Aye, Simon it's a fine night for a bit walk, I'm thinking," he mentioned. "Just a small bit stroll would be the thing."

"It would so, surely," he was allowed. "Just the thing."

"Yes, then. You'll be minding yon wire-netting you were to get me? Fine man, *Beannachd leat*, Simon."

The others followed him out into the glowing evening.

Kinlochalish and its hotel—which was the major part of it, indeed—stood squarely between the limitless western sea and the serried hills of Ross, and the silver sands of its tiny bay crept up to its front doorstep and the bracken and birches and heather of Beinn Garbh rose from its back, and between the two of them, it shared the narrow shelf of levelish ground with the white sandy road. It was a gallant road that, if narrow and tenuous-seeming, for it encountered and survived more obstacles on its course than any other road in all that country; it had a thousand hills to climb, some of them to dizzy heights, a hundred sea-lochs to circumnavigate, never once faltering fainthearted at a ferry even where a twenty-mile detour was the alternative, marshes to stride, rocky headlands to scramble round, passes to thread, and more headlong streams to cross by stout little right-angled stone bridges than arithmetic could cope with. And always it went under constant threat by the hungry sea on the one hand and the jostling mountains on the other, and, picking its heedful path between, persisted. A modest, unassuming, but remarkably adequate road it was, starting away down in the south, where the Great Glen slanted down to the western coast and ending only where the land ended far up at the grey edge of the northern sea—a good road and sole slender artery for the life's blood of a whole country. Where it rounded the headland of Ardruig, then, on its return to the coast after the long circuit of Loch Alish, the hotel-cum-Post Office-cum-store and the two-three slated houses stood, with a tumbled stone jetty, and a boat or two drawn up on the shingle—Kinlochalish. A small bit of a place, and modest, like the road, but with its own importance; there was none other in a day's walking.

Down that road, something less than a mile, beyond the headland and along the northern shore of the loch, where the land levelled and widened a little, a fair-sized stream came in. Over its bridge a narrower side-road turned off, to skirt the green haugh, pass the small croft-house of Balnacraig crouching under its great rock, and lift up through scattered birch-woods and a plantation or two, to the Lodge of Farinish. The Lodge itself was not visible, but a wisp of smoke from beyond the woods indicated that it was undergoing its seasonal occupation, the three months of July, August, and September when the Highlands are considered suitable for gentlemen proprietors to live in. And from down amongst the hazel and alders of the haugh another plume of blue woodsmoke lifted lazily this quiet evening. No house stood there, though a grass-grown track led down into it from the road. A shaggy garron, tethered by a long rope to a stake, grazed amongst Hughie Bell's shaggier sheep. That grass track we will follow.

Down beside the swift amber waters of the Allt Buie where the winter spates had scalloped out a level crescent of green-sward and gravel, a man sat before a small fire of birch logs, and the slender spiral of his pipe smoke, with the blue pillar from the fire, and the busy columns of the midges, rose to the vault of the evening. Opposite him, across the smouldering embers and perhaps a couple of yards off, another man stood, feet firm planted, in the well-filled substantial blue serge of the County Constabulary. He smoked no pipe.

The man who sat drew strongly, seemingly pondering. He was in no hurry to speak. When he did, his words came slowly, thoughtfully, as though he turned them over on his tongue and found them reasonable. "I understand you, yes . . . and I am not blaming you, at all."

The policeman blinked, and there was more than a tinge of relief in his surprise. "That's fine, then," he said. He was only slightly sarcastic.

"Aye. A man under orders must be doing what he is told, God's mercy on him. 'Tis not your fault, whatever."

The manifest and undisguised pity in the man's voice brought a flush of deeper red to the other's already high colouring, as he eyed him sharply. He saw only sympathy and regret on the face

7

opposite, with possibly even a hint of amusement behind those dark eyes—certainly neither deference nor apprehension. But then, it was not a face on which any man with eyes, even a policeman, would look for deference, apprehension, or any other like emotion. It was a long face, dark complexioned and prominent as to nose and chin, leanly prominent, with a mouth that smiled beneath a thin wicked scimitar of moustache, and brows that slanted obliquely. But it was the eyes that made the face—deep-set black eyes that smouldered, and could flare and flame without a doubt. An adequate, not to say masterful face, beneath the relic of a felt hat. There was an adequate body too, long and lean like the face, and loosely-knit, clad in patched and ancient tweeds, so faded and stained as to be nondescript as to colour and variegated as to shade. Altogether, a figure that anyone might eye askance. The policeman did so, and said nothing.

It seemed that they had a capacity for silence, both of them—both were Highlandmen, of course. The dark man puffed at his tobacco, the Allt Buie murmured and gurgled, quietly disinterested, from down at the loch-shore the piping of the redshanks came faintly, and no other sound broke the hush of the evening. The sitter stirred the embers of the fire with the toe of his boot—an excellently-made boot, by the way, and in good repair—and the tiny spurt and puff of the white wood ash was a thing to remark and consider.

The policeman it was that spoke first, and the words came rather abruptly. "You will be out of it then by the morning, Ross?" he jerked.

The other raised one of those eyebrows speculatively. "My name is MacIver," he mentioned easily, "and I will not be out of it at all, see you."

John Grant drew a deep breath, opened his mouth, and shut it again. "H'rrrrrm," he said. "I'm thinking you're no' being very wise-like, Ross."

"Never was I a wise-like man all my days—anybody will tell you the same," he was assured. "And the name is MacIver."

"Ross it says here"—and the constable produced a shiny

black notebook from his breast-pocket—"and this is official. 'Alastair M. Ross, tinker, of no fixed address.' That's yourself?"

The dark man rubbed his jutting chin with the stem of his pipe. "It could be," he allowed, "to such as knows no better. But MacIver's the name, as it was my father's, and his father's. One time it was MacIver of Strathalish"—and he jerked his head back and round to include all the spread of the land about the loch—"but that was a while back, two hundred years nearly." He smiled, and his teeth were noticeably white against the hue of his skin. "Mac 'ic Iver Mhor, it was, in those days, and no Speyside Grant would have stood before him at an Englishman's bidding!"

Grant stirred from one foot to another. "Maybe no', but this is police business, you see—and Ross the name is."

"Ross was a name we got in the heather—the MacIvers of Ross, the Ross MacIvers. Man, you must have the name right. That's the sort of thing it would never do for the police to be getting wrong, to be sure."

The other frowned doubtfully. That there was mockery behind the fellow's gravity, he had no doubt. But it was right enough that a policeman had aye to be careful. "Ross or MacIver, yourself it is that's meant, anyway," he maintained. His eye, following the tinker's sudden glance, lighted on a figure approaching down the grass track through the birches, a deliberately-striding figure with a dog at heel. Something of the aspect and carriage of the newcomer had its own effect on the policeman, and involuntarily his bearing stiffened and his tone hardened. "And you'd best have your mind changed about getting out of here by the morn, or—"

"Yes . . . ?" the other enquired interestedly.

"—or the worse it'll be for yourself," Grant ended, a little vaguely.

The tinker looked at him thoughtfully, and smiled.

Strolling, intently casual, Bert Clarke came across the haugh to them. Alastair Dubh eyed the turned-up toes of the man's great boots, almost with fascination. Those boots, most definitely keeper's boots, reacted strangely on some obscure part of

9

his brain, some deep-seated consciousness that was ages-old and impersonal. He hated those boots with a cold and elemental hatred. "It is a fine evening, whatever," he stated easily.

"Evenin'," the newcomer jerked, but it was not at the tinker that he looked. "Everythin' okay?"

Slowly Grant nodded. "Yes, then," he said heavily, almost defensively.

The keeper kicked idly at a piece of birch-twig. "That's fine."

"Aye."

The man Alastair glanced from one to the other, and his nostrils flared slightly in seeming amusement. He held his peace.

Pushing back the rim of his peaked cap with the tip of his pencil, and at the same time scratching a bald brow, the constable gazed at his notebook, sighed, and slapped it shut and buttoned it back into his pocket. "Aye, ihmmm. Very well so, indeed," he mentioned. He looked up at the sky and then at the ground. "Goodnight to you, then," he said abruptly, and turned about to stalk off.

"*Beannachd leat*, Mr. Grant."

The keeper stared after the retreating figure. "Lord, ain't he turnin' you out arter all?" he demanded.

"He is, and he isn't," the other informed. "A matter of opinion it is, entirely."

Bert Clarke hesitated, and he was not a hesitant man. "You're mighty cocky, ain't you, for a tinker," he suggested.

The other looked him in the eye. "I am as God made me," he said, ". . . like the rest of us. Yourself, you are not so blate—for a stranger!"

Blate! The keeper did not know just what blate meant, but the tone in which it was spoken gave him a fair idea. He came a pace or two nearer the fire. "When are you movin', Gippo?" he demanded.

"When I am ready. . . . Paid-man!"

"What d'you mean—Paid-man?" Clarke's lower lip, his whole jaw, thrust forward.

"Just that. You will be the new keeper on Inveralish, I'm

10

thinking? Marsden's man." The inference might have been plain.

"I dunno just what you mean . . . but I don't like your tone o' voice," the other decided. "When a gip gets cocky, it's time he was dealt with . . . and I know just how to deal with the likes o' you."

"Just as well it is, then, that you are keeper on Inveralish and not here on Farinish, or you might be thinking to try out your new authority . . . and I wouldn't like to be having any trouble, at all!"

Clarke drew a long breath. "You wouldn't, eh?" One large hand clenched tight, was lifting slowly. At his feet his dog rumbled deeply, remotely, in its throat.

"I would not, being a quiet man." The sitter had neither stirred nor altered his expression of easy interest.

"I've a good mind to wipe your dirty face in the muck where it belongs."

"You could be trying, surely," and as the other swayed on his toes, ". . . but you won't with yourself uninvited on this land, and me sitting here with Hughie Bell the tenant's permission."

And the keeper, properly-oriented man, swayed back on his substantial heels and took hold of himself, a good hold that it took him a couple of gulps to effect. "Perhaps you're right," he said slowly, after a moment or two. "I'll not dirty my hands on you . . . this time. But God help you if ever I see you on my ground!"

"And He will, maybe, too," the reply came, judiciously.

And that could have been the end of that, and should have been—two men of their minds willing in that way. But just then a woman appeared from behind the green screen of the junipers at the head of the haugh, and walked towards them slowly, a tall willowy woman, copper-haired and almond-eyed, with a stained tartan shawl about her slanting shoulders, suckling at her bare breast a naked child. It was the woman that did it; As she came up to them unhurriedly, almost deliberately, to pause unspeaking before them, the southerner's lip curled in a distaste, an offence, that was inborn, elemental. The child,

11

stirring, clawed voraciously with a tiny bronzed fist at the white heavy breast, and sucked noisily. With a combined shrug and toss of the head, Clarke snorted his revulsion. "Can't you find your bitch some rags," he cried, "the dirty . . ."

And like a steel spring released, MacIver sprang, straight from his log beyond the fire, in the one complicated movement covering the six feet or so that separated them, and his fist crashed full in the other's face. Another lightning blow, under the heart, and a third on the point of the jaw as the man sagged, and Bert Clarke crumpled and sank inert on the grass. Stooping, Black Alastair grabbed the man by his coat-collar and dragged him, at a strange trot, the few yards to the water's edge, and, with a fierce improbable strength that seemed to be effortless, picked him bodily off the ground, held him so for a second, and tossed him in. Without pausing, and with the splash of it soaking him, he strode back to the woman, took her arm gently and turned her around, and walked back with her whence she had come.

That is how the thing started.

II

THE early sun was just lifting above the serried ramparts of the eastern hills, flooding the strath with its brittle radiance, and spilling long inky shadows behind every eminence and projection and into each hollow, in a chequerwork of black and gold. From all the corries and folds and seams of the hillsides the white mists were streaming upward, coiling, thinning, dissipating, though fragile wisps of them still floated, steam-like, above the level waters of the loch, placid waters brushed only faintly, here and there, by a stripling breeze. Above, in the thin blue haze of the morning sky, all the larks were trilling joyously at their soaring, and already the soft hum of the countless questing bees was the prelude to the subdued undertone of the day, the quiet August day of a West Highland summer.

One other sound, and one only, prevailed in the golden morning along Loch Alish-side, the clop-scrape-clop of hooves on the sand and gravel of the white road, combined with the chink of metal-shod boot on stone—prevailed but never disturbed. The hooves belonged to a shaggy mild-eyed plodding garron, and the boots to Alastair MacIver, at its head. Walking behind, perhaps twenty paces, the woman Anna crooned some ages-old melody of the Isles, simple, unending, but she sang wordlessly, almost soundlessly, under her breath, for the child in her arms was asleep, and her singing near the subconscious. And her bare brown feet made no noise on the road, either.

The man moved unhurriedly, with the long slow stride that eats the miles, his dark eyes on the road, and his thoughts his own. The pony, black-maned, stocky, and wide-hoofed, paced deliberately under the balanced superstructure of its burden of household goods, head hung low, the epitome of drowsy resignation. A lean dog, part-collie, part-retriever, loped midway between the man and pony and the woman and child, scrupulous it seemed, despite half closed eyes, to so maintain

13

that position. So they moved through the morning, and left no wake behind them on its quiet surface.

It was at one of the many wooden bridges by which the road coped with the myriad headlong streams of that streaming land, that it happened—if the hesitation, pause, and redirection of the little cavalcade's even progress could be termed a happening. The garron it was that was responsible, faltering in its rhythmic pacing, raising its head, and with just the suggestion of a shake, turning in towards the cart-track that branched off, away from the loch, to follow the stream. And the man, pushed by the beast's shoulder, faltered likewise, lifted a hand to the rope bridle, started to press back, raised his brows and shrugged, in a curious whimsical gesture, and allowed himself to be side-tracked also. The woman followed, unspeaking, but a close observer might have noticed the expression alter in those almond eyes.

She had curious eyes, that woman, cloudy grey-green eyes that went strangely with the red glint of her hair whose heavy copper coils looped back without artifice, framed a perfect heart-shaped face. Whether it was the eyes that did it, shy and hooded, or the tight lips guarding a wide mouth, or the hint of disdain in the so-slightly curved nose, there was an aloofness about that face, a reserve, that seemed to speak of a spirit turned in on itself, timorous, or prideful, or just heedfully inviolate. Sadness there could be, too, the sadness implicit in a kind of beauty that woman had, fundamental, latent almost, and basic as it was unassuming. The beauty of all generations was based on just such foundation, though few today might have called her beautiful. And the rough homespun skirt and faded tartan plaid that, together, might have been all that she wore, as well as the child in her arms, were as elemental as the rest of her, and she followed the man in the passive resignation with which such women have followed their men throughout the centuries. That was Anna MacIver.

The track they followed bore the stream company through a little copse of larch and spruce, round a bracken knoll, to stop short at a house and farm-steading tucked under the first

14

wooded spur of a great hill. It was quite a small place, trim and compact, and the tidiness of it was noticeable in a country not noted for its tidiness. There was a cut grass space before the long low front of the house, and a flair of gravel, white and bleached from the loch-shore, at the near end fronting a range of outbuildings, reed-thatched, that ended in a heavy squat chimney-stack. By the wide open doorway in its whitewashed wall a cartwheel stood, and a plough, and from the dark interior the chink of hammer on anvil came pleasantly. Behind the house a long kitchen garden lifted up towards the birch-woods, under a scattering of apple-trees, and amongst the fruit bushes a line of washed clothes swayed lazily in the warm morning air. A settled domestic secure place, and a scene against which the incoming gipsies seemed strangely incongruous.

The pony halted of its own accord at the sweep of grass, dropped head for a tentative nibble, half-closed its eyes, and so remained, evidently content: a remarkable animal. The man Alastair stood for a little, still likewise, seemingly pensive, then suddenly, abruptly, he lifted his head and his voice, and his single bark-like hail shattered the quiet, to be taken up and tossed, echoing, amongst all the enclosing hills, an unexpected sound and somehow challenging.

Results were immediately forthcoming. From behind the house a black-and-white sheep collie came running, barking excitedly, and nearly knocking itself over with the fervour of its tail-wagging. From within the smithy, the tapping of metal on metal ceased, and in the wide doorway a burly figure appeared, shirt-sleeved and sacking-aproned, to grin widely if a trifle vacantly, and roar a cheerful greeting above the dog's yapping. He was followed by another, the frail shadow of a man, emaciated and bent, but still in frame a big man, tall, with a shock of almost white hair. He saluted, gravely, hand raised. "The top of the morning to you, Alastair Dubh," he greeted. "You are early on the road, surely?"

"And a good road to be on, any time, that passes your door, Ailean Fuirbeis." That was suitably said.

The burly man's smile embraced all the morning. "Strangers

15

you are, whatever," he cried happily. "How's the bairnie, Anna girl?"

"Well, thank you," the woman said quietly.

"Good, then." He strode wide-legged across the gravel to the grass, stooping as he went to clap the lean dog round which the young farm collie was romping boisterously, a massive eager figure of a man, youngish only, but somehow childlike. He came to Anna MacIver, and his great horny hand ran over her hair to slip down to the child within her arm, and tickle it under the chin. "My, oh my—liker his dad he gets every day that's in it, the little small devil," and his roar of laughter filled the place, and opened the infant's black eyes wide, wide, but unflinchingly. Man and child stared at each other closely then, a curious intense stare, eloquent of an affinity outwith years. Willie Maclay was like that.

The older man was speaking. "The door of Lagganlia is open to you, always"—Alan Forbes was a courtly man at any time— "though it's the bit meadow down-bye that you do be preferring most times, you barbarian you."

"It is a good meadow, and a good house too," the gipsy acknowledged. "Have I ever said different, Ailean Mor?"

"Well, I can just mind some of the things you were after saying a whilie back . . . when you were a bit of a school-laddie."

"And hadn't I the cause, you great tyrant . . . ?" MacIver's glance had switched past the other towards the corner of the steading, round which a newcomer had appeared. "Ah . . . *fail' ort*, Moireach."

It was a young woman who came, unhurriedly, from the direction of the garden, undoing an apron from her waist, and a mixed group of hens and ducklings followed at her heels, hopefully. At sight of the visitors she came hastening, a well-made noticeable figure of a girl, supple and shapely, clad in a trim short-sleeved woollen jumper of navy-blue and a crotal Harris skirt, that did her outline no injustice. "Alastair MacIver," she cried, "where have you been all this while?"

"Here and there, girl—just here and there," he answered her, and his dark eyes sought and found and held her blue ones, and his smile was strange, warm and twisted and understanding and sad, in one.

She stopped beside him and looked at him intently, almost perplexedly, and shook her head over him—as she had done many times before. "What have you been up to, Stair, this time?" she wondered. She had a pleasant soft Highland voice, with the lilt of the West in it.

"Nothing that I shouldn't, at all," the dark man protested, grinning rather like a small boy. And then, even more like a small boy: "At least, well . . . nothing, then, nothing at all."

"No . . . ?" Those lifted eyebrows betrayed no conviction. Martha Forbes's eyes were wide open, too—not the sort for pulling wool over—set under a broad forehead and above a short straight nose. The good mouth, not too small and upturning at the corners, might have betokened acquiescence, but the chin below it was firm and the jawline strong. It was not a beautiful face nor yet striking, but it was a bonny one, with sufficient of that indefinable quality that may be termed character or personality to be noteworthy. It was not a face that a man would forget quickly, under its tumult of wavy brown hair.

She moved over to the woman Anna, and held out her arms for the child. "Well, Anna *a graidh*, how is the little one?" she asked, and taking the naked infant from the other's unresisting grasp, she hugged him close. "My little golden trout," she crooned. "My little brown fawn of the woods. It's just a darling, he is. Proud you must be of him, Anna."

The girl beside her—for she was only a girl, that gipsy, despite the impression she gave of maturity, or perhaps agelessness might describe more aptly the quality that seemed to clothe her—did not speak nor move, but stood by impassive, waiting, though her eyes, those strange slanting eyes, beautiful but hooded, sought the questioner's, and for a moment were piercing, intense. Then, with the faintest lift of her sloping shoulders, she gave just the hint of a smile and a nod, as her glance dropped.

Martha Forbes gave her back the child. "And Ewan—where is he this time?"

It was Alastair who answered, quickly. "He is locked up

again, in jail," he announced. "It was the drink again, and him misliking the looks of a policeman—a sergeant. At Torrachan it was, three weeks back."

Alan Forbes shook a censorious head. "A pity," he said. "It aye makes for inconvenience, that sort of thing . . . with the Constabulary." And with a glance shot from under bushy white eyebrows: "There would never be a knife in it, this time, Black Alastair?"

The dark man's teeth gleamed white in a grin. "No knife was found, anyway . . . this time. Only three months he got." Then, like lightning, his expression changed, darkened, and his glance slid over to the girl Anna. "Ewan is a fool!" he stated and his voice was vibrant with emotion.

The woman, eyes downcast, said nothing.

For a moment there was silence in that peaceful place amongst the sunbathed hills, as currents and cross-currents of thought eddied and traversed, and the hum of Alan Forbes's bees came into its own.

"He who calleth his brother a fool is in danger of hellfire!" That was Martha Forbes, lightly, breaking the silence. And then: "But why don't you all come away in?—Willie, take the pony. I've got some scones new off the girdle."

As she turned towards the house MacIver stopped her. "Not for this morning, *mo charaid*. It is the top of the road we are on, today."

"You mean you are going away? You are not stopping?"

"Just that. I am a travelling man this day, with ground to be covering."

"But why?" They all stared at him. Always when MacIver came to Lagganlia he stopped there, for a day, for a week, for a month. Neither time nor any urgency was apt to affect the gipsies' mode of living. They drifted as the spirit moved them.

Gravely, Alastair Dubh considered them. "This Strathalish might be better without us for a small while, perhaps," he suggested carefully. "A pity it would be to get involved in any sort of trouble, see you. We are peaceable folk. . . ."

A bark of a laugh from Alan Forbes, and something like a

snort from his daughter. "You're not after telling us that Major Telfer has Alastair Dubh MacIver on the run?"

"Maybe he has, then!"

The older man shook his white head. "I'll no' believe it. Don't say you're after running away, man—you!" he marvelled.

The gipsy examined the toes of his good boots thoughtfully. "Never have I run away from any man yet," he told them slowly.

There was a pause while they waited. The dark man would say only his own say and in his own time, they knew.

And then Anna MacIver spoke, for only the second time in that foregathering, and her voice was low and husky and level. "It is for me," she said. "He put the new keeper on Farinish into the Allt Buie for me last night, and now he goes away . . . for me." Her eyes, smouldering now, swept over them all, to reach Alastair's and there remain.

Broodingly almost, he returned her gaze, and then, slowly, he smiled at her, but did not amplify her statement.

Willie Maclay's bellow of laughter broke the slight but undeniable tension. "He put the new keeper in the Allt Buie, she says!" he roared, slapping his thigh. "God Almighty, that's Alastair, whatever! Grand it is—just magnificent. In the Allt Buie . . . !"

The girl Martha looked from Alastair to Anna and back again, and a tiny furrow appeared between her brows. But when she spoke her tones were only flippantly chiding. "You too, Stair . . . and you complaining of Ewan! I'm ashamed of you, really, you, you ruffian!"

And her father, watching them all from wise colourless eyes, let his breath free in a long sigh. "Aye, very well so," he said. "Time enough there is for a drink, anyway. There's aye time for one for the road, whatever the stramash. Come away ben, will you."

They barely had reached the doorway within its wooden porch when the sound of horse's hooves halted them. Horses were only to be expected round about a smithy, but in that country visitors were scarce enough always to arouse interest. So they turned

19

and watched.

Along the track round the bracken knoll came a horse and rider, a tall slender high-stepping horse and a tall slender and probably high-stepping rider—an unusual sight to see in a Highland glen. The beast was a long-legged arch-necked chestnut, and a thoroughbred, obviously, from its flaring nostrils to its curving tail-root. The way it picked up and set down its white-socked hooves spoke eloquently to anyone who knew horses. And two of the men watching knew quite a lot about horseflesh, and looked heedfully. The rider was a long-legged up-sitting young woman, dressed in jodhpur breeches and a brief white open-necked shirtblouse. Her carriage, her long neck, the cock of her head and the superb line of her flaxen hair, told their own story. One at least of the men did not consider that his expert judgment was restricted to horseflesh. Their eyes were kept busy.

The girl rode on to the gravel in front of the smithy door, and dismounted with a fine easy swing of leg and torso. She thrust a hand into breeches pocket and brought out a lump of sugar to present to the nuzzling animal. Then she turned round to eye the group by the house levelly, coolly, and waited for attention.

She got it, too. Obviously she was in the habit of being attended to. Alan Forbes had advanced whenever she came on to his gravel, and now he moved forward to take the bridle, and his bow, dignified and natural, was an acknowledgement of what his eyes told him, and with nothing of servility to it. The other two men came on, too—Maclay to move around steed and rider to the open smithy doorway, grinning widely in frank admiration; the gipsy to approach the horse and stoop and run a knowledgeable hand over the glossy chestnut-and-white of its off foreleg.

"It is a very fine morning for the saddle, ma'am," Forbes observed politely. "Welcome too, after what's been in it."

She nodded. "Yes, very. Punch here has a shoe loose—the off foreleg. I want it fixed, please." Her voice was cool, like her glance, with only the merest hint of that weariness to it that fashion demanded.

"You would, then. You will be from Inveralish Lodge, likely?"

"Yes. I am Angela Denholm." That was an explanation rather than an introduction, mentioned casually but with large implication.

"So—the laird's niece!" Forbes had heard about Sir Charles's niece, daughter of the sister who had married Lord Somebody Denholm of the ducal house of Merton. Sir Charles was not averse to the mention of this connection. "Glad I am to meet you," he said. "I am Alan Forbes, Lagganlia, and that is my daughter Martha, and these are friends of mine."

Looking slightly surprised, she nodded briefly. "Will it take you long to do that shoe?"

"Not that long, at all." He sounded in no sort of hurry, whatever—but then Alan Forbes was a Highlandman, and it is doubtful if anyone had ever seen him in a hurry. "Will it be your first visit to these parts, ma'am?"

The girl was turning back to the horse. "To Strathalish— yes," she threw over her shoulder. Alastair MacIver was still running his hand up and down the chestnut's foreleg. "Watch that leg," she warned him, sharply.

Bent yet, he glanced up at her. "Just what I am doing, isn't it?" he enquired reasonably.

"Well, be careful how you touch it." That injunction had a suggestion of the defensive about it.

The gipsy straightened up. "Lady, it's your own self that would best be said to," he told her grimly. "That leg is strained, badly. The beast should not be ridden, shoe loose or firm."

Her frown came down like a bar across her features, fine regular features firmly-etched, and she opened her lips to speak, and then closed them again, firmly. "If I require your—assistance, I will ask for it," she said then, after a pause, and her voice was cold now, not cool.

"And it will be your's . . . for the asking," he gave back, easily.

Their eyes met, deep-set, dark, near-cynical, and violet, flashing, imperious—met and stayed. For a long moment they stared unswerving, while the others watched intently. Then

21

somehow, without any faltering in her gaze, the girl's expression altered, as though she had started looking with her eyes instead of just staring and interest succeeded mere hauteur. Moving now, slowly, her regard covered his features, his figure, down to his feet and back again, in a comprehensive survey that was frankness itself, frankly interested or frankly slighting. The man was not quite sure which. He tried to do likewise, being the man he was, but he was handicapped by a tradition of manners, from which she was free. So when, her inspection over, her eyes returned to his face, they were met by his own, steady, set, and the faint suggestion of a smile that had begun to lift the corners of a scarlet mouth faded. Instead, was it—could it be—the pale beginnings of a flush that mounted and spread from cheeks to brow? Abruptly she turned away.

Martha Forbes thought that it was time to intervene. "Will you not come in and take a cup of tea, Miss Denholm?" she invited. "The water's on the boil—it will not take a minute, at all."

Angela Denholm seemed to consider. "That is kind of you...." She turned to Alan Forbes. "How long will you be fixing that shoe?" she wondered.

That tall wreck of a man stroked his long chin, and his glance rested not on the horse, but flickered from his daughter to the laird's niece, to the gipsy, and back again. "Let me see, now," he temporized. "It'll take a wee whilie, mind you. There'll be the shoe to make as well as to fit—we're not after keeping shoes in stock, as you might say, for beasts the like of yon...."

"I see. I think I'll get back to the Lodge, in that case, and call for Punch in the afternoon. Thank you."

"There's no harm in having the tea and a bit scone first, ma'am—no time at all it'll take. The Lodge is a fair step away, whatever."

The young woman hesitated—a thing she was not noted for. "Well...."

Alastair MacIver spoke then, deliberately. "We are on our way, anyway," he said. The woman needn't lose her tea for fear of having to associate with such as himself. "Long enough we have wasted as it is, and the district unhealthy." He stepped over to his garron, and grasped the rope bridle. "Anna . . ."

"What hurry is there, man, at all?" Forbes began, when his daughter slipped over to the dark man's side. "Stair, what are you going to do? Where are you going?"

"Over the hills and far away. There is plenty of room in the heather, Moireach."

"Must you . . . ?"

"Why not, then—what is wrong with the heather, at all?" He smiled, and his hand was on her arm. "We will be back."

"He will be back," her father confirmed. "The season is not that long." He did not need to complete his reminder that once the fashionable shooting season had run its brief course and the sporting gentry had returned south whence they had come, life in the glens would return to its easy norm, and keepers would find their own level again—as indeed would tinkers and policemen. "Which road are you taking, boy?"

"We will just follow your burn up its bit valley—as good a way into the heather as any . . . and not that noticeable from the road! And once over the hill there will be all Ross itself before us." MacIver turned. "*Slan leat*, Moireach. *An la chi's nach fhaic. Madainn mhath duit*, Aileann Fuirbeis." He swung on the horsewoman and his ancient felt hat was swept off in a bow, elaborate and wicked. "At your service, ma'am . . . for the asking!" he assured, and his smile was dazzling.

They watched them go, as they had come, man and pony, dog, and woman and child, sped by Willie Maclay's shouted cheerful "Haste ye back!" down to the stream, to turn right-handed up into the jaws of the little valley it had cut for itself into the flank of the great hill of Carn Liath. Then, with a long breath, taken and expelled, Martha Forbes shook her head, and spoke brightly, politely. "Your tea, Miss Denholm," and led the way into the house.

Later, twenty minutes or so, Angela Denholm, walking down towards the road-end where the track from Lagganlia joined the loch-road, was aware of a car that approached, wavered, and

23

went on along the highway, to be lost to sight behind the birch trees. But turning into the road, the sound of hastening footsteps swung her round to await the arrival of a solidly-built youngish man in breeches who obviously was making for her.

"Mornin', miss," he jerked. "You ain't seen anythin' o' a couple o' tinkers about the road, have you? Gipsies, you know."

She looked surprised. The man seemed vaguely familiar—hadn't she seen him about her uncle's place? "You're one of the gamekeepers with Sir Charles Marsden, aren't you?"

"Yes, miss. Clarke's the name. These tinks I'm looking for . . ."

"A dark tall man, with a woman with a baby? Leading a pony . . . ?"

"That's them, miss. You've seen them?"

"Yes. What do you want them for?" People in Miss Denholm's position need not hesitate to ask questions.

Bert Clarke hesitated to answer her, though. He was a man with a fair conceit of himself. In the present circumstances he felt that there was no point in entering into a detailed account of last night's performance in the river. "It's just a small debt I've to settle with 'im, miss," he said. "Ross, he's called."

"I don't know anything about the name. But if you want him, they left that place up there where the smithy is rather less than half an hour ago. They were going up over the hill, I think, following the stream. They weren't going quickly—if you hurry you ought to catch them up."

"Thanks—we'll hurry," the keeper assured her. "Mornin', miss—much obliged, I'm sure," and touching his cap, he turned and hurried back whence he had come.

It was only a minute or so later that, walking on, the sound of an engine made the girl look over her shoulder. The car was coming back. At the road-end that she had just left, it turned, with the scrape of gravel, into the track for Lagganlia. And it was a powerful car, and beside the man who had just been talking to her two figures were sitting, noticeably upright figures dressed in black. Angela Denholm frowned a little, uncertainly. What were the policemen for, she wondered.

24

III

THE Courtroom at Ardwall was stuffy and very warm. The hollow ticking of an ancient wall-clock and the drone and bumble of a bluebottle against the dull panes of a hermetically-sealed window aptly interpreted the atmosphere of the place. Perhaps the Sheriff-substitute was affected by the afternoon's somnolence; certainly his questions and pronouncements, uttered from between lips that scarcely moved, were made at ever-lengthening intervals, and the tap-tap of his penholder on the desk was the complement of the clock and the fly. He was a long man and lanky under his black robe, and his grey wig was pushed back from a high shiny forehead; above a great fleshy nose, heavy-lidded eyes appeared to keep themselves open only with an effort. He was speaking now, and it was necessary to listen carefully to catch any more than just the gist of his words. "This question of motive," he mentioned. "It is not crystal-clear to me . . . perhaps I am obtuse. . . . Will Mr., ah, Anderson explain a little further? Am I right in assuming that this woman was in some way involved?"

The little Procurator-fiscal took off his pince-nez, turned them around and put them on again. "Indirectly," he admitted. "Indirectly, I suppose she was." This was annoying. He had managed to keep the woman pretty well out of it so far. Her entry would only complicate a perfectly straightforward case, without affecting the issue. "But I respectfully submit that the evidence produced is adequate to establish sufficient motive for the assault, the *admitted* assault. Albert Clarke, the game-keeper, was present at the interview when the constable John Grant warned the accused off the property—indeed, he offered to assist the constable in the carrying out of what might well have been a difficult and even dangerous duty. As your Lordship knows, these tinkers are not the easiest people to handle. Having made his pronouncement, the constable apparently considered that his duty was done, and left the scene." The little man coughed. "Whether indeed that was an adequate assessment of his duty is not for me to decide. But I submit that the witness Albert Clarke, being a gamekeeper, and having just heard the policeman's order, was fully justified in expecting to see some signs of it being carried out. When none were forthcoming and he enquired the reason, he met only with abuse and insolence which eventually culminated in Ross completely losing his temper and committing the assault."

"Quite." Silence. Then: "But this woman, Mrs. MacIver"— he pronounced the name as it was spelt instead of the accepted 'MacEefer'—"she *was* Mrs. MacIver or Ross or whatever the name is, I take it?"

That question was asked with what, in anyone less soberly correct, might have held just a hint of the slyly suggestive. "Good. It is the prosecution's contention that the arrival of the woman, then, had no direct bearing on the assault which, the evidence seems to suggest, coincided with the said arrival?"

"That is so." The Fiscal's eyes met those of the witness on the stand for an instant. The man in the dock, silent, seemingly almost uninterested, watched them both. "It is possible, I suppose, that her entry might have precipitated the attack—not that such a contention has been put forward by the defence?"

"Not specifically, I agree. But then there has been in reality no specific defence at all." The black-robed shoulders shrugged eloquently at the prisoner's extraordinary attitude. "You will admit that, I think?"

The prosecution was admitting nothing. "With the assault not denied, and the reason behind it, as I contend, clear enough, probably the accused is wise to, as it were, throw himself on the clemency of the Court, rather than to put forward any mere token defence."

The Sheriff-substitute stared at his blotting-paper and his pen tapped in time with the clock. The man's heavy rumination was in marked contrast to the terrier-like aggressiveness of the little Procurator-fiscal, and the withdrawn, faintly scornful, impassivity of the prisoner. From its window-pane the bluebottle still

26

buzzed monotonously, and below the judicial dais the scratch-scratch of the Sheriff-Clerk's pen went on unceasingly.

"All right," the Sheriff said suddenly, out of his musing. "The witness may stand down," to watch with hooded eyes while Bert Clarke, tapped on the shoulder by the stout and perspiring police-sergeant, glanced about him quickly, nodded a little uncertainly, and cap in hand, was led to the door, his hobnailed boots scraping loudly on the floor as he went, so that he walked almost on tiptoe. As the door closed, he went on: "It may be rather beyond the scope of my office, but I suggest that the ends of justice would not have been retarded if evidence in some form had been submitted by the accused's wife."

The Sheriff-Clerk looked up and half-rose to his feet. But Mr. Anderson spoke first. "There was nothing to prevent the accused from bringing forward such evidence, and . . ."—he smiled thinly—"to correct a slight—er—misapprehension—the woman referred to is not the wife of the accused, m'lud."

"Not! Eh—what?" The Sheriff actually opened his eyes. "Dear me." He glanced down at his papers. " 'Anna Gunn or MacIver Ross . . .' " he read out. "From the wording here. . . . And they were living together, alone, were they not? Do you mean that they are not legally married . . . ?"

"She is legally married—but not to the accused, m'lud. She is the wife of the accused's brother, Ewan, I understand."

"Indeed! I see. And where, may I ask, is her husband?"

The Procurator-fiscal coughed, glanced at the Sheriff-Clerk and took off his spectacles again. His hesitation was extremely correct. "He is at present serving a sentence of imprisonment." He looked legally apologetic. "On a charge of assault!"

The Sheriff opened his mouth. "Ha," he said. "Mmmmmm . . . hum! Is that so! Interesting . . . but, of course, quite irrelevant to the case on hand. Quite irrelevant." He pointed his pen in the direction of his clerk. "You understand, Mr. Baillie?" Returning to his papers. "It is as well, perhaps, to point out at this juncture, that this Court is concerned only with the assault labelled as committed at, ah, Balnacraig, Inveralish, on the seventh of August. Nor, ahem, is it a court of morals!" Sitting back, he

27

peered at the silent figure in the dock. "Alastair MacIver Ross, do you wish to call the woman Anna MacIver Ross to give evidence in your defence?"

"I do not." These were the only words that the dark man had spoken for a considerable time. There was no mistaking the decision behind them, nor the prisoner's attitude towards the Sheriff, the prosecution, and the proceedings generally.

The Sheriff-substitute's mouth tightened and turned down, understandably enough. "Very well," he said. "You have no further evidence to bring, Mr. Anderson? In that case the Court will adjourn for half an hour, whereupon I will proceed to the summing-up." He rose.

"Court adjourned."

"Alastair MacIver Ross," the Sheriff said, "you appear before this Court on a grave charge—violent assault upon the person of a fellow-citizen . . . and I may say that assault, physical attack upon a neighbour, is one of the most serious offences with which a member of an organized community may be accused, striking at the very roots of our civilization. If such is to be tolerated, then there is an end to all orderly dealings between men." He tapped his penholder sharply to indicate the depth of his conviction in this matter—as well he might; where would the Law, and the lawyers, be if men were to make a practice of settling their disputes thus out of hand? He went on. "Your attitude through-out has been unhelpful, frivolous, if not impudent, and you have persistently refused the services of a defending solicitor such as could have been made available under the provisions of the Poor Person's Legal Representation authority. Admittedly you have not denied the assault, but you have put forward no form of defence, and rebuffed any attempt on the part of others to bring one for you. I can only suppose that you do not yet realize the seriousness of the offence—indeed, your remark to the police that 'the man Clarke got just what he was needing, but too little of it,' confirms the impression given that you are neither repentant nor suitably aware of your responsibilities as a citizen." Justice appeared to have become considerably more wide-awake since the adjournment. "And yet you are not just an ignorant and uneducated vagrant. That is evident." Glancing down at his documents. "I see that you have had an education, a reasonable education, unusual in one of your, er, calling. If I may say so, Ross, it appears to have been wasted upon you."

The quiet man in the dock spoke quietly. "You may say so, indeed, since I cannot be stopping you, but I doubt your authority for the saying of it, just the same."

"H'rrrmmmmm," said the Sheriff.

The Clerk looked up at the police sergeant, and jerked his head, frowning, and the latter cleared his throat, and said, "Silence!" but without noticeable assurance.

MacIver paid no heed, but went on unhurriedly. "My business with the keeper Clarke was personal entirely, and no affair of any man besides our two selves, at all. Because I chose to settle it in my own way, you have no more right to be saying that my education is wasted on me than have I to say that because you are after reaching entirely a wrong conclusion on the cause of what I did—and more besides—your own legal education is wasted on *you*. I . . ."

"Silence!" cried the Sheriff and the policeman in unison.

It was to the sergeant that Alastair Dubh turned civilly enough. " 'Twas just the conversation seemed to be getting a wee thing one-sided, whatever," he mentioned.

"Order in the Court!" the Clerk squeaked, appalled, while the police rubbed a podgy finger between tight collar and bulging neck, and did nothing. The Sheriff hunched forward and raised an admonitory finger. "Such conduct, such insolence, will get you nowhere. I warn you, it will only harm your case. . . ."

"My case! Have I a case, at all?" he wondered.

"Be quiet. If you interrupt again, you will be removed," he was warned sternly.

The prisoner smiled then, for the first time in that place, and said no more. At least the atmosphere was now more lively.

His judge leaned back again, and waited for a few dignified moments. "To proceed. In extenuation, all that I can think of is that your mode of living, unsettled and unprofitable and in some degree antisocial, has blunted your perceptions as to decent conduct and the obligations of citizenship. At the same time it is my duty to impress on you quite definitely the importance and necessity of such obligations, in order that more reputable members of society may not be intimidated by your—er—indiscipline in future. In the circumstances I should be inclined to inflict a heavy penalty, but in view of the fact that this is apparently your first offence, or, at any rate, the first occasion on which *you*"—the 'you' was rather marked—"have appeared before a court for trial, I will limit the sentence to one month's imprisonment." Uncoiling itself, Justice rose to its feet. "And I think that you may consider yourself fortunate, young man."

The young man stared at the dull window. Suddenly he was aware that there were bars guarding it, as well as cobwebs and dust—iron bars. Involuntarily his hand lifted to his bare bronzed throat, as he was led away.

IV

IT was high noon when Alastair MacIver left the last grey stone house of Ardwall behind him and turned his face to the hills. The morning had been wet, with a heavy billowing mist, but a lightsome breeze had come sportively out of the west to banish all such gloomy vapours, and now the yellow September sun smiled genially over the glistening land and drew tiny coiling columns of steam from the metalled road. The man walked with a steady set striding, deliberate to start with, but which gradually increased in length of pace and in urgency as the road mounted in a long ascent with the lifting moors, towards the beckoning line of the first foothills, outstretched arms of the great mountain massif that was both the soul and the substance of that northern land.

Something of MacIver's expression altered with the tempo of his pacing. From the heavy fixed stare, glower almost, with which he had started, it graduated, through a dourness that was entirely foreign to a face that, whatever else it was, was vital and keen, to a growing eagerness, a hunger, as he made for the heather. It was not entirely a new hunger that was upon him; the same surging longing, that was a pain indeed, he had known as a child cooped within the four walls of his schoolroom and staring dark-eyed through the window at the blue line of the hills—freedom, and his birthright. Under the shoulder of one of those, in a cave contrived between a fallen larch tree and a great outcrop, he had been born. But this hunger had an edge to it, a sharp angry edge, ground and sharpened during thirty evil suffocating days in a box-like cell. And the hunger was only half of it; there was hurt and bitterness, resentment and stark anger. There were hard lines about his mouth and jaw that had not been noticeable a month ago.

The road that the man was on had started out from Ardwall swackly enough, with width to it and tarmacadam and telegraph poles, but as the miles passed and the small grey farms it fed grew fewer and smaller, it narrowed in, and its tarmac was replaced by sand and gravel dug out of a succession of tiny roadside quarries, and its telephone wires dwindled to a single pair which persisted bravely but at length gave up and turned aside into the haven of a black pine-plantation ringing a whitewashed shooting-lodge. Thereafter, mounting steadily through open birch-woods and lifting shelves of bracken and junipers, Alastair Dubh had the road to himself, and the hills, austere but welcoming, drew ever closer.

For all his striding it was the bitterness and the anger, rather than this eagerness, which preoccupied the man's conscious thinking, thinking that had been turning, boring, into his mind like a screw into wood, deeper and deeper during the endless days of his waiting—and that had not been eased by the valedictory address of the police Inspector who had released him from his cell. "And see you keep away from Loch Alish," he had been told. "You're not wanted there, either on Farinish or Inveralish. Sir Charles Marsden as well as Major Telfer won't be having you about the place. So I warn you . . . !" Not wanted—won't be having him! Telfer . . . and Marsden! Glorified tourists, summer visitors, with their money stinking of factories and Midland slums. God damn them!

So he was to keep away from Strathalish, he, Alastair Dubh MacIver, who was of Strathalish, every tree and stone and pool of it—the Southerners said so! He, who knew just where the roebuck went to drink, the golden-eagles had their eyries, where the trout lay under the rocks and the mallard nested. He, who had harvested on every holding, clipped at each sheepshearing, who knew the history and troubles of every family. *He* was to keep away. The Major-man wouldn't have him; Marsden the company director agreed—and his fine niece did her part in getting him off the premises. That was to be the way of it. That was the Englishry's wish, and the Law would see to it. Aye, so! MacIver's jaw had a forward thrust, leading the way. And the way it led was north and west, towards the watershed and the sea-lochs and Strathalish.

After perhaps seven miles of stout walking he left the last of the long braes of the Carse behind him and entered into the quiet fastnesses of the high hills, and almost at once a new emotion began to grow on him, an elation, to add to the others, but not calculated to soften them, for it was fierce, not soothing. The age-old spell of the mountains had had its way with him often enough before, but never more swiftly and more potently than this. It was strong and wild and brave, this land of rock and torrent, peak and chasm, sternly beautiful, vigorous, not softly lovely or patient or gentle. And always it had made its mark on him and his kind. Had not his forebears drawn their spirit from it, proud, independent, uncompromising, back to Roderick MacIver of Strathalish who had followed his prince into the heather, and farther back than that, a thousand years! It was a vivid country and at its most vivid on this day of early autumn, with the bracken turning to gold and the birches to palest yellow, with the junipers staining rust-red against the black of pines, and all the leagues of heather flaming into fullest bloom. From here and there quartz in naked rock dazzled the eye, and from all around, everywhere, water that rushed and leapt and fell and lay, caught and flashed and mirrored the sun, while near and far the shadows were bold and strong under the vast cloud-flecked heaven, outlining peaks and ridges range upon range to seeming infinity. It was a gallant fighting country, and Alastair MacIver was of fighting stock.

Such elation, wedded to the hard core of his resentment, could bring forth only stormy offspring. It did, too, as the man followed his dwindling road, only a track now, through the afternoon.

It was early evening before his climbing brought him out on to the great watershed, the vast area of high mosses where the rivers were born. Up here the colours were more sombre and the shadows less sharp but more prevalent, deeper, and growing. About him the heather flowed in endless waves, pitted by the black patches of the peat-hags and the steely surfaces of the countless pools and lochans, and on every hand stone showed greyly, outcrop and boulder and gravel. No sound of water broke this place's silence, womb of waters though it was, but only the thin whisper of wind amongst the heather stems and the lonely calling of curlew.

Alastair Dubh walked into the eye of the sinking sun, but his frown was at more than the sun's level dazzling. The projects and plans that his mind turned over may not all have been the progeny of the new-found resolution that the hills had put on him, but it added decision to them and crystallized them. His mind had been busy in the cell also, too busy, but it had taken the challenge, the twin challenge, of the Inspector's warning and the hill's virility, to define and shape and clarify thoughts and urgings into plans. And if his thinking brought an occasional twitch of a grin to the corners of his mouth as well as the glowering and frowning, it did not necessarily indicate any softening in his purpose.

On reaching the wide expanse of the watershed his track had split into a multitude of paths, sheep and deer paths, branching like the veins of a leaf, but the man had held to one surely, exactly similar to all the others as it had appeared, and circuitous as its course proved, amongst the bogs and peat pools and tussocks. And when, in the centre of it all, this path, too, faltered, MacIver did not, but pushed on unhesitant, not straight—since that would have been folly in that terrain—but obviously with a definite line in view. So he went, while the sun sank behind the westernmost peaks, and the afterglow filled the sky with opal and saffron barred with orange, and all that great basin of the hills with violet gloom, a small and lonely figure in a vast waste, but determined in his smallness.

The soft Highland night was almost upon him before he won out of the hags and hummocks and ghostly pools of the watershed, and over its lip by a gap, pass-like, in the long crest of a hog-backed scarp. Pausing, deep-breathing, amongst the boulders in the summit of the gap, he stood and looked out and down, and praised his God for what he saw. Beneath a sky of deepest cobalt above him fading through dove-grey to sheerest colourlessness, emptiness, the mountains rose out of the dark mysteries of their valleys, ridge after ridge, in every shade and half-shade of blue and purple, remote and outwith all measure of distance, preoccupied with the night, and beyond them, visible in two V-shaped glimpses, was the burnished pewter of the western sea. The man stood a full minute in the stark beauty of it, watching, and then he nodded twice, as if in confirmation, and slipped quietly down into the soft obscurity of the valley.

At what time in that timeless night Alastair MacIver emerged out of all those winding glens between the silent watchful hills into the sleeping strath of Alish, is not to be known nor has it any significance. He was tired, but not distressfully so; indeed, for the last hour he had as good as slept on his feet, walking companionably by a murmuring burn that had talked sooth-ingly to him from its pebbly bed and lulled him into somnolence with its ageless, endless story. So that though he had covered since noon all of thirty-six miles of as rough going as any in these islands, his mind was in greater quiet as he stood above the spreading inky stain that was the loch, than it had been for many days.

Skirting a black wood out of which an owl hooted twice, he slanted through some sloping pasture where mountainous ani-mals heaved themselves up from beneath his very feet and lumbered away in ponderous fright, and across a field crisp under foot and dotted with obstructions which turned out to be corn-stooks. So Alan Forbes had cut his oats—the first time Alastair MacIver had not been there to lend him a hand.

Slipping round the looming bulk of the steading of Lagganlia he made light-footed for the back-door and the dairy-cum-larder-cum-store that adjoined the kitchen there, and his quick authoritative word stilled the growl that rumbled in the throat of the young collie sleeping in the passage. Inside, he tiptoed to the shelves, and with lighted match selected what he wanted; some scones which he stuffed into his pockets, a large hunk of dripping cut out of a basin with his penknife, a few handfuls of oatmeal wrapped in newspaper, and some tea. From a large bowl he drank deeply of creamy milk, and munched two or three more scones. Also he found the remains of some rabbit-pie which he ate rapidly—for he had a hunger commensurate with his great walking. In place of all this he left only a single bracken frond tied into a knot, that he had brought in with him. Martha would know.

Patting the watchful dog, he left that treasury and made his heedful way out and across the stubble again, pausing in its midst to glance back at the uncertain outline of the house below, thoughtfully. Then, feeling his way along the dry-stone wall of the field, he found what he wanted, a broad flat stone projecting from the rest to form a stile, giving on to a little path that led steeply down through the birches to the haugh of the Allt Liath, the same murmurous stream that he had listened to earlier. There, he quickly knew that his surmise had been correct; a towering shape over to his right turned out to be his garron, and with a few swift steps he was at the door of his tent, lean-to against a frame of birch boughs. Bending, quickly, his hand was about the cold muzzle of his dog, and only the faintest smothered yelp of excited greeting escaped. Stooping still, he slipped inside, to crouch on one knee over the dark pile of bedclothes, out of which...was it? Yes...out from which two eyes watched him, wide-open and unblinking. "Alastair," she breathed.

His hand smoothed her hair and he kissed her brow. "Anna, *a ghraidh*."

She did not move, there, under his hand, nor speak. Only her gaze was intense, vital, sensibly so, even in the darkness

He spoke quietly but urgently, in the soft Gaelic. "You are well, Redhead? They have not troubled you? And the Pigeon, the little one? Good, then. If they had troubled you, my God ...! Listen, now. I am going into the heather, and I will teach these people whose place this Strathalish is. Time it is that they learned what their money won't buy them. There are many things that I can do, and I will do them all. They will see who they locked up in a cell. You will stay here, and if they trouble you Alan Forbes will tell you what to do. But they will not I think, if they are wise! I will take a few things in my pack. I will take Rob—you will not need him. And I will send you messages—I may come and see you sometimes. You will be all right, my dear,

36

never fear."

He stroked her hair, as her hands came up to grip his collar, to touch his cheek. And still her habit of silence persisted. Was it a cloak, a shield, or a weapon, in that woman?

Alastair went on, but he had moved slightly and his eyes were darting about the gloom of the tent questingly. "I have taken a few things that I will be needing from Lagganlia. I will take my little rifle and shells, and the glass and my knife, and matches.... I will carry them in my pack."

"Over there, in the corner," she directed, her voice a whisper. "Alastair, you will take care? You will not let them catch you again? You will not be foolish . . . ?"

"I will not then, my sorrow," he answered. He was already gathering together the things that he wanted, bent on hands and knees. "I have learned that lesson. That is why you cannot come with me. Where are the hooks, the fly-hooks? I have the lines here...." The child stirred in its bundle of blanket, and for a few moments he was all hushing elaborate caution. The woman smiled her own fleeting smile. Presently he was finished, the old canvas pack found and the odds and ends bundled in. He returned to the woman, where she lay. "Lie still now, woman dear. I will be fine and grand—and so will yourself and the small fellow. You will see."

He stooped to her again, and the girl rose on her elbows, her hands on his shoulders, and her eyes searched his in the dusk, and whatever those eyes said, her lips did not question the wisdom of what he did. So they stayed for a moment, silent, and the only sound in all the night was the gurgle of the stream nearby and the thump of the dog's tail at the tent-door. "Alai," she breathed at last, "you will do what is in your mind, and I will be there when you need me, always. But you will have a care, a little care . . . won't you?" At his nod, her fingers gripped tightly, and then she thrust him from her strongly. "Go, then—go you with God."

Outside, he straightened up, slung his rifle and his pack, and patted his bulging pockets. Then, with a word that brought the anxious-eyed dog joyfully to his heel, he raised a hand in salute, grave-faced, and turned away quickly, upstream, whence he had so lately come.

Only the paling stars watched him climb back into the heather, his heather. Alastair Dubh was home again.

V

MAJOR JEFFREY TELFER sat down at the side of the track, and lit a cigarette. Far below him, on a track winding up over the shelving moor to join his own, quite a cavalcade was climbing, fully a score of slowly mounting figures, and a large concourse to be seen in that country. He eyed their approach with satisfaction; it was not the first time that he had played host to Marsden, but on the other occasions there had been no such scintillating house-party as this for Sir Charles to bring with him. He'd got the Duke of Merton himself, for once, and the Cabinet Minister fellow, and a brace of lords as well as sundry other notabilities. Marsden certainly did things in a big way—easy enough, of course, when you were a millionaire, or as near as dammit. All the same, it was a pretty impressive party . . . and it would make a very pretty paragraph in the right newspapers. "Shooting over his moors at Farinish, Ross-shire, Major Jeffrey Telfer and party, including the Duke of Merton, the Rt. Hon. Sir John Clark, Dominions Secretary, Lord Millwall, etc., etc., bagged so many brace. . . ." Major Telfer, as has been indicated, was only in his second season as a Highland proprietor, and was concerned to build on sound foundations. He had reason, too, to feel satisfied with the sport that he could offer his guests. Though Farinish was only a small place compared with its great neighbour of Inveralish, a mere corner of barely two thousand acres clipped out of the strath, nevertheless, it had on it some of the best grouse ground in the district. It lay in rolling heather moor, set on the flanks of a wide corrie that ran up from a great terrace perhaps three hundred feet above the loch, deep into the side of the hill rampart that enclosed the strath, a fine sheltered place, draining itself excellently and with a good undergrowth of blaeberries and cranberries below the heather-stems. The birds were there all right. And the weather was right, too—not wet, like it had been for so long, but not too sunny and hot, fetching out those accursed flies. And he had organized everything as it should be—he had rather a flair for organization, he knew—the beaters were all in position, the butts numbered and allotted, and gillies to them, hampers prepared, and the whole day planned. Well could he look down, satisfied, at the oncoming column of sportsmen.

Sir Charles's party had come up the floor of the valley or corrie—since, tailing away as a wedge eventually, into the great hillside, it was no valley—in three half-track shooting-brakes, Marsden-style. The Major wouldn't mind owning a couple of them himself. These they had left down near the burn-side and about half of the way up the corrie's length. The beaters were still farther up, right at the head, and the drive would be back towards the strath and the loch, in two bounds. That would take till lunchtime, and in the afternoon they would shoot the other side of the hill, lower ground, requiring less energy.

Telfer, a slight dapper figure, even in tweed plus-fours, rose up to meet his guests, backed by his other guns, his brother and another military gentleman, stolid-seeming and named Scobie. Sir Charles Marsden, a large man of ample girth, as befitted a great industrialist, could do little by way of introducing his illustrious but breathless company. A few names gasped out, in the midst of spasmodic comments on the steepness of the path, the warmth of the day, and his advancing years, had to suffice. An impressive tower of a man in vigorous checks seemed to be Sammy, the Cabinet Minister could be recognized from photographs and the wart, and a depressed-looking individual towards the rear appeared to be the duke. There were two or three women as well, tall and angular and loud-voiced, the one looking very like another. A little way behind, a group of silent mask-faced men, underkeepers and loaders and so on, completed the party.

After a short pause for the newcomers to recover their wind, during which Major Telfer ran over the day's programme and dispositions, a move was made towards the butts. These were quite nearby, a line of well-made turf-built breastworks, shoulder-high and stretching right across the moor from top to bottom, at, roughly, two-hundred-yard intervals. In these he placed his guests, singly and in pairs, with loaders apportioned to those who wanted them, and then, toiling back up to the high ground, he chose an eminence, and climbing it, blew on a whistle loud and long, and waved his hat back and forth. He was rewarded in a minute or so by an answering whistle and wave from the head of the corrie. All was ready.

It was not long before the shouts and halloos of the beaters, nearly a mile away, came faintly down to the waiting guns, an exhilarating sound. Men flicked open the breeches of their weapons and popped in cartridges, shutting them with a satisfying click. One or two practice throws to the shoulder gave added confidence, ensured that the limits of the butt were appreciated, and looked well, into the bargain. Loaders, quite unnecessarily, were given last-minute instructions, and spare guns moved from where they were to somewhere else. The birds would be over any time now.

One or two had indeed come over, sailing fast and true on down-bent wings, and an odd shot or so had saluted them along the line of the butts, when Major Telfer first noticed the blue haze in front. At first he thought that it was an untimely wreath of mist, left over from the night, the more so as it seemed to rise from out of one of the little ravines that scored the face of that sloping moor. But a few minutes sufficed to banish that theory. It was smoke, coiling, drifting smoke, and, moreover, it was thickening and spreading. Telfer stared, dumbfounded. It had started up half-left of the topmost butts, about four-hundred yards out, and exactly to windward. Now it was running farther down the lip of the ravine, and the breeze was beginning to blow it across, all along the line of the butts. The acrid tang of it was in his nostrils now. Good God, this might spoil the drive . . . ! He looked about him anxiously. His keeper was forward, superintending the beaters. Should he send word down the line to stop all shooting, and go forward with a party to stamp out the fire? But would there be time? The birds would be coming over in numbers any moment . . . it would be a tragedy to miss the best of the drive. He waited, his fingers beating an impatient tattoo on the stock of his gun.

From the next butt Lord Millwall hailed him. "Something on fire, Telfer," he pointed out helpfully. "Bit late for heather-burning. No aid to marksmanship, what!"

He spoke truer than he knew, for in a little while what had been only a film of smoke had grown and swollen and darkened into billowing murky clouds that bore down on the waiting guns on the morning wind, enveloping them in its drifting gloom, setting eyes streaming, noses sneezing, and cutting down visibility to fluctuating yards. Heather and blaeberries burn smokily. Confusion reigned. Eyes smarting, and coughing and swearing by turns, Major Telfer stamped forth to consult with Sir Charles. Humiliation.

Most of the guns had left their butts and were stumbling about waving arms and hats before their faces in a vain attempt to clear the air. Some, more sensibly, had not been long in following their loaders' and gillies' example in tying handkerchiefs, damped if possible with whatever came to hand, over nose and mouth. None were attempting to shoot at grouse, which was wise—anyway, few if any birds were now coming over. They were swinging away downhill and across the valley, rather than enter the barrier of smoke, being sensible creatures. The Major found Marsden amongst a bewildered and red-eyed huddle of his guests. His apologies, his imprecations, and his wonderings, were inextricably mixed, and for such a notable organizer he was distressingly uncertain what to do next. Sir Charles, at least, had no doubts about that. "Let's get to hell out of this confounded smoke, for a start," he cried, and led the way back and downward. It was some little time before the depressed individual in the rear—still the duke, actually—could get his suggestion considered that it might be wiser to go uphill rather than down, which, after all, was the way that the smoke, blown by the wind, was rolling. It was a short-breathed, short-tempered company that eventually won out of the path of the billowing pungent smoke-clouds, up on to the higher ground near where they only recently had foregathered. And even there, ruffled brows were hardly smoothed when the Cabinet

Minister, laying his gun down, blew away a swathe of heather and grit, as well, nearly at his host's foot into the bargain, as a result of having omitted to unload or apply the safety-catch, in the excitement.

Heavily they turned to stare down at the conflagration. Already, fanned by the breeze, the creeping tongues of flame had reached out perhaps thirty yards from their apparent genesis at the lip of the ravine, leaving a black belt of charred and smoking desolation behind. It was not entirely an even belt, seeming to have started in patches. The lower-most patch, indeed, was not connected with the rest at all. The Major was remarking on this when David Kennedy, his keeper, arrived, an affronted man, having halted his beaters and come to reconnoitre. "My God," he cried, "isn't this a fair scandal! Was it a picnic you were having, or what? To be lighting wee fires out in front o' the butts just afore a drive . . . !" Hopelessly he shook his grizzled head. "Eh, sir, it's right ridiculous."

Telfer stared. "Good Lord, man, you don't think *we'd* anything to do with this! We were just starting the shoot when it happened. What's the meaning of it?"

The Highlandman turned to look back at the source of the trouble. "None o' you was out there lighting ceegarettes and sich-like?" he demanded suspiciously.

"Don't be a bloody fool," his employer said irritably. "Nobody's been near there . . . unless some of your dam' beaters . . . ?"

"The beaters has been under my own eye the whole o' the morning, Major Telfer," Kennedy stated frostily. "There's no blaming the beaters."

"Then who *is* to blame? You don't suggest that it was spontaneous combustion, do you?" Telfer was sarcastic.

"I couldna' say, sir—but it was all by way of happening two-three hundred yards in the front o' you gentlemen. It's a wunner none o' you was after seeing anything, at all!"

At this Parthian shot there was a brief silence, while everyone concentrated on the smoke.

"Well, there's no use standing here," the Major said, at length. "We'll have to get that fire put out. You'd better get your

43

beaters on to that right away, Kennedy."

"Och, you can just leave it, sir. If a fire there'd got to be, it was in as good a place as any. It'll burn itself out in half an hour. Yon strip just in front o't was burned at the moor-burn in March. It'll die out when it reaches there, see you, and no harm done."

"Except that it has ruined the day's sport!"

"Och, not the whole day. There's still the afternoon, whatever. We'll away round the other side o' the hill, sir, after you've a' had your bit lunch, and we'll have a crack at the braes yonder. There's plenty birds there to give you a grand bag yet . . . if you'll be after using your guns right, gentlemen!" and his glance just flickered over the Cabinet Minister and down to his gun lying in the heather. He had a remarkably keen eye, had David Kennedy, and the tongue that went with it, into the bargain.

"Right, Kennedy," Major Telfer nodded. "We'll start the afternoon's programme half an hour earlier than was arranged." He turned to his guests. "We'll go down to have lunch, now, and later we'll make up for this, er, unfortunate mishap. Follow me, please."

Unfortunately, circumstances over which Major Telfer had no control, prevented him from making up for the forenoon's mishap as adequately as he would have liked, indeed, from making it up at all—unless the excellence of the cold lunch with which his housekeeper had treated them and surpassed herself, was to be taken as an end in itself and not just an incidental. For, as he was leading his party of guns from the shooting-brakes up through a birch-wood to the appointed place for their afternoon's battle, David Kennedy came hurrying to meet them. If he had been an affronted man at the morning's debacle, he was appalled now. Red in the face, almost with tears in his eyes, he came to them, half-running along that woodland path. "It's no use, sir—it's no use at all," he cried, broken-voiced, waving them away rather as though he was shooing off trespassing poultry. "You might as well away back and play bools, for there's devil the bird in it this afternoon, whatever. The braes yonder is just in a stour wi' sheep and dogs!"

"What!" Telfer stopped and stared, and the company behind him did likewise. "What the hell are you talking about?" That was almost a shout.

"Just what I say. The place is full of sheep, with dogs herding and chasing them, any amount o' dogs. It's like a bloody trials." The keeper took off his hat, stared at it, and then clapped it on his head again. "Och, it's a right stramash."

His employer opened his mouth, but no words came. This was too much. He gripped Kennedy's arm, and shook it violently. "Whose sheep are they?" he demanded, practically in a whisper.

"They'll be just Hughie Bell's, up from the low ground—what other?"

"Then God help Bell when I get my hands on him . . . !"

"Och, Hughie's nothing to do wi't, whatever—he's one o' the beaters up-bye. They've been gathered from a' the haughs and brackens at the foot o' the hill, and driven up through the gate into the heather, and then damnt if they havena' been split up into three-four wee flocks wi' a dog at each, and sent charging about the place setting up every bird that's got wings. Losh, it's right devilish!"

"But who's doing it—have you got the men. . . ?"

The other shook his head helplessly. "That's the queer thing—there's devil the sign o' a man anywhere. He—or they—must be there somewheres, but there's no seeing him. You could hear whistles on the dogs, early on."

"But what have you done, man? Good God. . . ."

"What is there to be done, and every bloody bird on the wing?" David Kennedy's Highland temper was well-disciplined through years of keepering, but it was not dead. "There's nothing to be done once a moor's disturbed, as well you know . . . sir." That last seemed in the nature of an afterthought.

"At least you shot the dogs, I hope?"

"Och, we couldn't do that—two o' them were Hughie Bell's own dogs; they'd been cried away from his steading. You can't be shooting the man's dogs because some blagyird's been after taking a lend o' them. But I've got the bit moor surrounded, and

45

if whoever's in it shows himself or tries to be making a run for it, the boys'll have him."

"I hope so!" the Major snapped. He kept his mouth tight too, as though controlling himself with difficulty.

At his elbow Sir Charles Marsden spoke up. "May as well call it a day, Telfer," he decided. "Can't do anything now. Looks as though there's somebody about the district that's not very fond of you, eh?"

"Ye-e-e-s. Somebody that Bell's dogs know!"

The two men's eyes met. "You think it could be . . . him?"

"Who else? He was due out of gaol two days ago, wasn't he? Wasn't it from Bell's meadow that I had him turned out—blast him! Damn it, he'll suffer for this. I'll teach him to interfere in my affairs, the low-down skulking gipsy."

"Aye, sir." David Kennedy nodded approvingly. "Just that . . . when you've catched him!"

Master and servant stared at each other for a moment, and then turned and went their several ways out of that birch-wood. The silly sound of baa-ing sheep rang flagrantly in their ears.

VI

SIMON CAMPBELL stood outside the doorway of his hotel, his arms folded across his ample front, and looked out over the darkening sea. He had just said goodnight to the last of his customers and watched them disappear along the grey mystery that was the road and the night, and already their footfalls had merged into the soft drawing sigh, regular, inevitable, and sad, sad, that was the waves breaking on the shingle. Apart from the occasional cry of a night-bird from the hillside behind, that was all the sound there was, and the peace and stillness of it, and the cool evening air, was grateful after the stuffy atmosphere of the low-ceiled bar. Most nights he came here to stand thus, before locking up, to let the burden and clamour of the day slip from him, and to listen to the great quietude that surrounded and enfolded them, whence they came and whereinto they would go. For Simon, though a busy man, was a Highlandman also.

Tonight he stood there longer than was his wont, staring out to where the nearmost of the islands was fading out behind the curtain of the dark. Perhaps his mind was more active than usual, less readily lulled by the hush of the night; certainly it had been a lively evening, with great talking and fair drinking, and the bar packed tighter than he had known it for many a day. A profitable evening it had been, by the same token, which just went to show that it was the truth that it is an ill wind that blows nobody good.

His ruminations may have had the effect of dulling his hearing, despite the quiet of the place, for when a voice spoke softly from just at his elbow, within the wooden porch, he jumped manifestly, and swung round. "What's that?"

"My own self and what else, Sim Caimbeul," came out of the shadows.

The big man gasped. "Man Alastair, where'd you spring from? I wasn't hearing you." Swiftly he glanced right and left,

47

quite unnecessarily indeed, and stepping back into the porch he took the man's arm and opened the door. "Come away inside, will you."

"I took the back door and through the house," MacIver explained, "the timid man I am."

"You are, and very well so." He led him through the empty bar and into the little private room at the back. He lit an oil lamp and drew the curtain. "We'll be fine and quiet here," he said. "You'll have a drink maybe?"

"I will so. What with one thing and another I've been a busy man this day, Simon."

"Aye, I daresay. Will you have the water in it, or splash? Just as you say, Alastair." The big man lit his pipe. "So you're not just finding the time hanging on your hands, then? No' like the beaters today."

"You're not telling me that the shoot wasn't a success?"

"Well, no' just an unqualified success, maybe. There was things got in the way, as you might say."

"Ah!"

"Aye, it was unfortunate. The toffs were right annoyed, so they tell me. Who would have thought the two nights ago when I was after telling you about the grand shoots that was to be in it, and the great folk at it, that this would have been the way o't!"

"Who, indeed," MacIver agreed. "You'd be hearing all about it, Simon, from the keepers and the beaters?"

"Aye, they've a' been here this night. It's been a grand night for the liquor—and for the talking."

"Good. Davie Kennedy would be having a thing or two to say, I'm thinking?"

"Man, you're right—you should have heard the threatenings and slaughterings that was in it. But, mind you, he was after seeing the funny side o't, too—all of the lot o' them was."

"But not the toffs, eh?"

"Not the toffs, no," Campbell confirmed. "Get off with you, dog!" This to his black Cocker that had padded through from the bar and was now sniffing interestedly at Alastair's old pack, lying on the floor at his feet. "It's an inqueesitive brute, is it no'," and he added his toe to his voice, by way of persuasion.

The dark man grinned, and stooped to undo the pack. "The Campbells aye were a long-nosed crew," he observed, and from out of a bed of bracken-fronds he drew a fish, and then another, big solid silver fish, and red where the heads and tails had been cut off. He handed them to his companion. "You could be using these, Sim?"

Beyond a couple of quick blinks the innkeeper showed no surprise. "I daresay I could, then." He took the first salmon in his two hands, balancing it. "A nice fish, man—all of twelve pounds in it, too." He laid it down on the table and took up the other, and if he noticed the jagged gash of the gaff high on the belly, he made no comment. Nor did he ask why the heads and tails were off. He was a discreet man was Simon Campbell, as befitted one of his responsibilities. "I'll take these through to the larder. They'll come in handy, no doubt. Anything you'll be needing from the store, Black Alastair?"

The other looked thoughtful. "Yes—soap, razor-blades, oatmeal, sugar . . . and matches. And throw in some fat while you're at it, will you?" He called the other back as he was closing the door. "You'll have some wire in that shop of yours, Simon?"

"Wire, is it. What kind of wire?"

"Well, brass snare wire would do well enough."

"I've no doubt but it would," the big man allowed, and escaped before his visitor could think of anything else.

Presently he was back with his packages, and MacIver took some care in stowing them away in his rucksack; he had had more than just the two salmon packed therein. "And what other news have you got for me, Sim Mhor?" he wondered.

"What news would I have, at all!" the other protested. "There's nothing happens hereabouts . . . except maybe a heather-fire, or Hughie Bell's sheep straying!"

"And future sporting events, man?"

"Och, how should I know. I'm not a gamekeeper."

"But the keepers come here, and they talk. It's here they collect their gillies, often as not. Come on, Sim—out with it."

"Well," Campbell's show of reluctance was not so very

convincing. "Donald Shaw was here tonight, head-stalker on Inveralish. He's not often about the place. He was after having his flask filled up."

"Ah!"

The big man nodded. "When I saw that, I reckoned he'd be for the hill, so I, h'm, I made enquiries. It's Friday, the morn's morn, and he's going out with one of the lords, not Sir Charles himself, and they're expecting to kill in the corries of Beinn Gaoith. He's hoping to make a good day o't—there's a beast with a rare head in it, up there, he was saying.'

"There is." Alastair nodded briefly. "Friday, eh? Anything more, Simon?"

"Not a thing. Will you have a droppie more? I had Anna in the shop yesterday . . ."

His glass empty, pointing out that he had other calls to make that night, the dark man did not delay long, nor did the innkeeper seek to detain him. At the back-door, a slight movement amongst the shadows revealed where Rob, his half-bred collie, lay waiting for his master. Shouldering his pack, MacIver held out his hand. "Goodnight, Sim Caimbeul. Thank you."

"Goodnight, Alastair Dubh. God bless the work."

Dog at heel, MacIver made his quiet way back over the coast-wise braes and down through the sleeping woodlands, by paths of his own and no-paths, till the sound of rushing water brought him to the rocky banks of the Allt Buie. It was dark there in the valley; it was a darker night indeed than was usual in that northern land, with heavy clouds obscuring a sky that the pale memory of the day never really forsook, but the man seemed to know his way instinctively, never hesitating over which branch of a many-forked path to follow, even when distinguishing any path at all called for the exercise of faith rather than sight; nor yet when to leave an erratic path altogether when it failed to take him just where he would go. And he disturbed nothing of the quiet of it all in his going.

He crossed the stream by a narrow fragile-seeming suspension-bridge of wood and wire that swayed ominously and drew the faintest whimper of reluctance from the otherwise silent dog stepping uneasily behind him. Then a few hundred yards on a fair path that led up out of the trough of the river, and he was at the intermittent fencing and looming mass of the Balnacraig back-premises. No gleam of light showed from house or steading, and, signing to his dog to lie still, he crept forward silently. There was no need to wake anybody up, at this time of night. It was not the first quiet visit he had paid to Balnacraig that day, anyway. Softly he made for the rough wooden porch at the back door, where a couple of cats made quiet welcoming noises and jumped down to rub round his ankles. From the other side of the door a low rumble of a growl began, to stop at the man's urgent whisper. "Hiss, quiet—Luath—Roy!" Then carefully clearing a space, his fingers feeling their way like antennae, on the topmost of the many shelves of that place, he drew another small salmon out of his pack, headless and tailless like the others, and placed it there. He was searching for such covers as he could find to be adequate against the attentions of cats and the like, when his hand came across the stiff canvas of Hughie Bell's gamebag, hanging from its nail. Into this he popped the fish, buckled it up, and, tying a frond of bracken in a knot round the sling, he hung it from the door-handle. Then, turning about, he left that place as silently as he had come, picked up the patient Rob where he had left him, and set off again on his walking.

Still he was not finished with his calls that night. Through all the dim uncertainty of the juniper glades, the bracken slopes, and the birch-woods, he picked his way, parallel with the loch-shore but high above it, a persistent flitting shadow, seeming to be possessed of purpose rather than substance. Numberless small burns he crossed, a tall deer-fence he climbed, helping the dog over first, and presently the pitch black of a pine plantation rose before him. Through its murky thickets he edged and sidled his way cautiously. It was only a belt, and before long he was out and his boots crunching on gravel. This he crossed—a fifteen-foot carriageway—and turned to follow up the grass verge on the far side. Soon the vague expanse of a large whitewashed house glimmered palely before him. Alastair MacIver had reached his last place of call.

It was fully an hour after midnight, and here too no light was visible in all the range of building. Leaving the long-suffering Rob, where the drive expanded to a broad sweep in front of the house, he tiptoed across the gravel, utilizing a flower-bed in the centre as he went. At the wide steps that mounted to the pillared portico of the front door, the man stopped, off-slung his pack and took out more fish. But this time it was the missing heads and tails that he produced, four sets of them, large and sticky, and placed them carefully in a row on the topmost step. It was the work only of a minute. Retiring, over beyond the gravel, he looked back for a moment, and saluted the great shadowy house ironically. It was all as it should be. Those were Sir Charles Marsden's salmon, taken out of the rivers that Sir Charles had bought and paid for. And there they were on Sir Charles's doorstep, for it was Inveralish Lodge.

Satisfied, the man turned again, and slipped back into the empty hills.

VII

ALAN FORBES had visitors again. They came in a large sleek open car, black and gleaming, now parked unsuitably amongst the inquisitive livestock of the Lagganlia steading. It was not a social call, obviously—the composition of the party indicated that—and Forbes made no attempt to usher them into his house. Now they stood in a group at the open door of the smiddy and stared into the middle distance, drew designs in the pebble gravelling with walking-sticks or concentrated on the suddenly furiously busy Willie Maclay, severally as they would. There were four of them, Sir Charles Marsden and his head-keeper John Robertson, and Major Telfer with David Kennedy.

It was Marsden that was doing the talking. The weather and the lateness of the harvest he had got over briskly, and now he was getting down to business. "I understand that the tinker Ross or MacIver or whatever his name is, is something of a friend of yours, Forbes?" He did not believe in beating about the bush in dealing with his tenants.

The Highland man, a head taller than the other, stoop and all, nodded easily. "Alastair Dubh MacIver," he said. "That is so."

"You've been in the habit of seeing a good lot of him?"

"I as good as brought him up, the lad."

"Indeed! And when did you last see him, Forbes?"

The older man turned his pale eyes full on the other, consideringly, and if no anger was discernable behind them, at least there was regret that manners should be so ignored that such a question should be asked. "I have said that he is my friend, sir," he reminded.

"And he appears to have constituted himself my enemy! When did he last visit you here, please?"

Carefully Alan Forbes made his reply. "I have not seen Alastair MacIver for some time, for quite some time."

Marsden's eyes narrowed. "How long?" he demanded. He

53

was not a great industrialist for nothing.

His tenant shrugged ever so slightly and lifted up his voice. "Willie," he called, "when would it be since Black Alastair came to see us? More than a month's in it, eh? Damn't, wasn't it the day that they were after dragging him off to the gaol?"

"My God, it was!" Willie roared. Willie Maclay usually roared. "That was just the day, whatever."

Sir Charles coughed, and frowned. "I'm afraid that I have a pretty shrewd idea that he has been here since then. I would remind you, Forbes, that it is hardly in your own interests to run counter to *my* interests in this matter."

"I can well believe it, sir. Is Alastair back in the district then, think you?" That was politely said.

The stout man's snort was eloquent. "In the district! Who d'you think wrecked Major Telfer's grouse drive? Who poached my salmon and left the heads on my doorstep? And who ruined Lord Millwall's stalking yesterday, absolutely ruined it, and then had the damned confounded insolence to dump the head of the best stag in my forest—a royal, mind you—at my front door during the night, with a blasted haunch into the bargain? By Heavens . . . !"

"D'you tell me that!" Alan's astonishment was striking. "Goodness preserve us, what a scandal! You're not telling me that the one gipsy-lad was after doing all that? Sounds more like a regiment to me. Have you seen him at it, the boy?"

The other ignored that. "He is asking for trouble in a big way, and he's going to get it. He may have some more of his tinkers helping him—I don't know. But he's a fool if he thinks that he's going to get away with this."

"By God, he is!" That was Major Telfer, stabbing his stick into the ground. "Anyone who interferes with an Englishman's sport is heading for disaster."

"So damned un-British."

"That's it—quite outside the pale."

Marsden became businesslike again. "His woman's here, living on your ground, Forbes. We've just been to see her. You're not going to pretend that you didn't know that *she* was there, are you?"

"I wouldn't do that. Why, Anna comes here for her milk and the like. Always they have camped in my haugh there. And she is not his woman, see you, sir. She is his brother Ewan's wife, and he has been taking care of her, and her husband not able."

"Well, whatever the relationship, the woman is there," the other shrugged. "He visits her, no doubt?"

"You will have asked herself that, sir—and it her own business?"

Sir Charles looked at the tall frail man that was his tenant thoughtfully. That his answers were unhelpful, obstructionist, verging on the insolent, was only too evident, yet the fellow's manner, civil, polite even, made it difficult to deal with him as the situation required. It was ridiculous the way these people, uneducated peasants, crofters, mere farm-hands and occasional-workers, adopted airs and graces and a veneer of manners, with an attitude of equality with their betters. Damn it all, none of his foremen, his managers, his heads of departments even, would speak to him with the easy assurance of these ragged Highland gillies with their confounded carefully-correct English. Sir Charles's own English was still not quite innocent of the broad vowels of the North Midlands.

"The point is, Forbes," he said abruptly, grimly, "the man must be caught, and the sooner he is taken the better for all concerned. I expect the assistance of all my employees and tenants. We don't want to bring in the police if we can help it, as you will appreciate."

"Indeed I do, sir." There was no trace of a smile to be seen on Alan Forbes's face, there, sharply as Marsden looked for one.

"H'rrrrm. Well, what about it, Forbes?"

Alan looked from one to the other of his visitants, from the impatient-seeming Telfer to the two rather pointedly disinterested keepers and to his determined proprietor. "And just what is it that you're expecting me to do, Sir Charles?" he wondered, speaking slowly.

Marsden had the grace to sound just a little uncomfortable, though as determined as ever. "I'd like to hear your ideas of where the fellow is hanging out." He coughed. "You under-stand that the longer he is at large, the more damage he is likely to do, and the worse it will be for him in the end. Any friend of the man's must see that. Where d'you think he's hiding out—it can't be very far away?"

The older man remained strictly civil. "Your keepers, I would have thought, you'd have asked that."

The two gamekeepers shifted their stances, and the points on the surrounding hilltops that they were examining.

"Your information might be rather more, er, definite than theirs, I think."

The two men's eyes met. "The pity, and me with no informa-tion to give you . . . sir."

In the silence that followed, the scraping of Major Telfer's busy walking-stick and the clink of Willie Maclay's hammer were very evident. Maybe Maclay was not so simple as he appeared, for he straightened up, and into the quiet he cried. "Losh, he's a lad is Black Alastair! And sly. Man, he'll be living in your own backyard, like as not . . . or on a bit island in the loch . . . or on top o' Gaoth. What a borach! You'll never catch yon one in a snare. I mind when he was a small bit of a boy. . . ."

"Quite," Marsden said. He turned back to Forbes, and if he felt just a shade of gratitude for the interruption, his voice did not reveal it. "Another thing," he went on quickly, "the fellow must be getting supplies—provisions and so on—from some-where. It would not surprise me at all if he got some of them from here. That must cease immediately. Do you understand?"

Alan Forbes opened his mouth, shut it again, and took a deep breath. He concentrated his gaze on the top of a larch tree above Marsden's head, and he spoke slowly and distinctly. "Sir," he said, "I am an old and done man and a quiet man and peaceable, and this is my house as it was my father's and his father's . . . though the property is now yours. I would not like to be saying anything, with yourself at my door, that was not suitable or that I might be regretting later. What you have said I have heard, and I will not forget it. That being the way of it, I think, sir, it would be best if you were to go now." And his long arm rose almost wearily, and the emaciated hand that pointed past the car and down the road shook noticeably.

It was the other's turn to open his mouth. He closed it again, almost with a snap. "Very good," he jerked, and turned about abruptly and strode across the gravel. Silently the others followed. With no waste of time and much banging of doors and revving up of engine, the big car swung round, crashed into reverse, and then roared off down the narrow road. Alan Forbes stalked straight into his steading and commenced to fork hay into a shed, vigorously.

Martha Forbes picked her way through the yellowing birches and brackens, down the little path that led to the Allt Liath, chuckling through its green haugh. She walked quickly, and she frowned as she went, an urgent lissome figure that would have blended effectively, but for her urgency, into the dappled sunshine and golden-brown of the autumn woods, with her high-necked fawn jumper and the rust-coloured crotal of her homespun skirt. Her frown was of the pensive considering variety, but, nearing her destination, at a corner of the green meadow-land by the waterside, its quality changed suddenly, as she stared and faltered in her step, changed to something more positive, angry. She had sharp eyes, had Martha, and once she had seen the large boots projecting, she had no difficulty in tracing the outline of the man hiding behind the fallen birch tree and the gathered bracken fronds. A few steps farther, and she recognized the man too, though his back was turned to her. It was one of Marsden's underkeepers, a small wizened man from the Lowlands, Rennie by name, and unmistakable. Her first impulse was to climb up to him and demand his business there, but a moment's reflection changed her mind. Without further glance at the hiding watcher, she proceeded on her way.

Anna MacIver was sitting at the door of her dark tent painting a new basket. Behind her, in a wicker cradle, the child slept quietly. Nearby, the black-maned garron cropped the grass with a rhythmic monotony in time with the steady long swish of its tail's unending contest with the flies. It was a peaceful scene, not lost on Martha as she approached the little encampment, and she knew deep regret to add to her other emotions.

The gipsy girl looked up but did not move nor speak. Passivity that was outward and physical rather than mental, clothed that young woman like an uneasy garment, a hair-shirt assumed for some woman's reason of her own, and tight-clutched now, lest without it she were naked. But there was no hostility in her strangely-beautiful green eyes as she watched the other's approach.

Martha carried one of the gipsy's own baskets. "I have brought you your eggs, Anna," she smiled. "The apples are from Willie. I'll put them in the box, there." She came round and stood in front of the other girl. "Anna," she said troubledly, "you'll have to leave here, I think."

The other's eyes widened and then went cold, cold as only green eyes can, but when she spoke, her voice was quiet and calm as ever. "That is the laird's wishes, then?"

Slowly her companion shook her head. "No, it is not, I think, Anna. I'm thinking he would rather that you stopped here. Did you know that you were being watched?" The gipsy's lifted brows showed that she did not. "Well, you are, then. Peter Rennie, the keeper, is hiding behind a tree back yonder, watching you."

Anna's expression changed swiftly. "Alastair. . . ?" she breathed.

"Yes. They guess that he visits you. They want to trap him. That is why I say you should go, right away from here, out of the district altogether."

The other said nothing.

"He must not risk coming," Martha went on. "The laird and that man Telfer—they're desperate to catch him. They'll do anything. You should have heard them at my father—as though he'd be giving him away. . . . They were at you, too, I hear." She looked at the other girl thoughtfully. "Alastair will have to be warned. Have you any idea just where he'll be hiding?"

Anna MacIver seemed to consider that at some length. "If he's to be warned, I can warn him," she said at length.

"And them watching you . . . and you with the baby?" Martha wondered. She shook her brown head. "It wouldn't do, Anna, at all."

The gipsy stared at her basket, her glance hooded.

The girl at her side stooped suddenly, and her hand went out impulsively to touch the other's. "Anna, word must be got to him, and quickly, or he may come here soon, tonight, and walk into their trap. I know you would want to do it yourself, but you cannot do it safely—you must see that? But there's others of us are Alastair's friends. . . . Do you know when he was likely to be visiting you next?"

"Alastair does not tell when he comes or goes. He is like the *earba*, the roe-deer, a shadow." Anna smiled a tiny secretive smile. "He is here, and then he is gone. They will not catch that one."

"But they might, if he was walking into their trap. They have guns, those keepers, and they might well be using them, with the laird and Telfer and the like behind them, and Alastair new out of gaol." Martha's lifting bosom testified to an agitation in marked contrast to the tinker girl's uncanny calm. "Where is he to be found, Anna?"

"He has not told me. He does not say where he hides." She paused, and the piece of willow wand that she was holding cracked in her fingers, twice. Perhaps she was not so calm, after all. "But I know where he is. . . . I think." She threw the broken pieces of stick from her, in a gesture that was final somehow, and strangely eloquent. "I have said it already. . . . he is like the roe, *earba*. Where would he go but to Am Fasach?"

"Am Fasach!" Martha Forbes stared, and her hand went up to her throat, tell-tale hand. Hers was a frank nature, though far from simple—if any woman's nature could be called simple. But Am Fasach, Am Fasach nan Earba in full; literally the Wilderness of the Roe, that unchancy place, bogeyland of her childhood! "He wouldn't stop in there!"

"Why not. Where better?"

"It is a long way, too. . . ."

"Not to Alastair. He has long legs."

Her companion pondered. It could be . . . and Alastair in it. If anyone knew the place, he did. If anyone could make use of it, defy the ill of it, he could. And distance had never meant anything to Alastair. It could be. . . . "Thank you, Anna," she said, at last. "I am grateful. It is a bad business, altogether. These men . . . !" She sighed. "Is there any message for him?"

The other girl sounded weary. "You can tell him that I have gone to the Munros at Corriemore; he will know. Tomorrow, I will go."

"You will be all right alone, Anna? Willie could help . . . ?"

"I will be all right." And suddenly, without warning, she whipped round, eyes blazing. "But I will come back," she cried fiercely.

Martha Forbes nodded gravely. "He will know that, too," she agreed, and took up her empty basket.

VIII

THE girl saw the long twisting weal of the glen before her with relief. Once in its deep shelter she could relax, straighten her shoulders and walk upright, her own woman again—though somewhere at the back of her mind she knew even now that all the recent stooping and head-bending had been really quite unnecessary, mere ostrich-like surrender to the fallacy that where one does not see, one is unlikely to be seen, so universal with all beginners in the art of stalking, and productive only of cricked muscles and a false sense of invisibility. But the instinct had been strong and her concentration fully engaged on covering the roughest country that she could find as inconspicuously as might be, in the shortest possible time. For hours, it seemed, she had been dodging and crouching and scuttling amongst hummocks and outcrops and peat-hags, creeping down burn-channels, seeking to make the heather swallow her. At the outset, leaving Lagganlia, to avoid suspicion Martha had taken her bicycle and pedalled along the loch-road towards Kinlochalish, shopping-basket prominent on her lamp-bracket. But beyond Farinish, where the birch-woods came down across the road to the very waterside, she had left the cycle hidden, and struck up through the trees, up and up till she had come out on the open hillside, high above the loch, with the lodge of Farinish and the croft of Balnacraig like tiny toy-houses below her. Bearing right, then, she presently had found a watercourse to provide her with an erratic stepladder and some degree of cover right up to the summit of the ridge that was the northern wall of the strath. Once over the crest it had been easier, with the climbing over and less fear of observation, but still she had to be careful for now she was nearing the best deer ground on Inveralish Forest, and an odd stalker or keeper with his inevitable telescope and eye for movement on the hill, could ruin everything. So she had zig-zagged warily down the long slant of that shelving hillside, feeling in the glare of the afternoon sun like a fly on a vast sloping windowpane, and the great hills had looked down at her from every hand, as though alive with eyes. Now, at the foot, the narrow glen of the Allt Luinn offered her shadow and a covered route, the longed-for impersonality. Perhaps her detour and precautions had been over-elaborate, but this was an errand on which Martha Forbes preferred to take no risks.

Down in the cool green floor of the little valley, beside the shouting amber stream, the going was easier and progress faster—as well, too, with her watch reading four-thirty and her not much more than halfway to Am Fasach, and Alastair still to find at the end of it. If she was to get back before dark. . . . It was a long glen, with the sides of it so steep as to block out all but occasional glimpses of the great hills through which it ran, and already the afternoon sun failed to penetrate to its floor. It was narrow, too, and there was not much room in the floor of it for more than the boisterous stream with its boulder-margins and the precarious sheep-track that kept it company, now high, now low, but always persistent. Along this path Martha hastened, limber, eager, picking her way amongst the rocks, leaping the multitude of the tiny burnlets draining from the scarp above, flitting light-foot over the green uncertainty of bog, an adequately-made young woman with limbs as useful as they were decorative.

Perhaps a couple of miles from where she first joined it, with the glen trending rather sharply north-westwards, the first changes in the land-formation began to become evident. The high walls drew further back, the flowing slopes began to break up into folds and creases, and the valley to climb steadily, to become shallower, while its flanking escarpments crumbled with the disintegration of the moors above. And then the trees began, just an odd one here and there at first, with hundreds of yards between, crooked ancient trees, with now and again a weathered stump jagged and naked and semi-petrified. All the way up the glen there had been an occasional tree, a lonely scarlet-decked rowan springing from between the rocks, or a couple of hardy birches, stunted and lichen-grown; but these were different trees—conifers, gnarled and twisted Scots pines, relics of another era, of the days when the Caledonian Forest was a forest indeed, and the tree-level did not falter at one thousand feet.

And now the girl began to hesitate in her fine striding, in some degree, perhaps, because her childish bogeys were not yet quite dead in her, but mainly because more than mere stout walking was now required of her. Eyes and wits now rather superseded legs in their usefulness—though it could be that her equipment in the one respect was as adequate as in the other. So, presently, where it bent sharply right-handed, she left the waterside and climbed out of that valley and up on to an eminence nearby.

It was a strange vista that lay before her, strange in that it was not to be expected, in that it did not conform to the accepted pattern of all the surrounding terrain. Ahead of her, in a wide arc to north and west, the peaks and ridges had sunk and dwindled and retired, and in their place a great plateau spread itself, a lofty table-land clothed in a black mantle of these aged pines. But though at first glance it appeared to be a high but level plain smoothed out amongst the hills, further inspection revealed it to be not level but rather the reverse, a vast succession of low, rounded hillocks, identical, monotonous, rising heather-clad under the sparse canopy of the trees, wherein no one appeared to be higher or lower in any degree than its fellows. And this strange outlandish forest of ancient trees and serried knolls stretched apparently into infinity; owing to the peculiar configuration of the surrounding country, with the ground falling away gradually to east and west and lifting imperceptibly northwards into the wide desolation of the great watershed over which Alastair MacIver had picked his way on that first night of his freedom, there seemed to be no end to it. Formless, without bounds, it sprawled upon the face of the land—Am Fasach nan Earba, the Wilderness of the Roe.

Martha Forbes stared long at the still and silent spread of it, dark and inimical under the yellow flood of the westering sun. Never had she been close to the place before—indeed, only once previously had she set eyes on it at all, and that from pony-back,

63

in her early teens, and from several miles away. But its name she knew, and its fame—ill-fame—little spoken-of as it was. There were stories about Am Fasach, ancient as the hills themselves, and others not so ancient. None were kindly. It was said that there was a curse on it, that a great treachery had been wrought there in a far-off age. Men had shunned it, even when the glens and sheilings were populous with men . . . and it was told that some who had ventured therein had not come out again. There were no streams there, reputedly, no water, though the place was far from barren and the heather grew, dense and twisted, to the height almost of a man. No birches grew or rowans or hazels or other kindly trees—only the stark and sombre pines, seared and ungentle, and all of them old, old with never a sapling amongst them. The sheep avoided the place, too, which was strange, for there was better grazing there, as Highland grazing goes, than in the moorland and peat-hags around it; no other life moved in all its wastes, it was said, save only the silent shadowy roes and a myriad of flickering bats. For the rest, silence, brooding silence was its emanation and its cloak. Such, and more, was reported of Am Fasach.

Facing the prospect before her, the girl knew her confidence to be ebbing. She was a Highlandwoman, and by no means impervious to influences such as these. But apart altogether from that aspect of the matter, the sheer physical problem facing her stood revealed in all its formidability. It had been simple enough, on hearing that Alastair was using Am Fasach as his hideout, to come here to look for him; but now she had to find him, and confronted with all the spreading wastes of the place, she saw her task as well-nigh impossible. How could she hope to trace him in that vast wilderness? Even if, as was likely, he normally lurked somewhere near the fringes of it all, to search them alone might well take hours and hours. Suddenly, what with one thing and another, Martha Forbes felt very much like going home, just as quickly as possible.

But she was made of sterner stuff than that, and she stayed where she was. What should she look for—where to begin? There were no paths, nothing to indicate a likely line. If this had been a story in *The People's Friend* now, there would have been a column of smoke, at least, to guide her. . . . Ah, well, she would just have to make a start somewhere, and she could shout as she went, which might help—it would also help to keep her courage up where it should be! Should she start by going down into the glen again, or by making her way across the peat-hags? She turned speculatively to look back downhill, turned, and gasped. "Oh!" she choked, and her hand flew up to her mouth and her knees sagged and only held her up precariously.

Below her, not ten yards off, Alastair MacIver sat quietly on a grey outcrop amongst the heather, watching her. "Good afternoon, Martha *a graidh*," he said.

With the girl still staring, the man went on, smiling. "A fine day it is for a walk, and a long walk you're having, lassie." He drew his pipe out of his pocket and put it between his teeth, empty. The calm, clever, capable man he was.

"Alastair, how did you get there?" she jerked. "What a shock you gave me. Where did you come from? How long have you been there?" Like a spate her questions burst forth. Then she took herself in hand—and him. "What do you mean by creeping up on me like that, Alastair MacIver? You were just trying to frighten me. I've come all this way on your account, and then you do a thing like that."

The gipsy's teeth gleamed white in a grin. "My, oh my!" he observed mildly. "Isn't she the chatterbox . . . and her with never a one to wag her tongue at for hours and hours!"

She stamped a tentative foot, found her legs to be functioning satisfactorily again, and stamped once more. "Don't sit there being rude," she cried.

"Save us, what a wull-cat, what a randy . . . !"

Martha drew herself up. "And you can save your tinker's manners for someone else," she declared loftily. "I'm not Anna MacIver!"

"Ah, oh, um!" the man nodded to himself. "So that's it, is it." He shook his head over her sardonically. "The sad thing it is, with women." He mocked her frown. "And how is Anna, at all, then?"

"She's gone . . . away north to Corriemore," she said swiftly, and then paused, and her blue eyes meeting his, she shrugged and sighed. "At least, she's going tomorrow, and not wanting to," and her voice had altered. "It was myself asked her."

"Why?" That was sharply put.

"For your sake . . . the same as why I'm here."

"What d'you mean?"

The girl came down and sat beside him on his outcrop. "They are desperate to catch you, Stair—the laird's people and Telfer. They're waiting for you round Lagganlia, and they set a man to spy on Anna—Peter Rennie, Altfar. They know you'll visit Anna, and us, likely. So we thought it would be best for Anna to leave the district for a whilie."

"I see." The man sat silent for a little. "And she did not want to go, you were saying?"

"No . . . but I convinced her it was best for you that way." Martha Forbes's eyes were fixed on the distant blue line of the hills south of the strath. "She would have come up here to warn you herself, but watched as she is, and with the baby. . . . So I came. Anna said to say she would be back, but"—a pause— "you could go with her to the north, Alastair!"

He removed his pipe and looked at it intently. "Well, now," he said, and then, "How did you know I was here?"

"Anna told me . . . after a lot of asking. She said it would be Am Fasach."

"So you came to look for me in Am Fasach, Moireach!" His voice went deep, and his hand closed over hers for a moment.

Martha Forbes sat very still and said nothing.

"That was kind," he went on. "A long road to come, a risk to take, and little profit at the end of it."

Quickly she looked at him. "What do you mean—little profit?"

"What profit is there in putting yourself out over a tinker, a gaol-bird, a wanted man?" Abruptly he got to his feet. "Come on down," he said roughly. "The top of a hill's no place for talking."

The girl followed, her brows furrowed a little. He led down and round, and presently his "Sssss—ssss!" brought the dog Rob out of the heather, slinking to his heels. "How did you find me, Stair?" she asked.

He turned and looked back over his shoulder, and his smile broadened again. "I was watching you ever since you were after crossing the ridge yonder."

"Oh . . . !" she said, and shut up.

In a short while, twisting amongst hummocks and hollows, the trees began to thicken around them and they were in the outskirts of Am Fasach. MacIver did not penetrate further, but under a dark pine on the flank of a hillock he stopped and turned. "We can talk here," he told her.

She looked about her. "But you don't live here," she objected.

"No—but this will do us fine. It's deeper in I stay."

"Take me there, then, Alastair. I'd like to see it."

"But it is just the same as here. All this place is just the same."

"Yes, but I'd like to see where you live. I've come all this way. . . . Please, Stair."

He frowned at her. "And what woman's ploy have you got on you, Martha Forbes? There's nothing for you to start tidying up or fussing over, at all," he cried, half-angry, half-joking. "I am fine and comfortable by my own self, whatever."

But she only smiled sweetly on him. "Yes, I know," she agreed. "But I think I should know just where you stay, in case I have to be bringing you up another message or food or anything. Much better, don't you think, than to stand outside somewhere shouting?"

"God forbid that!" the man said fervently, and surrendered. "Come on, then."

So they went on, unspeaking, into that strange uncanny wilderness, and the brooding silence of it enveloped and pressed down on them like a blanket, heavy and impenetrable. Alastair had said that it was all just the same, and the truth of what he said was, in its substantiation, weird and improbable and somehow terrible. The sameness of those rounded hillocks, rising to perhaps thirty feet, each with its four or five sable trees

67

lifting out of its shaggy heather, was almost unbelievable. Round and through and between this sea of knolls they picked their way, man and dog and woman, high-stepping in the pathless heather. After perhaps ten minutes of this progress, in a direction and for a distance alike, to the girl, uncertain in the extreme, the man brought her to a mound, identical apparently to all its fellows. Halting, Martha looked about her, back to the gipsy and then to the knoll again, enquiringly. Alastair eying her, could not quite keep the pleased-schoolboy grin off his face. But still he made no move. It was the collie, Rob, that gave the show away. Ploughing through the heather, with only the white tip of its tail visible, it suddenly disappeared beneath a veteran tree. In a couple of moments its pointed foxy face was peering out whence it had gone, pink tongue lolling and ears cocked, in an expression so blatantly pleased with itself as to set the man and woman into frankest laughter.

"Fool beast!" That was Alastair, who could not be expected to know that the dog's expression was almost a replica of his own a few seconds previously, as he led the way up.

Stooping below the tree, he pulled aside a lot of loose tall heather-stems to reveal, beneath the spreading roots, a cavity dug out of the bank. Something of it, undoubtedly, was natural, but more had been excavated, to form a cave perhaps five feet wide and six feet deep and high enough for a man to kneel in without bringing a shower of sandy soil down the back of his neck. It was dry in there, and floored with heather tips, and the few necessities that made up the man's plenishings lay, reasonably neatly, in one corner: a rifle, a gaff, some lines and wire, a mug, a few tins, a billycan, and a biscuit-box. "There it is, then—all of it," Alastair gestured, with a bow.

The girl looked in, delighted. "Stair, isn't it grand!" she cried. "It's just like the ones we used to play in under the alders in the haugh. Do you remember? May I go in?"

"I wouldn't like to be stopping you, and you determined."

She bent down and slipped inside, getting her face licked by the collie as a welcome. A quick exploration, and she turned round and squatted near the entrance. The man still stood outside. She held out her hand. "Are you not coming in?"

He thrust his hands deep into his pockets. "I'm fine here, where I am," he said casually.

"Oh, don't be an idiot, Alastair MacIver!"

He started and stared at the sudden vehemence, the spark of real anger, behind her few words. He was surprised, and yet knew that he should not be; all his life he had known this girl, and yet he knew that, any time, she could surprise him. "Well, now," he said, since words were necessary, and sat down. But still he sat outside the dugout.

There was silence for a little, broken only by the dog's contented panting.

The gipsy spoke first, his eyes on the tree tops. "So they are taking it hard, the Sassenachs? They're not liking their sport interfered with, at all?"

"What would you expect?"

"Just that, indeed," he agreed complacently. "Maybe they'll be liking it less still before the finish o't, whatever."

The girl pulled a heather stalk to pieces with busy fingers. "Then you're going to go on with it, with your . . . campaign?" she wondered. "Must you, Alastair? You have been very clever. You have made proper fools of them. That grouse-drive, and the way you shot their best stag from under their noses. . . . But isn't that enough . . . ? Won't you call it off now . . . be wise as well as clever?"

"Wise!" he mocked. "Is this Moireach Forbes in it! Wisdom, is it? Always I've to be the wise man . . . and me Alastair MacIver! Don't be upsetting them too much, in case they're angry. A wee bit poaching, maybe a fish, a bird, or a haunch, but don't be offending them, at all, the great folk from the south, and them buttering our bread for us! Is that it? I've heard that before, but never from Martha Forbes!"

"You do not hear it now," she reminded him, patiently. "I would not ask you to do anything that a proud man could not do. . . ."

But the fire of his own words that he had lit was not quenched so easily. "They buy the land with their money and the people

69

with the land. All is theirs, the land and the folk, and the Law in their pocket, all for the signing of a cheque. But they have not bought the MacIvers, my God! I will show them what their money is worth, see you. I will . . ." Abruptly he stopped, took a deep breath, and fumbled for his pipe again. "I am sorry, Martha," he said quietly.

Gravely the girl looked at him. "You do not change, Alastair," she told him, and the faintest smile followed her words. "I was only saying that now you've paid them back for what they did to you, you should go away, out of the district. They'll be away south in two or three weeks, and then you could come back. They'll do anything to catch you if you stay. You've angered them, and . . . well, they must not catch you, Alastair."

The man shook his head at her, but gently. "They will not, either," he assured. Clasping his arms round his knees, he went on. "I have angered them, you say, but I'm for more than angering them, *a graidh*. I'm going to teach them something, the stiff-necked ones, and I am not going from here until I have taught them . . . or afterwards either, maybe. I must do what I must, you see."

Martha Forbes knew that when he spoke like that there was no point in arguing any more. She sat quiet for a little, and the silence of the place surrounded her and weighed down on her. Suddenly she felt tired, weary. "I must be going now, Alastair. It is time," she said, and she rose and crept out of the cave. "I have a long walk home. It will be dark before I'm back. . . ."

Lifting to his feet, he helped her in the same movement. "No hurry," he claimed. "I will see you home, lassie."

"No need. I'll be all right. It would be foolish to run any risks."

"There will be no risk in it . . . and the darker the better. So there is no hurry at all, you see."

"All right. But let's go away from here, Alastair." She glanced around and above her, and shivered, though it was not cold. "I do not like this place. It is horrible, somehow evil. I don't know how you can live here."

"Where better?" he demanded, shrugging. "You don't want

to believe all you hear."

"But it's queer—you must feel it?"

"Maybe," he admitted. "But it does me no harm. And I'm not the first MacIver that Am Fasach has sheltered." Legend had it that the MacIver of the Forty-five had found a refuge there, while the Redcoats turned a province upside-down for him.

"No—and what became of *him*!" The self-same legend rather suggested that though the Chief of MacIver thus escaped from Cumberland's dragoons, he was never known to have escaped from the grip of Am Fasach nan Earba.

Alastair's eyes flickered ever so slightly. He was a Highlandman, after all. "I am not superstitious, at all," he said, and he meant it, too. "Anyway, I don't stop in here most of the time—I'm fine outside in the open heather. This place is just a refuge, a kind of sanctuary like the stags have. They'd never catch me in here." He was stooping, replacing the heather curtain that screened his den. Almost he laughed. "I'd like to see them try."

"I dare say—I never could be finding my own way back here, myself." Her hand sought his arm, urgent to be off. "How am I to reach you again, Alastair, if I need to see you?"

"You couldn't find this tree again, then?" and he grinned.

"No." That was definite.

"Then I shall have to come to *you*, whatever."

"Don't be stupid." She frowned. "No—I could come to the edge of this, this place, and make some sort of signal, and if you were here you could come to me. If not, we could choose a tree for me to leave a message in. Now, what signal could we have . . . ?"

He glanced at her obliquely. "I seem to mind someone who used to beat the roes themselves at the barking?"

Martha looked pensive. Then she turned her back on him, and suddenly a series of short, deep, cough-like barks, sharper than a dog's, defiant, tense, shattered the hush of that place, challenging, even if ending in something of a choke. The man and the woman turned to each other, and both were cowering under the noise and the sensation of outrage that succeeded it;

without realizing it, both had been talking almost in whispers for some time.

Martha hunched her shoulders and set off down into the hollows without further delay. "Come on, Alastair," she threw back. "Let's be getting out of this!"

The man stared after her. "Not that way, Moireach," he cried, and then he shook his black head and plunged after her. The great hurry she was in, and her off in the wrong direction, entirely!

It was a long glen, the glen of the headlong Allt Luinn, but not so noticeably long going down as it had been, to Martha Forbes, on the way up. Though, indeed, length had little relation, nor time, to their passage through the quiet reaches of that valley. Evening, grey and softly insistent, was settling on all the hills, and down in the gut of the valley, so deeply remote from the last glow of the setting sun, the gloom was a cogent thing that played its own games with that glen and all within it. The close at hand was blurred and indistinct and things far off came close and changed their size and shape. The rocks lost the edge of their outline, and shadows were not cast but welled up out of every hollow and fissure and fold. Even the stream seemed to have changed its character, sly instead of boisterous, murmuring and chuckling instead of shouting. And through the blue-washed uncertainty of it the man and woman picked their way awarely.

For most of their journey the path's narrowness constrained them to walk in single file, man and dog and woman, and their voices only seldom intruded on the Allt Luinn's monologue. But their communion was none the worse for that; a glance now and then, a hand across a muddy patch, the shared reaction to the lost cry of some bird of the night—all these, within the close embrace of the valley walls, could speak as loud as any words.

They had a good four miles of that glen, before its eastward trending forced them out on to the braeside. But this way they had no great hill rampart to cross to reach the strath of Alish; the Allt Luinn had its own route through the massif, and had they clung to it, eventually it would indeed have brought them to the loch and the road, but a long way east of Lagganlia. By cutting over a small hill-shoulder and across country by the birken aprons of the foothills, three miles could be saved that were well worth saving, with the night upon them—if the cutters knew their country and were not to be daunted by the darkling woods. Martha Forbes would not be daunted by much in that man's company, and Alastair MacIver was to be daunted by nothing but the devil within him and the God above him.

So, the man leading still, they climbed by erratic sheep-tracks over the broad shoulder of the hill of Cárn Ruadh, pausing for a moment at the summit to stare wordlessly down into the wide shadowy trough of the strath with its black loch and gathering mist wraiths, before slanting across thin heather and deer-hair grass till the dark glades of the birch-woods opened their arms to them.

On some sort of a path, apparent to the man at least, they entered those quiet aisles of the trees, and sometimes they walked side by side and sometimes one behind the other, but always they walked close together, at the bidding and decree of the wood and the path. And sometimes their shoulders would meet and their arms brush and their fingers touch, but neither cunningly nor questingly, and imperceptibly their pace slackened to an easy drifting, in tune with the place, and still they did not speak more than a quiet word here and there; and that was the wood's decreeing likewise.

It was the sudden breathtaking explosion of a capercailzie from a thicket almost at their feet that upset the even tenor of their way. Behind them, the dog yelped, once. Gulping, her heart in her mouth, Martha grabbed the man's arm, as the great foolish bird beat its way off through the dim lanes of the birch-boles, he responding almost as quickly and as good manners if nothing else demanded, with a reassuring clasp of her hand and a generally-protective attitude, in close support. And though he did not continue with his courteous gesture for more than a few moments longer than the situation required, and the girl's slightly breathless laughter betokened the passing of that crisis, yet something of tension remained with them and between them. Their further progress was not just a continuation of their former equable drifting. They walked perhaps a little more rapidly. They spoke a little more frequently yet less spontaneously. And the girl's hand remained within the man's arm.

Before long, noticeably before long to them, the sigh and lap-lap of the wavelets on the loch-shore proclaimed their approach to the road. Martha's steps faltered, and within the last fringe of the trees she stopped. "No further, Alastair," she decided, low-voiced. "The road is too risky for you . . . and there's no more than half a mile in it now, anyway."

"Less, lassie," he told her. "But I may as well be finishing the job. No thick-necked keeper's going to be putting a hand on Alastair MacIver this time of the day . . . or any other!"

"Maybe not, boaster—but I'm better not to be seen in your company . . . even if your legs are as long as your tongue! I'll keep my good name as long as I may." That was unevenly said.

"The cruel tongue *you* have!"

"Yes." Suddenly she knew nothing more to say. Yes."

He looked down at her intently. "Thank you for coming to me, Martha. It was kindly done, and will not be forgotten."

She shook her head wordlessly.

"It was a long road to take," the man went on gravely. "Only a stout heart would have taken it, at all. But then, always you were that." He lifted his shoulders expressively. "But I'll not be starting on what I think of you, *a graidh*, and me maybe saying the things I should not. I have to watch my tongue . . . and it that long!"

"It is not always long," Martha said slowly.

"Long it is," he assured. "But often I fight with it, and sometimes I win, see you."

"Need you . . . often?"

"Yes then, I do so." His voice was deepening, and suddenly his hands lifted and caught her shoulders, and gripped. "Thank you, woman dear, for all of your kindness . . . and you are very kind." His eyes, holding hers, even in the half-dark, were very sombre. The hand tightened, tensed, as though to pull her forward, and then abruptly, surprisingly, twisted her right around, and pushed, not roughly, but firmly. "Go, now," he said, and it was a command, yet with pleading behind it. "Go, and may the good God go with you."

The two or three steps she took, and then she looked back. "Alastair . . . !"

He shook his head. "Goodnight, Moireach," he said, and turning, plunged back into the gloom of the trees.

And watching him go she had no words, no words at all.

IX

THE Corriemore Fair was not only a fair, a bazaar, and a local holiday, it was a social occasion, the last event of the season indeed, before everybody that was anybody departed for the civilized south. Everyone went to Corriemore, and from a wide area: the seasonal occupants of the shooting-lodges and their keepers and stalkers, the fly-by-night patrons of the little fishing hotels and their gillies and boatmen, the farmers and crofters of the glens, the shepherds of the hills and the fisher-folk of the iron-bound coast—all arrived with their women and children, to mix there with the drovers and the show-people and all the tinkers and gipsies of the north-west, in a seething, robustious and vociferous round of business and carnival and sociability, inextricably mixed, that was the tonic, vindication, and annual improbability of that remote seaboard. From a radius of fifty miles they came, out of a seemingly empty country and a rock-dotted sea, on foot, by pony, by boat, and awheel, people and cattle and sheep and dogs, all at their most eloquent. That was Corriemore Fair.

It was the latest in the year of all the Highland fairs, and it had developed from being merely the autumnal assembly of all the sheep-flocks from their summering in the shielings and high grazings of the mountain pastures, preparatory to their voyage south to the winter hirsels—this, in the middle of the last century. Corriemore had been the selected gathering-place mainly because it possessed the only harbour deep enough to accommodate the vessels for transporting the sheep—since overland droving was well-nigh out of the question—and partly because there, also, was to be found sufficient levelish green-sward to permit the flocks to be penned and grazed while they waited on the vagaries of the shippers and the weather. In time, lamb sales had been added to this assembly, the occasion being convenient, and gradually other livestock had become included, and more than livestock. Sales, of any kind, are thirsty work, as everyone knows, and one thing leads to another. When royalty started to patronize Highland Meetings, the gentry began to put in an appearance, and sometimes even a lordly steam-yacht was to be seen lying out in the Sound amongst the humble coasters and puffers. So Corriemore Fair had grown to its present stature, and around the twentieth of September Wester Ross could be seen flocking thither.

Corriemore itself contained but the one street, and that only one-sided, for it fronted the harbour in an open crescent, a fine, wide, generous place of cobbles and gravel and sand and living rock, and of its two-score whitewashed houses approximately one-third were licensed. At the north end of the street the stock-pens began, surrounding the sale-ring, and behind them, inland, across the level machar, stretched the folds and common graz-ing, now somewhat encroached upon by the show-ground. And behind and flanking it all, the hills came down, steep and rock-strewn, in a jealous grudging semicircle.

In the thronged street, hostelries, fairground, and purlieus of Corriemore, then, it was not surprising for any indweller or sojourner in that countryside to meet any other, be he friend or foe, or merely relative. Everybody did so, and made the best of it. But, that the Inveralish Lodge contingent, on a showery day of that September, was surprised to come upon Alastair Dubh MacIver, casually and quite definitely non-furtive, was not to be denied. Indeed, surprised only partially describes its reaction.

They had just left the car park, two carloads of them, with Major Telfer and his brother picked up as an appendage, and were making for the entrance of the fairground, when it hap-pened. Sir Charles Marsden leading the way and in animated, loud-voiced conversation with a tall, seemingly bored young woman—he had to shout to make himself heard above the high-pitched clamour of the rest of the party—rounded a corner and came face to face with MacIver, at ease, sitting on the rail of a cattle-pen and chatting to Archie McKillop out of Kinlochalish.

Sir Charles stopped in his stride, and it was this, rather than his barked expletive, that imposed the silence on his talkative following. He took a few more paces forward, and stopped again. "My God!" he said. "You!"

"Good day," the gipsy acknowledged equably, and then, because there were ladies present, he raised his shapeless hat. But it was not at the speaker that he was looking, at all, but at the young woman beside him, and his eyes were not as equable as his voice.

The girl, tweed-costumed in dark olive, and bareheaded, stared back, and the initial surprise changed swiftly to another stranger expression that MacIver, even had he been in a mood to diagnose, would have had difficulty in placing. At any rate, she was no longer bored.

Marsden gulped. "What impudence . . . insolence!" He looked over his shoulder. Major Telfer was there, glaring. "Look at him," he cried. "In a public place . . . !" Righteous wrath and affront—with just a trace of uncertainty—were never more clearly demonstrated.

"Well, I'll be damned!" Telfer agreed. Then he smiled, grimly. "We've got him now, anyway."

The stout man nodded. "The blasted nerve of him!" The unsuitability of it all seemed to be affecting him most forcibly: that this poaching scamp, this outlaw, should be sitting there brazenly, openly, for all to see! To a law-abiding man it was an outrage. MacIver sat still. When he spoke, it was to McKillop, uncomfortable at his side. "And wee Jessie—is her knee right again now, Archie?"

"Och, she's fine, yes." He glanced right and left, a trifle anxiously. Evidently, he would not be sorry to be elsewhere.

Marsden and Telfer stared at each other. This was too much. "I advise you to mind your manners," Sir Charles rasped. "You'll find insolence expensive now." He turned round to his interested party. "Sammy, and you, George—flank him in case he makes a bolt for it."

As the two bechecked stalwarts made to do as they were bid, confidently vocal as to their ability to handle any and every such effort, Alastair, as soon as he could make himself heard, spoke up, but reasonably. "Is it myself you're talking to, at all?" he

78

wondered. "What for would I be doing any bolting? I am by way of talking to a friend of mine, see you, sir . . . and my manners are those God gave me."

Marsden did not intend to start an argument with tinker riff-raff in a public place, especially as passers were beginning to look interested, politely but distinctly. Beyond a snort, he ignored the man. "Telfer," he said "there was a policeman back at the car park, I noticed. I think, if you were to fetch him . . . ?"

"Yes, I agree—definitely. . . ."

Another voice broke in, a languidly-modulated woman's voice, and though it was not upraised nor insistent, Sir Charles at once paid heed to it. "Isn't this all rather absurd, Charles?" the girl asked. "I thought we came all this way to see cabers being tossed, and all that—not to brawl in the street?"

"I'm sorry, my dear—this is unfortunate, I know, but it is not a thing I can pass over. This is a case for action, Angela, believe me, or I would not dream of—er—causing a scene. I suggest that you go on ahead, all of you ladies, and we'll follow you later when we've disposed of this, this specimen."

His niece shrugged. "We'd better stay," she decided. "Lord knows what you'd be up to otherwise. But, for Heaven's sake, don't be long about it. . . ."

Archie McKillop was a quiet man and with no aptitude for a quarrel; moreover, Sir Charles Marsden was his landlord and, for three months out of the twelve, his employer. To him it seemed that the present might be as good a time as any to be getting on his way. "That's John Angus," he decided suddenly. "I'll be having a word with him. I haven't seen him since months." He nodded quickly to Alastair, "Good day, then," touched his cap vaguely towards the gentry, and was gone.

MacIver, smiling, was heaving himself off his rail, when Marsden snapped, "Hold him, or he'll be away!"

The gipsy stiffened, tense, and his two arms stirred slightly, slowly, in a circular movement, as though preparatory to further violent motion. He used his deepest voice. "If any man lays a hand on me, I'll not be responsible—I will not!"

At the quiet ferocity behind his words the two valiants drew back a little, prudently, with one accord. Even Sir Charles blinked. The three other ladies of the party made ineffectual protesting sort of noises and vague moving-on gestures, but Angela Denholm stayed still, interested unconstrainedly—she was not a constrained person at all, indeed. Again her eyes met Alastair's in a searching glance, and did not flinch under his contemptuous glare; for that matter, there was something not unlike mockery in her own regard, searching or not.

So the police found them, as they rounded the corner, heedfully dignified behind the hurrying Telfer.

Marsden cleared his throat authoritatively. "I am Sir Charles Marsden, of Inveralish," he announced, "and I want this man taken into custody—er—officer." He cleared his throat again, glancing from one to the other of the two policemen. There seemed to be nothing to choose from between them, neither wearing any chevrons or other mark of seniority. Yet he could not address them collectively as 'officers' or 'constables', in the course of his remarks. Difficult. A small thing, but irritating. He selected the elder-seeming, and held him with his eye.

"Yes indeed, sir," and "A very good day to you, sir," his statement was politely greeted, with the elder ruddy-faced constable making something between a nod and a bow, and the younger ruddy-faced constable saluting military-fashion. Two identical shiny-backed notebooks were extricated from breast-pockets, and, with more difficulty, two stubby short pencils. "Sir . . . Charles . . . Marsden," it was repeated, "Inveralish . . . Aye." A watch was produced and consulted. "Two-forty then, John?" the younger calculated. "Just about, Alick. Twenty to three, I make it." Both wrote steadily, having taken the precaution to moisten their pencils.

Sir Charles frowned impatiently, and Major Telfer tap-tapped the toe of his shoe on the ground. Alastair MacIver reached into a capacious pocket and drew out his old pipe and older tobacco-pouch. "Afternoon, Mr. Grant," he mentioned pleasantly.

The older, plumper policeman looked up innocently. "My, is

80

that yourself, Mr. Ross?" he said. "Showery it is, but it's the back-end after all, yes."

"I've seen it worse for the Fair," his colleague put in judiciously. "Last year it was bad, d'you mind?"

"Aye, that is so, Alick. Wicked, it was, just wicked. . . ."

"Constable," Marsden observed heavily, "might we dispense with the formalities? I am in rather a hurry. I want this man," and an accusatory hand pointed in a fashion that could leave no doubts whatever, even to a West Highland policeman.

"Yes, indeed, sir. Just that," Grant concurred heartily. "Ross, the name is, they tell me," and the writing started again. "Alastair . . . Ross . . ."

"MacIver," the gipsy corrected gently. "The name is MacIver."

"Eh? Oh, aye. MacIver . . . or Ross. So it is, then. Ross . . . or MacIver. Och, man, we'll just call it Ross, will we no'—it's easier . . . ?"

"John Grant!" That was almost thundered. "I don't give a tuppenny damn what you're after writing in yon wee book—it's no matter. But to my face you will call me MacIver. It is the name I was born with, as it was my father's before me. . . ."

"Right—right you are, then. MacIver it is, indeed. Yes. MacIver . . . MacIver with an I," he added for his colleague's benefit. "It's just that it would have been easier, see you, and the first charge under the name of Ross. . . ."

"The first charge!" Alastair had changed from thunder to ice. "What first charge would you be meaning?"

"Och, just yon time you were after putting the man Clarke in the watter, you mind . . ."

"And what has that to do with this, at all?"

John Grant looked up, rather troubled by the deliberate enunciation of these last two queries. "Well, it's handy for, for reference, you see." He nodded. "For reference," he repeated. "Having your name on the books, as you might say. . . ."

MacIver eyed him narrowly. "You're sure you're not making a mistake, Mr. Grant?" he wondered. "When a case is finished and done with, it's by way of being an offence, I've heard, to be bringing it up in connection with another charge. Prejudice, or some such thing, it's called . . . ?"

"Och, man, there's nothing like that to it, at all," the other assured him hurriedly. "Nothing at all. Never a thing—is there, Alick? It's just handy for reference, you see. You wouldn't get me doing a thing like that. This charge will be quite separate, indeed. . . ."

"And what *is* this charge, then, I'm wondering?" The gipsy looked at the policeman significantly, and the policeman looked at Sir Charles almost thankfully.

That gentleman, who had been fretting rather apparently for some time, exploded into vigorous accusation. "I'll tell you the charges! Trespassing in pursuit of game on Inveralish. Poaching deer and maliciously spoiling the sport on my forest. Stealing salmon from preserved waters. . . ."

". . . interfering to ruin a grouse-drive on Farinish." Telfer took up the tale. "Deliberately setting fire to moorland, illegally driving sheep belonging to one of my tenants, out of enclosed land. . . ."

"My, oh my!" Grant shook his head, shocked, his pencil almost out of control. He looked at his companion, brows raised. "Bad," that more stolid man agreed, writing heavily, "mal—iciously . . . spoil-ing . . . sport . . ."

"And the witnesses?" That was Black Alastair, level-voiced.

"Oh, aye—the witnesses, sir." Grant licked his pencil. "Two-three names will be all I'm needing for just now."

Sir Charles frowned. "What d'you mean—witnesses? This isn't a Court of Law you're conducting, is it, constable—though the proceedings appear to be just about as protracted. All that is required is for you to take this fellow into custody now—the formalities can be dealt with later."

"Aye—uh-huh." The police looked doubtful.

MacIver did not. "You could tell the man, Mr. Grant, that since this is still officially by way of being a free country, one party can't be getting another party locked up without some of the formalities . . . even if one's a manufacturer of tin-tacks and the other's a tinker, a gipsy, or a common second-hand tramp . . . !"

The sudden single and unexpected laugh drew all eyes for a

moment to the young woman at the stout man's side. The prosperity of the firm of Marsden and Bull had been largely founded upon the extensive production of non-rusting wire-nails. It was a very short laugh, but it made its impression.

John Grant, looking a little harassed, scratched the back of his head with his pencil. "That is so . . . in a manner of speaking. The charge must be . . . must be . . ."

"Substantiated?" his colleague suggested.

"Substantiated, yes. The charge must be substantiated, sir. We're not doubting that the charges are right enough, you will understand . . ."

"Damn it, I should hope not. Look here, Major Telfer and myself are responsible people. I am a magistrate, as it happens. . . ."

"The more reason that he abides by the law, then," Alastair interjected piously.

". . . and actually, we have a member of the Government in the party." Marsden looked round and over his company for the Right Honourable gentleman, but that astute legislator had quietly disappeared, not being a politician for nothing. The fact that his defection had been more than made up for by the adherence of a large number of more interested if less illustrious spectators, did not help Sir Charles. "Anyway, we are not such as would make frivolous public statements or bring unfounded charges. It is all a perfectly straightforward case. You can't let this man, this known disturber of the peace, go free just because we don't happen to have a witness on hand . . . ?"

"You can so—and must, whatever . . . unless the gentleman has a warrant for my arrest in his pocket!" Black Alastair sounded supremely confident, now, sure that however sketchy his own knowledge of the law, these others knew no more, besides having so much more to lose by making a mistake than had he. There were advantages in being a vagrant, an irresponsible Hie'land cateran, a dog with a bad name, after all. He was beginning to enjoy himself, and took small pains to hide it.

"A warrant . . . ?" Grant repeated hopefully.

Marsden brushed such a suggestion aside. "This is absurd, and a waste of time. There is no question of the fellow's guilt—

he can't deny it. . . ."

"He doesn't have to." The dark man was grinning now, cheerfully. "I'm just not admitting it. Not one of your charges do I admit at all. You'll be noting that, will you, Mr. Grant? Not one—and the man there . . ."—he corrected himself carefully—". . . the *gentleman* there, can't substantiate one, either. You see, he'll not can produce a witness to something nobody's seen me doing. That's all there is to it, see you, and you should tell him so, John Grant, and not be wasting the gentleman's time any more. The lady, there, is in a hurry—she was saying so not that long ago."

Sir Charles's knuckles gleamed white, his fists clenched.

"Blast you, you insolent oaf . . . !" he began, when his niece's hand touched his arm. "It's true, you know Charles—I *am* in rather a hurry. I don't see that anything is to be gained by staying here . . . apart from providing an extra show for the Fair." Her voice was cool and throaty and somehow inherently mocking. "I think, if the policemen were going to arrest your gipsy for you, they'd have done it before this—wouldn't you, Constable?"

Grant looked unhappily from one to another of the contestants, and wished that his duty lay somewhere else entirely, that the sergeant would be putting in an appearance, that folk would act in a decent peaceable manner and not be putting other folk in difficult positions. "If only you'd had a warrant, now, sir. . . ." he lamented.

"You see!" Angela Denholm pointed out.

"You're not going to do as I ask, then?" Marsden demanded with a show of finality.

One policeman looked at the other, and then at the distressingly assured MacIver. "Well, not exactly, sir," the elder said. "We can't just be doing a thing like that out of hand, as you might say. It's not as if you were a Justice of this county. I'm sorry . . ."

"That is so," the younger confirmed with sudden heartiness.

Sir Charles glared at them both. "Bah!" he cried, and without another glance at the gipsy turned on his heel and marched off. "Come on, then," he threw back, to niece and party alike, an

84

indignant man.

From his railing the dark man spoke conversationally to no one in particular. "If I wasn't a mild-like man myself, I could be after reminding the police that there's a bit law about making public accusations against other folk that cannot be proved or . . . substantiated, is it? Slander, I think they call it. And look at all the witnesses I have, whatever!" His smile was kindly, embracing all there—and there were many, now. "Very well, so," he said. "*Dia!*—a fine afternoon it has turned out, after all."

It was perhaps quarter of an hour later, with Black Alastair chatting to the Munros, drovers and cousins of Anna, near the cattle-pens, that Angela Denholm found him.

The curious glances of his companions stopped the dark man in his talking, and he turned round to find the young woman at his back.

"Tinker-man, may I have a word with you?" she asked.

Warily he eyed her. "I could not stop you, lady—even if I wished," he said slowly. "But wasn't it yourself that was in a hurry to be away, just a few minutes back?"

"Perhaps it was . . . with enough foolishness listened to for one day."

"Ah!" His wariness was not decreased. As a stopgap he bethought him of his manners—hadn't Sir Charles advised just that a whilie back? "Colin and Dougal Munro, friends of mine," he mentioned. "The lady's name I do not know, but she is rich, for sure, and proud and beautiful, as you can see, and far above the likes of us." His dark eyes held a glitter. "And I do not think she loves tinkers."

The young woman inclined her head ever so slightly, a bare flaxen head faultlessly groomed, climate or none, in the direction of the two drovers, but her level glance never left MacIver's face. "My name is Angela Denholm," she said with a sort of cool patience, ". . . and I see no reason why I should love tinkers."

The Munros touched their caps doubtfully, not altogether liking the tone of her voice, and one mentioned the fine weather that was in it after the showers. And they had business beginning to call them elsewhere, obviously.

"You do not!" Alastair agreed with her. "The pity it is."

The girl waited, and, as the dark man made no move, raised her eyebrows. "This word I was going to have with you," she reminded. "I think it might be best said privately."

"Might it, then?" The hard fleering tone behind his mock civility was not softened at all, for all her patience. He looked about and around him elaborately. "Safer here, I think, ma'am, where there's folk about. Some of your friends, or the police even, might just stumble on us by chance, as it were, in a quieter place. Stranger things have happened . . . !"

She shrugged. "As you will. You are entitled to your suspicions, I suppose."

The Munros withdrew.

Alastair waited. He was giving that young woman no assistance . . . and her requiring none.

When she spoke she did so carefully, picking her words, which, had the man known her better, would have impressed him more than a little; she was not usually so careful of what she said. "I have wanted to speak to you for some time," she said, "ever since the day I heard that you had been arrested and taken off to prison. I came through here, to Corriemore, to try to see you, that night—my uncle said that it would be here that the police would bring you. But they had taken you straight to Ardwall. Then I had to go South. While I was there I got a letter from Sir Charles mentioning, amongst other things, that someone had told him that you had cursed me in your—er—general denunciation, for giving you away to the police. I came North again, just as soon as I could."

"Well?" His voice was cold, unhelpful.

"I felt that it was important that I should see you, to tell you just what happened."

"Why?"

"You had gained a wrong impression. I felt that it ought to be corrected. So I came . . . for my own sake, I suppose, rather than yours." She laughed shortly, a jerk of a laugh. "It must have been, to bring me all the way from Town, twice in one year, to this Godforsaken country!"

Still he eyed her, inimical, unspeaking.

"I wanted you to know that I didn't knowingly give you away to the police that day. The keeper, Clarke, came up to me, described you, and asked if I had seen you. He only said that he had a small debt to settle with you. I saw no police then, and he did not mention any. I had no reason to suppose that they were involved—I had not heard of your little argument of the night before."

She paused, and, meeting her eyes, he took her up. "Why are you telling me all this? What matter how it was done . . . now?"

"To you, none, probably. To me, quite a lot, I think. I may be several kinds of a pest—I've been assured that I am, frequently—but I am not an informer. It may be of no consequence whether you imagine me to be one or not, but I could not be comfortable while I feared that anyone thought so . . . even a graceless tinker!"

Alastair could understand that, even if he admitted the fact to himself only grudgingly. "And you, a lord's daughter, came all this way just to be telling me that?" he wondered.

"Shall we say that I came for the sake of my own peace of mind? If you prefer to think that it was because I was so overwhelmed by your personality in the few moments that I saw you that day, you may, of course." She half-turned to move away. "Not that what I was doing in the South was of earth-shattering importance, anyway!" and she smiled at some thought of her own.

In some way this woman thought along the same lines as himself, MacIver recognized—and might well be the more dangerous to him, therefore. He was not without his masculine conceit, the man. And he could not but admire the way she used her tongue. "You are a strange niece to your uncle, I'm thinking," he mentioned.

"Perhaps I take after the less reputable side of the family," she suggested. "My Uncle Charles is a good soul, but afflicted with a tidy mind . . . that runs to making fortunes and disliking stray gipsies and poachers and so on." She paused. "But he is a pretty able man, too, you know, and with a habit of . . . disposing of things he doesn't like!"

Alastair, rather surprised, found that he had half-turned also, and was now walking slowly by her side. Ahead was the thronged village street and the open harbour. "Is it you trying to warn me off, now?" he demanded.

"No-o-o." Angela Denholm shook her head. "No, I don't think so. I'm rather interested to see the outcome of all this, actually. One so seldom gets the chance of watching an honest-to-goodness fight nowadays—we're all so damned respectable. I just mentioned it—my uncle's efficiency at getting his own way—in case you got a bit above yourself over your success this afternoon."

Alastair, not unaware of the attention that his progress in present company might well be attracting, nodded a trifle sheepishly, for him, at Hughie Bell's passing greeting and lifting eyebrows. "Does your uncle know you're here, talking with me?" he asked suddenly.

The girl shrugged. "I don't know. If he doesn't he soon will do, I've no doubt. Does it matter?"

"It might." He was noncommittal.

"You're a suspicious devil, aren't you! Are you always like that, or is it just my company that does it to you?"

"Ma'am." The dark man stopped in his tracks. "I was after spending thirty days in a cell for not being suspicious enough of folk such as yourself, locked up inside four walls eight feet apart . . . and I did not like it."

"I thought that you were locked up because you maliciously assaulted one Albert Clarke . . . ?"

"I was locked up because your folk were not wanting me about the place. Clarke was only an excuse."

"But you did throw him into the river, didn't you?"

"I did, yes—and him asking for it. But if Telfer and Marsden hadn't been wanting rid of me there would have been no case brought, for sure. And if the trial had been fair, there would have been no conviction in it, either. The man Clarke's case smelt heavens high. What was he doing at Balnacraig anyway—it was not his land? The policeman, Grant, was not wanting his help—he left him there. The man was just looking for trouble. He threatened me. He was for turning me out, himself. And then he called Anna, my brother's wife, an ill name, my God, and said other things besides. So I put him in the river."

"Naturally," she nodded, with half a smile.

It occurred to Alastair MacIver that they were more ken-speckle standing still in the middle of the street, than walking. So he started to move on, and the girl moved with him. He frowned. Damn it, that was Willie Maclay! The whole province was here staring at him and this woman.

She was speaking again. "But you didn't tell the judge all this?"

"What use, when I saw the way things were? And I was not having Anna mixed up in it, at all."

"You are fond of your Anna, eh?" she said, looking at him out of the corner of her eye.

"She is my brother's wife, and in my care," he answered shortly.

"Of course."

They were by the water's-edge now, at the rough stone and timber of the old harbour, and the man, staring down, watched the yellow spreading seaweed rise and fall with the swell of the tide, and said nothing.

Angela Denholm was not finished with him yet, however. She flicked a pebble into the water with the toe of her shoe. "You seem to be a very well-known man hereabouts—famous, perhaps? A large proportion of the passers-by appear to be interested in you. Does my presence enhance your reputation, do you think, or merely complicate matters? Though, probably, you're so used to the company of admiring females that you're quite unaffected! I thought I caught a glimpse of one of them, just now, watching you anxiously from a shop-doorway—the young woman Forbes, that thinks so much of you. . . ."

Alastair glanced up and round quickly, and his companion laughed. "She is rather pretty, in an ingenuous sort of way, don't you think?" she went on. "A bit strapping, perhaps . . ."

Alastair reacted as was to be expected. "Martha Forbes is a friend of mine," he said stiffly.

"Ah, yes—just what I was saying. I wonder what she thinks of all your activities?" That 'all' might have been just slightly stressed.

"I have no idea." The man glanced about him, a trifle wildly for him, and then his eye gleamed more typically. "I do not know," he reiterated deliberately, "but I will go and find out, whatever! Good afternoon, miss," and swift as the words came out, he turned and left her.

He hurried across that wide place. It was time that he got away from that young woman, high time. Never had he run away from a woman before, but it was time he left her. She was cunning and dangerous and damnably attractive, and devilishly quick at reading a man's mind. And as he went, hastening, he heard her laugh behind him. "Be careful, won't you, Alastair MacIver . . . or Ross!"

Curse the woman!

X

RAIN held the land in its leaden grip: chill, steady and persistent rain, curtaining the hillsides beneath the heavy grey canopy of cloud that hid all the high tops and peaks under its scowling shroud. For days the earth, sodden and sullen, had cowered beneath its relentless downpour, and everywhere water triumphed, whether noisily rushing, or grimly, sibilantly flooding, or silently soaking and seeping; every burnlet was a torrent, every watercourse a cataract, every stream a swirling spate. Under it all, life fell silent and oppressed, man and beast and bird; only the curlews called wearily, wearily, out of their abiding sorrow. Winter was not far away.

In Strathalish, as elsewhere, the tempo of men's activities dwindled and sank. The crofters, fatalists always, watched with resignation their meagre harvests of scant-eared oats, still ungathered, wilt and droop and darken. The shepherds drove their flocks out of the low pastures, and, eyeing the rising waters askance, retired to their firesides and hoped for the best. The keepers and stalkers stayed indoors and plagued their wives, or sought Sim Campbell's bar and impoverished them. And the gentry, such as had not already gone South in their wisdom, did so forthwith and thankfully, save only the ardent deerstalkers whose season only now was approaching its best. At Farinish, Major Telfer remained, with stags to shoot—Marsden's if not his own. Sir Charles also stayed meantime. His reasons were varied. He would like to see a task here completed; he was fond of a shot at a stag himself, though he was not the man, these days, to go stalking them in their inaccessible fastnesses amongst the high peaks, preferring to let the onset of harsh weather drive them down into the more approachable low ground, thereby sparing himself much unprofitable labour; and his niece Angela, who was the somewhat tart apple of his eye and the only relative that he cared a damn for, surprisingly seemed determined to stay on under his roof; far be it from him to dissuade her. But the remainder of his guests had gone, with the exception of a young man named Bowden, and Sir Charles had little difficulty in reaching a conclusion on whose account he had stayed.

Nor was Alastair MacIver unaffected—not unnaturally. In the soaking woods, the streaming hillsides, and the dripping stillnesses of Am Fasach, he found the fine flame even of his righteous anger damped—but not quenched, never quenched. There was little that he could do to further his campaign, with the rivers beyond any kind of fishing—even such as did not rely on hook and line—the mist blanketing all the stag country, and no sporting activities of any sort to interfere with. Sundry minor assaults he did make, mere pinpricks, such as scuttling the three lodge boats on the loch, levelling the high deer fence for some considerable distance at the extreme northern limits of Inveralish Forest, thus permitting the deer to drift over into the adjoining forest of a Hebrew peer should they be so inclined, and seeing that the floods carried away a couple of plank bridges on the recently-built stalker's road leading up to the high ground of Beinn Druim; for the time being sportsmen would walk thither instead of riding in a shooting-brake. He shot an odd roe and a bird or two, of course, for the pot—and more than his own pot—but that was by the way. As the chill days of rain wore on, Alastair MacIver had to cherish a grievance that thus far had needed no nursing.

It was with some satisfaction, then, that on an unadvertised visit to Sim Campbell's hotel one night, in quest of warmth, company, and a droppie of whisky, he heard that Major Telfer was planning a stalk, on Marsden's invitation, just as soon as weather conditions permitted. There were some corries amongst the high buttresses of Beinn Druim that had not been stalked that season, and Jeffrey Telfer was the man to do it, it seemed— Davie Kennedy had told Campbell so that very day. Just as soon as the weather cleared. And MacIver had trudged back through the driving deluge that night, his mind busy once more.

When, two days later, after a wild night of boisterous wind, the day dawned quiet, exhausted almost, but rainless, and presently a pale sun came out to smile thinly over the cowed and sodden land, the dark man sniffed the air and decided that the new state of affairs would last, and made his plans accordingly. Down at Kinlochalish that night confirmation was forthcoming—from two sources Campbell had the word: from Hughie Bell, Balnacraig, and John Robertson, head-keeper on Inveralish. On Friday, two days hence, the Major would be after the stags on Beinn Druim, with Donald Shaw stalking for him, if the weather held. Sim's whisky seemed to have a loosening effect on quiet men's tongues.

Alastair looked forward to Friday with some pleasurable anticipation.

Martha Forbes was collecting the windfalls from under the sadly battered apple trees of the Lagganlia garden when Willie Maclay, grinning hugely, brought her a visitor. Martha, flushed somewhat already with her climbings and stretchings, flushed a little more, and a quick hand went up to pat and smooth her exuberant hair. "Good afternoon. It's nice to see the sun again, isn't it?" she greeted, in a rush. "Very wet, it's been."

"I could put it a little more forcefully, perhaps," Angela Denholm suggested. "Do you often get weather like that in this country? It might account for a lot." She was dressed in jodhpurs as she had been on her first visit to Lagganlia, but this time she wore with them a close canary woollen jumper, severely simple and cunningly fitting. To the other girl, nevertheless, very much aware of her apron and the green smudges that she had collected from the fruit trees, she seemed to be most distressingly smart.

"Och, yes," she said. "We get it wet like this now and again, at this time of the year—and other times, too. It's been bad for the crops and the beasts."

"It's been bad for the humans, too. I've never been so bored in my life . . . and that's saying something."

Martha glanced at her quickly. "I was thinking you'd have been away South, then?" she suggested curiously.

"No," the other said briefly. She paused just for a moment.

"A good thing I'm not, perhaps, for some people." That was said significantly. Glancing around, to make sure that Willie Maclay had quite gone, Angela Denholm came a step nearer. She never was one for beating about the bush. "Miss Forbes," she said, "I want to speak to your tinker friend, Alastair MacIver. Do you know where he can be found?"

Martha stared, and unwittingly she drew herself up and her chin lifted a little. "Do you think, ma'am, that if I knew, I'd be telling you?"

"I do . . . if you had any sense. I have something important to say to him."

Martha said nothing, but her blue eyes flashed.

The other looked her over with a cool, detached scrutiny. They made a strangely contrasting pair standing there beneath the apple trees, the flushed vital Highland girl, wide-eyed, tense, but natural, and the slender, assured aristocrat, languid-seeming and aloof. Both of an age, both good-looking—but so very differently—both able . . . and not liking each other.

"You are fond of the man, aren't you?" Angela Denholm demanded.

"We were brought up together," she was answered shortly.

"Then you will want to help him, and it is important for him that he hears what I have to tell him."

Martha said nothing.

"It is urgent that I see MacIver soon, right away—urgent for his welfare."

"*His* welfare! Late you are, ma'am, in your family, thinking of Alastair's welfare."

The other ignored that. "Will you tell me where I can find him?"

"What makes you think that I know where he is, then?"

Her visitor looked at her with a sidelong glance almost of amusement. "I would . . . if I was in your position," she said pointedly. "Don't come all innocence, Miss Forbes."

Martha felt that she was flushing again under the other's calculating eye; she hated her traitor reactions that would not let her dissemble, as was surely her woman's right. "If you are so sure, why not give me a message for him, then?" she suggested.

"Because you are watched—you would be followed. They are pretty sure," and her flaxen head nodded back in the direction of the Lodge, "that you have been in touch with him already."

"And you?" That was swiftly put.

"I will not be suspected. I have brought my pony. It is perfectly natural that I should bring it here, to the smithy, and then go, well . . . wherever it is, for a ride."

Martha stooped and picked up a couple of bruised apples.

"I cannot think what you can have to be seeing Alastair about that is so urgent?" Her voice was troubled.

Angela Denholm tapped at her long leg with her riding-crop. She did not speak for a few moments. When she did, her speech was jerky, for her, less coolly controlled than was her normal, and her unwillingness to speak was obvious. "They have set a trap for him, my uncle and Major Telfer, and if he is not warned he will probably walk right into it. It is tomorrow. Major Telfer is supposed to be stalking the high corries of Beinn Druim. They have let word of it get to a few sources from which they think our friend gets his information. If he falls for the ruse and goes to try and interfere, he will find himself in a trap—they're going to have the whole area surrounded. He won't have a chance." She shrugged. "So you see, he must be warned, today."

Martha's eyes had widened at this disclosure. Already she could see Alastair, pursued and cornered and at bay fighting and going down beneath overwhelming odds. Her hand crept up to her breast. But she spoke steadily, nevertheless. "If all this is so, why are you telling me—why are *you* giving it all away . . . ?"

Angela Denholm took a pace or two back and forth, her eyes on the ground. "Because, shall we say, I like to see a fair fight. I don't like to see a mob against one man. Whatever the pros and cons of the case—and both sides being men, have acted like complete idiots—so far, Alastair MacIver has put up quite a good show in this ridiculous battle; I think this is a case where the odds against him should be evened a little. Those are my reasons, and . . ." she glanced up quickly, her expression changed, ". . . he has such fascinating eyes, hasn't he!"

Martha, forthright soul, had been ready with expressions of agreement, not to say gratitude, at the other's unexpected views, but that last remark shut her up like a clam. So she stared, wordless, indignant, while the girl opposite mocked her with her eyes.

Since she got no reply, Angela went on. "So, you see, your secret will be safe enough with me."

"Will it? How can I be sure?" The Highland girl spoke more coldly than she knew. "How do I know that it's not just another trap?"

"If your common sense doesn't tell you . . ." The other shrugged. "I give you my word, anyway."

Hating her as she did, Martha accepted that. "I would much rather be taking him the message myself," she said shaking her head. "But . . ."

"And probably be followed, and have his hiding-place disclosed?"

"No." Slowly she looked up. "Will you promise that you will not tell anyone, not a soul, where he is if I tell you?"

"Don't be absurd—of course I won't. What do you take me for?"

"I do not know, at all," Martha confessed truthfully. "But I will trust you . . . in this, anyway."

For a moment the two young women stared at each other, eye to eye, in silence. Then Martha sighed. "This is how you get there, then. . . ."

Later, as she watched the other ride off not on the chestnut this time, but on a hardy shaggy hill pony, more suited to the job on hand, the Highland girl bit a troubled lip. Nor did her frown relax, as, turning in her saddle, Angela Denholm raised a hand and waved derisively. "Shall I give him your love?" she called. "A pity for him not to know . . . !"

Alastair MacIver had spent the day on Beinn Druim, spying out the deer, mapping routes and distances, memorizing burn-channels and hiding-places, trying to gauge wind-currents, and reconnoitring every slope and scree and corrie and watercourse of that high landmass—all with the patience and circumspection of a man who knows and respects the noses and ears, if not the eyes, of his deer. Reasonably satisfied with what he had seen and decided, he was returning to Am Fasach, by devious ways, when he saw the pony, where no pony should be. Sinking down into the heather he had his glass on it in a matter of seconds—it was a good mile off—and what he saw formed his lips into a soundless whistle. My lady Angela, the dangerous one! What was that young woman doing on his doorstep, what did she want and how had she got there? He did not know, he did not know at all—but he would discover. Heedfully but without hesitation, he started to find out.

Half an hour's circuitous travelling—such as had become second nature to him now, anyway—brought him, undiscovered, to within a hundred yards or so of his objective. Creeping round the flank of a heather knoll, he saw, and considered.

The pony, a garron, saddled and bridled, but otherwise not unlike his own, was standing, head adroop, tied to one of those ancient pines, outposts of the forest of Am Fasach. And nearby, beneath the next tree, Angela Denholm sat and smoked a cigarette. Very much at ease she seemed sitting there, back against the bole, long legs crossed, a hand behind her head tightening the line of her jumper, watching the tobacco-smoke drift upward. The man could not but admire. But even as he watched she glanced at her wristwatch, raised her head to search the vicinity, and, opening her mouth, produced unexpectedly and unsuitably a series of short improbable barks, ending prematurely in a choking gasp. After a cough and a long breath she did it again; the effect was like a lapdog much frightened, the expression ludicrous.

MacIver's grin, if wide, was short-lived. Under that tree with the peculiar right-angled bend in it, the only such hereabouts, and barking like that, poor imitation of a roe as it was, there could be only one explanation. Martha Forbes had told her. But why? Why?

He made a quick reconnaissance of the neighbourhood, and

assured himself that the girl was alone at any rate. He sat and pondered for some time, and then, with a shrug, he did the only thing to be done; he rose out of his hiding place and walked forward, straight across the old heather towards her. "Good afternoon, ma'am," he said, touching his hat. "Is there anything I can be doing for you?"

If Angela Denholm was anyway startled by his sudden appearance, she did not show it. She let him come to within a few yards before she stirred herself. Then, lazily hoisting herself to her feet, she stretched and yawned. "You've been the hell of a time, Alastair MacIver," she complained.

The man stood before her, wary-eyed. "Sorry I am to have kept you," he said. "You should have let me know you were coming. I would not keep a lady waiting. Have you been long?"

"About an hour. Too long, with that devilish row going on." She jerked her head, over towards Am Fasach, from whence drifted a distant mournful howling, infinitely depressing. "What in heaven's name is it?"

MacIver grinned. "That is my dog's answer to your challenge. He is tied up there, and the noise you were making has been too much for him, whatever. He is not a very clever dog, Rob, and has not recognized that you were after being a roe-deer!"

The girl looked disappointed. "Only a dog," she commented. "From all accounts this place of yours ought to be able to do better than that. I'd expected a banshee or a kelpie, at least." She silently ignored his implied commentary of her barking. "What are you doing?"

The gipsy had moved over to the pony, and was now loosening the reins that tied it to its tree. "With your permission we'll be moving down into the woodie, a bit," he told her. "I'm a retiring sort of man by nature, and if I was seeing this beast of yours a mile off, others could be doing the same."

Carelessly she nodded agreement, and followed him, as Martha Forbes had done not so long since, down between the hummocks and the peat hags, and into the quiet precincts of Am Fasach nan Earba.

Alastair MacIver, leading the pony over difficult going, kept his questions to himself, and got little enlightenment from the young woman behind him. But once within the cover of the woodland he stopped, and fixed her with his glance, a determined glance. "You have been talking with Martha Forbes?" he put to her, bluntly.

"I have."

"I'm wondering what made her tell you where I was to be found?"

"I did." That was casually said.

"It is not like Martha, whatever. I wonder what you told her to make her speak?"

"I told her it was to your advantage that I should see you, your very real advantage . . . and she has your advantage very much at heart, of course, has Miss Forbes—as have we all!"

He ignored that last. "And is it true—about this advantage?"

"Do you think it might not be?"

Taking his time, he answered: "I think that if you were wanting something badly, you would not be too particular about the way you were after getting it."

Thoughtfully she regarded him. "You are very clever Alastair MacIver or Ross," she said. And then: "Perhaps we are fellows in that?"

They moved on, in silence, and the queer hush of Am Fasach surrounded them, broken only by the intermittent woeful howling of the tethered dog. The pony was nervous, jerking its head and frequently sidling, but perhaps the dog's baying accounted for that. Alastair faltered in his step. Why was he taking this woman deeper into his sanctuary? There was no need. . . . Yet the dog should be shut up. . . . He turned abruptly. "What was it you had to tell me . . . to my advantage?" he demanded.

"Just that you should not go to Beinn Druim tomorrow."

"Why not?" That was sharply said.

"So you do know all about it, then! Uncle Charles was right. . . ."

"Never mind what I know, then. Why must I not go to Beinn Druim tomorrow?"

"Because it is just a trick to get you where you can be caught. It's a trap. Jeffrey Telfer will be stalking, right enough, with Shaw, but the whole area will be surrounded—they're gathering men from far and near. You're to be cornered . . . at any price!"

"So-o-o!" The man nodded his head slowly. "I see. I might have known that there was something queer to it and me hearing about this ploy from the three different folk. Aye, then, I might have known it."

"Yes," she agreed, "they were determined that you should hear all about it. I'm afraid your bush-telegraph system is getting a bit suspect."

"Aye." He stroked the garron's soft nose pensively. "And why should you be telling me all this, ma'am?" he wanted to know.

Angela Denholm lifted her shoulders. "Because I like to see a fair fight, not one man against a mob, was the reason I gave your friend Martha Forbes," she said, picking her words. "And for Mike's sake, don't call me ma'am!"

And since it seemed to be the easiest thing to do, with his mind fully occupied, he turned and moved on.

But now she was walking, not behind him and the pony, but at his side, and it was not long before the changed circumstance penetrated his preoccupation. Nor was she noticeably keeping her distance. Presently the man halted. "No point in taking you on farther, at all. You'll just have to come back," he pointed out. "I am grateful for this word you've brought me, very grateful. Just why you've done it I'm not rightly sure, but you have my thanks, whatever. There's nothing more you've got to tell me, is there?"

"What more would you like to be told, tinker-man?" she wondered slowly.

He glanced at her, and then away. "Just if there was anything more about tomorrow that would be worth my knowing."

"All that you need know about tomorrow's affair is to keep away from it, I should say."

"Aye . . . ih'mmmmm . . . just that," he agreed, and she eyed him curiously. "We may as well be getting back, then."

"But aren't you going to show me where you live . . . ?"

The man smiled to himself ruefully. These women were all the same. " 'Tis only a small bit hole in the ground," he told her, but scarcely hopefully.

"I would like to see it, just the same," she insisted. "Anyway, that dog of yours needs quietening."

And that was true. Rob's suspicions were still being bayed to the listening wilderness. It was seldom, indeed, that he left the brute tied up, but today, inspecting the deer-ground of Beinn Druim, the dog's presence would have been an embarrassment and its scent a liability. "All right, then," the man shrugged. "But you will have to be getting back soon, or the dark will be catching you."

"And that would never do, would it!" Angela Denholm said, smiling her own smile.

"You are pretty snug here, aren't you?" the young woman commented, from inside the refuge beneath the pine tree. "Were you here through all that rain?"

"Some of it, anyway," the man said cautiously.

"What . . . ?"

"I said I was here for some of it."

"And did you manage to keep dry?"

"While I was inside it, yes."

"What . . . ?"

"I'm saying while I was inside it . . ."

"Well, don't stand outside there muttering, for Heaven's sake. It must have been a ghastly bore—it was deadly enough indoors." When she got no answer, she glanced, one eyebrow raised, to where he now crouched at the entrance to his cave. "How does this thing work?" she demanded.

"What thing?"

"This thing here."

"I can't see what you're meaning."

"Of course you can't, sitting away out there!"—which was

true enough, the girl keeping her body between him and the object of her enquiries.

MacIver sighed, and proceeded to crawl into his dugout. A different proposition this woman was from Martha, altogether, for all there was some similarity in procedure. He demonstrated the working of his collapsible gaff, but her eyes were roving.

"Are those books, under there? Strange to find books here—somehow one doesn't expect tinkers to be readers."

"Why not?"

"I don't know—it's just unsuitable, upsetting the gipsy tradition, you know. This popular education has a lot to answer for." She was watching him out of the corner of her eye—and she had not far to watch. But he held his peace. She picked up the books, well-read copies of Hugh Foulis' *Para Handy*, *Wild Sports*, by St. John, and an old Johnson's *Tour*, by Boswell.

"Never heard of any of them," she commented, and it was the man's turn to smile.

"A queer thing, education," he observed.

Angela Denholm turned and sank down on the shelf of heather-tips that was his bed. "Tell me about yours," she requested. "Tell me about yourself, altogether."

"That would take some time, I doubt," Alastair said soberly, "—and you having to be on your way soon if the dark isn't catching you." And then, as an afterthought: "Why should I, anyway?"

"Because I'm rather interested." She laughed shortly. "And it isn't often I'm interested. There aren't many interesting people about, I find. Anyway, you owe it to me, after the news I've brought you."

"Yes, then." That was entirely noncommittal—a very useful Highland phrase.

"Your friend Martha Forbes told me you were brought up together. How was that?"

MacIver eyed her doubtfully. They were very close in that place, and this girl's presence was not to be readily ignored, mentally or physically. Nor was she at any more pains to play down the latter than she was the former; the long line of her

102

neck, shoulder and bosom, hip and thigh and calf, breeches notwithstanding, was flauntingly, challengingly feminine. Sedulously casual, she sprawled at ease on his couch, and Alastair Dubh MacIver was a man, virile and not in the least cold-blooded. So he talked, since he recognized danger when he saw it, and was concerned that if he played it would be his own and no woman's game.

"A lot of my childhood I lived in Alan Forbes's house of Lagganlia," he said, then. "My mother, God rest her, had been no tinker, and she never took to the life at all. When she was dying, two-three years after I was born, my father, Colin Bán, promised her that I should have the chance of living her own kind of life, one day, if so I wished. So each winter I lived with Jean Forbes, Alan's wife, who was my mother's friend, and when the days lengthened, my father came for me and I took to the roads with the tinkers. And I went, with Martha, to the small bit of a school at Inshbeg and learned a little, and up and down the land with my dad and learned more, but the most I learned from Alan Forbes, who is a man of parts, and who taught me to love books. He is a good man, is Alan, and he has taught me other things besides. . . ."

"And his daughter?" came from the heather couch at his side. "She has taught you a thing or two, besides, I shouldn't wonder?" The girl's elbow rested against his knee, with her hands clasped behind her head.

Alastair sought in his pocket for pipe and tobacco, and, perhaps unnecessarily, his knee moved away. "Maybe she has, then," he agreed quietly.

"Were you a willing pupil, I wonder—quick to learn?" she asked. "I dare say you would be—there is a gleam in your eye . . . !"

He filled his pipe methodically. "I learned from the Forbeses one way of living and from my father another way. . . ."

". . . and in the end you chose your father's way?"

The gipsy nodded slowly, unspeaking.

"Yes," the young woman said after a moment, "I should think, for a man like you, that would be almost inevitable. I

103

don't see you sitting down to be just a crofter, or a smith, like Forbes. . . ."

"Alan is more than just a smith, see you," the man pointed out. "He is the best metalworker in all of Ross. You should see the things he can make, in silver and copper, besides iron."

"I know. I have a badge he made for a hat, and a brooch. And my uncle has a little dagger, that he uses as a paper-knife. . . ."

"A *sgian dubh*—one with the stag's-horn handle to it?" Alastair chuckled. "I made yon my own self. Alan was after teaching me his craft, too . . . but I have not his touch, at all. Aye, Alan has taught me a lot, man and boy . . . and with never once a hand lifted to me—which is more than I can be saying for my own father, whatever," and he smiled.

She turned a little on her side, to watch him, busy-eyed. "Tell me about your father," she said.

"Colin Bán! He was a man of parts, too, was my father, but different from Alan Forbes, yes." He sucked at his pipe strongly. "God, he was the boy! Give him a fiddle or a knife or a rifle . . . or a bottle, and no man on this seaboard would touch him— more especially the bottle! And the stories he was after telling! He was the one for a *ceilidh*—he could sing sweet and true as a blackbird and dance like any whittrick. There was never a wedding nor a burying from here to the Kyle that didn't seek him . . . I have his fiddle down-bye, but I was never the fiddler like himself. And there was not a parish north of Ness that he hadn't fought in—he was a terrible man to fight. That was my father, a wild, generous, laughing devil of a man, Colin Bán MacIver."

"A man, most definitely," Angela Denholm agreed. "Well might your mother turn gipsy for him . . . though I'll bet he wasn't faithful to her!"

MacIver said nothing, and the girl laughed softly. Casually an outflung arm fell across his leg, and her hand ran down hard knee and calf and ankle, in a caress and mockery combined. "How much are you your father's son, I wonder?" she murmured.

He sat very still. "Enough to be my own man, anyway, thank God," he told her as quietly.

She raised herself on an elbow to stare at him. "I wonder?" she said, "I wonder?" So they remained for a time, moments, the woman's violet eyes meeting the man's, dark, black almost, and holding. Then she laughed again, and threw herself back on the heather, and her voice lifted, lightened, once more. "The proud tinker, eh?" she scoffed. "... though I understand that you claim to be descended from a Highland chief, or something of the sort?"

Alastair drew a deep breath, and nodded. "That is so," he said briefly.

"Tell me." She was good at saying that.

He considered her, lying there, all the abandoned lazy insolent grace of her, and he spoke through his teeth that tightly clenched his pipe. "It's a right mannerless . . . vixen you are, a proper ill-tongued shrew. . . ."

"Say a bitch and be done with it," she told him cheerfully. "Of course I am—manners are for respectable middle class nobodies, not for such as you and me, Alastair MacIver. You'll be posing as an upholder of the conventions next. Now tell me about your Highland chief."

The man took the pipe out of his mouth, looked at it, and put it back. "Aye," he said doubtfully. He made a mental note of something that he had just decided that she needed. "And overdue it is, too," he decided out loud.

"Eh—what's that?"

"Just something I was thinking." He smiled grimly. "But I'll tell you about the MacIvers. Always they have been in this country and MacIver of Strathalish was the chief of them. One time these glens were full of folk—they say there were five hundred croft-houses on Alish-side alone, before they were driven out, to the shore and across the sea. Mac 'ic Iver Mhor was a power in the North—and more than the North—in those days, with a hundred fighting men in his tail, and five times that if he wanted them. From the time of the great Somerled to the luckless Stuarts, then, the Clann Iverach held its own, and a bittie more than its own, maybe, with a good marriage now and again, and a bit tulzie oftener, to keep the name respected, whatever. Then came the bad days, and the lad from France, the young Tearlach, Charles Edward, after seeking his throne. And that was the end of the MacIvers. When the clans were beaten at Culloden and the slaughter began, MacIver wounded and with just two-three of his tail left, came limping back to his own place, and when the Butcher's redcoats came after him he took his wife and his son with him into the heather before they burned his house down and raped the strath. And in the heather they stayed, with some of his people, they say in this very place—Am Fasach nan Earba. And though the woman died and the lands were sold and the clan scattered, MacIver lived and his son lived and *his* son after him, and the heather got into their blood . . . and is in it still. That is why I did not stay with Alan Forbes, I'm thinking."

"So!" Angela Denholm nodded presently. "Well, the romantic Colin's story-telling ability is not entirely lost, I think!" Her eyes were on the sandy roof above her, where the tree roots turned and twisted, and one breeched leg swung rhythmically across the updrawn knee of the other. "It accounts for a lot, you know, all that story. . . ." Almost she might have been talking to herself.

"It is true," the man interrupted harshly.

"Did I say it wasn't?" she went on imperturbably. "I wondered what it could be. . . . You see, we come of the same sort of stock, you and me, Alastair MacIver—though my family has become sadly prosaic of recent years, almost suburban, Lord help us! But we Denholms used to be folk of some spirit—you didn't win dukedoms three hundred years ago by being respectable! Actually, the first of them was not unconnected with your Stuarts, unconventionally if very naturally—at least, his mother was. And we kept our place thereafter by a mixture of hard fighting, polite brigandage, card-sharping, and judicious blackmail. So the House of Merton survived while righteous folk faded into mediocrity and disappeared—and serve them right! But now! Lord, it's just as well you don't have to hold your position by the quickness of your wits these days, or I reckon my spineless cousin would be a commoner pretty sharp, playing a tin-whistle in the gutter!"

"With the dukedom rescued by his female relation, whatever!" the man finished for her.

She turned and looked at him, eyebrows raised. "Thank you, tinker-man," she said, and fell silent, still looking.

Alastair kept his eyes to the front. He was not quite sure of her expression—it was getting dark in that dugout—and a man had to watch his step with this young woman. It was thus that he came to a realization of the fading light, and his decision was immediate. "Time you were on your way," he announced briskly. "It'll be dark soon." And knocking out his pipe on the heel of his boot, he rose, stooping, and slipped outside. It was quickly done; he hoped, at the back of his mind, not too quickly. . . .

The girl lay still. "No hurry," she said. "I'm not afraid of the dark."

"Maybe not—but your beast is. It'll never make that path that you came up, in the dark."

"Then I'll lead it, if need be."

"You will not . . . though maybe you deserve to have to."

She laughed provocatively.

"Come on—it's a long road you've got in front of you, mind."

"And whose worry is that?" she asked. "Anyway, I'm very comfortable here, thank you."

"I dare say. But I've got work to do this night—and you are going down the glen now," and Alastair turned and strode over to the fretting horse where it was tethered to another tree.

When he faced round, the beast unhitched and eager to be moving, she was outside his refuge, standing wide-legged, stretching her arms up and back and yawning frankly. "Your sudden he-mannishness is encouraging . . . but not very convincing," she jeered. "A bit late in the day, isn't it?" And when he made no comment: "And what work have you to do, anyway?"

"My own work—tinker's work," he answered briefly. He looked over at the collie, Rob, crouching anxious-eyed in the heather, and spoke a few words in the Gaelic, soft but authoritative. Disappointment in every drooping line, the dog got up and slunk into the dugout, its long lead trailing after it. Then, turning, he led the pony downhill without another word. Smiling faintly, the girl followed.

Through and between all the hollows and the hummocks of that quiet brooding place they went, and apart from the scuffle and swish of the garron's hooves against the heatherstems and the faint creak of its harness, they made no sound. When the trees thinned, MacIver turned left-handed and slanted across the open moorland, zig-zagging his sure way amongst the black peat-hags, the green of bog and the fading tussocks. Soon they were at the lip of the infant glen of the Allt Luinn, and down into its shadowy trough he plunged, to halt at the sodden narrow sheep-track that partnered the brawling stream. "There you are, then," he said, as the young woman came up with him. "Follow the burn all the way down, and it'll bring you to the loch-road. Less than the hour it'll take you. You'll be there before it's right dark." And in a different tone: "And thank you for the word you brought."

Surprised, she stopped and frowned at him. "And you . . . ? Aren't you coming? I thought you had work to do . . . ?"

"I have, yes—but not on your road."

"And you're going to leave me here—let me go back all that way alone . . . !"

"You came alone, fine and well, whatever. And I'm telling you it won't be dark before you get to the road." The man was smiling a little grimly.

"Oh!" Angela Denholm took a deep breath. There was sudden fury in her eyes. It was something new to see this young woman showing her feelings. But in a moment she was herself again. "Your father wouldn't have done that, I think," she said softly. "He was a man . . . if there was any truth in your story!"

He did not answer her, but stood quiet, eyebrows raised.

"But it wouldn't be true," she went on, taunting him. "MacIver of Strathalish! The blood of chiefs! Stories, tinker's tales. You're just a tink, Alastair MacIver, like your precious father before you, born in a ditch . . . and a coward at that. You're frightened of me, my bold gipsy, just scared to death . . . !"

And like a flash, from his easy lounging, he acted—as he had acted that other evening by the other wider stream, with another Sassenach in need of a lesson. In the twinkling of an eye he was beside her, and an arm like a steel bar was behind her shoulders, had twisted her round and forced her down, bending, in the one swift movement. Over his bent knee she stumbled, and was held, struggling, while his free hand beat a sharp tattoo on the adequate prominently-rounded seat of her breeches, open-handed lusty smacks, wholehearted and sincere. A dozen of these, perhaps, he rained on her, and then the taut left arm jerked her up again, and without pause, its place was taken by its neighbour, which, acting exactly in reverse, pulled her round and bent her also, but backwards this time. And over her wide-eyed upturned face he stooped, and kissed her full on the open lips, a long, hard, angry kiss, that was an insult rather than a caress, before he straightened up and pushed her away, so that she staggered backwards against the waiting pony.

"Since an hour ago I was thinking you needed that," he jerked. "Overdue, it was," and without another word he swung about and went up the tilt of that bank long-strided. Nor did he look back once to where the girl stood, rigid, fists clenched. It was a long time since Angela Denholm had shed tears.

XI

THE new day, breaking gently out of the clasp of the night, found Alastair MacIver sitting on an outcrop of granite below the great vague bulk of Beinn Druim, awaiting with an inanition that was beyond patience, what the dawn would bring. For so often the dawn brought with it a questing wind or a change of wind, and to him this day, as to others, the wind was vital. But for this doubtful element he would have been up amongst the corries of the mountain before him by now, safe under the cover of the dark; but with deer to be circumvented as well as men, he must bide his time. No liberties could be taken with the noses of the red deer of the high tops.

He sat, a lonely grey-brown figure in a wide grey-brown desolation, and he was very small under the stark colourlessness of the dawn sky, his features grey also and drawn and shadowed deeply about the unshaven jaw and chin. It was very still and silent as the grave, and there was no warmth in the air nor in the land nor in the man. Even his eyes were dulled, without their normal gleam and life, turned in on himself to where his mind was sunk away in the depths of a half-consciousness outwith and beyond thought. His plans were made, intricate plans, his object clear, only his course to it was uncertain, dependent on what wind the dawn would bring. So he waited.

Somewhere a curlew called, long and clear and infinitely sorrowful, its weary trilling tailing away in an ecstasy of loneliness. It was the first sound that the man had heard beyond his own heartbeats and the murmur of waters, for hours. Slowly, as though returning from afar, his eyes livened and he turned to face the east. Still there was no sign of a break in the heavy curtain of the dark, but the bird had spoken true and even as he looked a breath of chill air, like the touch of cold fingers, brushed across his cheek. It was only a single tremor, a mere whisper of air, but for the watcher it was enough. It came out of

110

the south-east. Whence it came more would come; moreover, it was from the same airt as in the last two days. Relieved, the man rose stiffly to his feet to face the steep lift of the brae-side, and as he did so another drift of air sighed across the heather. He was satisfied.

Beinn Druim was a great mass of a hill, an isolated slice of a lofty plateau actually, with sides that were steep, rocky and scree-lined, and a summit that was bare and flat and half a mile in length. It lay perhaps four miles due north of Inveralish Lodge and rather less west by south of Am Fasach nan Earba, from which side it had by no means so impressive an appearance as from elsewhere. And in a great crescent, facing south and west, green wedges running up into the mighty buttresses of rock that supported the summit, were the high sheltered corries that the deer loved, quiet oases of grass and herbage amongst the desert of scree and stone.

Alastair MacIver had planned this day's work thoroughly— but all might not go according to his planning, just the same. Besides the all-important wind, there was the men's reactions— not to mention the deer—to consider. He could not be sure; he could only assume and forecast. But he had a pretty shrewd idea as to the probable trend of events. . . . God being good. Given a little grace, he would take a hand in this day's ploy, so he would!

His steady climbing, lifting the ache of cold out of his bones and setting the blood running warmly, soon brought him to the cloud-level. Thereafter he clambered on through the chill clammy obscurity, less steadily but still unhesitant; with the steep pitch of the slope to move diagonally across he could not go far wrong. He was climbing the less notable eastern face of the hill, and heading north-west, his objective a commanding position above and to leeward of the corries on the farther side. The newborn breeze, meantime, was at his back, sending the murky blanket of the mist streaming and eddying past him in a strange secret soundless progress, out of nowhere into nothingness, and stumbling amongst the blocks and aprons of stone, he kept it doubtful company.

Only the gradual levelling of the ground, after the last boulder-strewn confusion, informed the climber that he had reached the summit. The mist slipped past a little faster here, perhaps, and the chill of it was more keen, maybe, but nothing else indicated that it was the top of three thousand feet of mountain. It meant that the man was too far to the south; he had intended to slip round the high northern shoulder of the hill, and so to turn in to face the wind. It was as well that this cloud would dull the scent of him—if the deer were anywhere near where they had been yesterday, he might well be too close to them now. Turning right-handed, MacIver moved off along the ridge, cautiously, an eerie proceeding with no certainty about it, and only the wind at the nape of his neck to give him his direction.

Presently he was amongst tumbled rock once more, with the ground falling away in front of him. Swinging over to the left again, so that the air was now on his cheek, he started to descend, picking his way with due care. Suddenly he stopped. Instinct rather than sight or any certainty of knowledge warned him of danger. This would do well enough. He would wait here amongst the jagged stones for what the day would bring.

And that, without any comfort, he did.

For long he waited, an hour, two hours, and more. To the rest of the world the day had come, but here, on this mountain-top that could have been the first to spy the rising sun, the flowing cloud still reigned supreme. It had been getting lighter steadily, of course, through leaden greyness to sullen pallor and now a pearly opaqueness, silvery-white yet as impenetrable as ever. But at long last a new quality became apparent in the mist, a leaven of yellow in the white, that grew and deepened and permeated it all, seeming to thicken the haze rather than lighten it. Then, presently, this yellow changed to gold, vital, gleaming, and intensified till the radiance of it was a pain to the eyes, with every tiny particle of vapour a dazzling mirror. And then, in the flicker of an eyelid, it was gone, mist obscurity and brilliance together, lifted like a curtain, swiftly and entirely, gone as though it had never been.

112

The man blinked in the sudden clarity, the terrifying immensity of the view that burst upon him. Far and wide under the infinity of the dome of the sky the land stretched away, boundless, with every feature picked out and etched by the smile of the eager sun, ridge over ridge, range upon range, rolling moors and shadow-stained valleys, clear-cut land and gleaming water. From the constriction of the mist to this dizzy immensity was unnatural, frightening. But what lifted the man's eyebrows was not so much the distant prospect and far-flung background as the immediate foreground—or lack of it. For, just a yard or so below his halting-place, the rocks stopped short, suddenly, entirely, and after them, nothing. Sheer and abrupt the land fell away before him, to a drop of hundreds of feet to the corries beneath. He was perched on top of the most northerly of the buttresses that towered above the west face of the ben. It was as well that his instinct had been working, a while back.

But MacIver did not waste long contemplating the soundness of his intuition. He had work to do, and that belated mist had held him up too long already. Producing his stalker's glass from his pocket, he scanned all the corries below him. There were four of these, green rifts in the dun flank of the hill, out of each of which a stream was born. In the first two he found nothing, but on the third, after an initial sweep, his glass faltered and stopped, and his breathing likewise. When his breath came out it was in a sigh of relief. The beasts were there, and in a good position too, down near the wide mouth of the corrie—a better position than he had been prepared for. Yesterday they had been scattered in two corries, and higher up. It would be the mist that had sent them down, likely. As well that they had not gone much lower, though. Four, five, seven, eight, of them, all stags, two of them with not bad heads—eight-pointers. The ten-pointer that he had seen yesterday had cleared off, evidently, which was a pity—a fine wide head it had, an old beast for sure. Good, then. Now for the rest of the party.

He raised his telescope for a wider sweep, altering the focus slightly, and starting far down in the floor of the valley below, where the burns from the corries had united into a sizable stream, he began methodically and patiently to scan all the spread of the ground, searching, prying, probing with his glass, yard by yard, back and forward, up and down. For a long time he found nothing; no life seemed to manifest itself down there, save a loping blue hare and a bird or two. It was a flash of russet and white across his lens that made him sit up; he followed it and in a few seconds had a graceful bounding roebuck in his glass, a lovely creature, all limbs and ears, that made for the shelter of dark woodland over towards the north. After a little it halted, wide-legged, alert, and looked back whence it had come. Knowing that look, Alastair looked back also, and it was not long before he had found what scared the roe; in a hollow among peat-hags a man lay, a keeper obviously, with a shotgun by his side, though the gipsy could not recognize him at that range. Moreover, he was waving his hand in a beckoning signal to somebody, and looking over his shoulder. Soon MacIver had placed a second man, and, intensifying his search on either side, a third and fourth. So! The girl had been right, then. The stage was set and this hill was surrounded. It was just the other principal players, two he hoped, that he had to wait for now. He made a last careful scrutiny of all the approaches to the corries from the low ground, but nothing could he pick out there. Laying by his glass for the moment, Alastair Dubh settled himself back more comfortably amongst his rocks and stared up at the deepening blue vault of the heaven. He would await Major Telfer's pleasure.

So he stayed, still and relaxed, and thought his own thoughts up there on his mountain top, and occasionally he smiled to himself. He was taking a big chance in this game, more than one chance, but it was a big game and the stakes were high. A modified success was probable, complete success problematical, and the risk to himself great. So much depended on Telfer doing the expected thing—or, rather, on his correct anticipation of Telfer's reaction to circumstances. If Telfer did not so react, then events might be merely tame, or definitely difficult. Shaw, the head-stalker, who would be with the Major, had to be considered, too—but Alastair felt more confident about that

114

lean man's attitude. Other factors there were, as well, to be taken into account—notably the instructions to the gang below on the subject of firearms, their enthusiasm for the task, and the efficiency of his own legs and lungs. Very well, indeed; these questions would be answering themselves, in due course.

Twice MacIver spied out the land again, before, perhaps an hour later, his eye caught sight of a couple of ponies, stationary, near the edge of the same long wood into which the roebuck had fled. Ponies meant only one thing; the stalking-party had arrived. Those garrons, left in the charge of a gillie, were to carry back the venison should the stalk be successful. Diligently he quartered and counter-quartered with his glass all the hill-face lifting up towards himself and the deer. They must be in there somewhere. He knew where to look, for he knew how deer so placed should be stalked, and how Donald Shaw would advise that they be stalked. Yet the very essence of their approach was that it should be inconspicuous, if stags were the quarry. So he searched on, patiently. But it is to be doubted whether he would have found what he looked for, hoped for, as soon as he did, had it not been for that brief gleam of light. He knew what that was—the reflection of sunlight on a carelessly handled telescope. That would be Telfer, for sure, with the shade not pulled out. Yes, b'damn . . . yes, it was, with Shaw alongside him. He frowned thoughtfully. It was not just where he had expected them. They were farther over to the south than he had thought likely—taking a risk, they were, with the wind, or would be when they got on a bit. Well, that was their lookout. . . . Grimly he closed and pocketed his glass, and prepared to move. It was action now . . . and might the Good One smile on him, and him needy!

Alastair MacIver's subsequent progress down the long western shoulder of Beinn Druim was carefully planned and well thought out, however much of a mad scramble it might have appeared to an uninitiated observer. And it would have to have been a succession of observers, in widely-scattered points of vantage. That was part of the planning.

His first move from his high stance amongst the rocks was a discreet unhurried retiral, with the importance urgent that he should not be seen or detected either by the deerstalkers or the deer stalked. He had crept cautiously away to his right, worming his way amongst the jagged boulders and avoiding the skyline of the summit at all costs, till the curve of the hill had intervened between him and them. Then, after another swift examination, through his glass, of the northern face of the mountain, he got to his feet and set off downhill at a long-strided lope, still keeping on the far side of the ridge of the ben's shoulder. Thus he still was invisible to the watchers he had spied in the main valley below the corries—whatever he might be to any others who perhaps were helping to surround the hill on its eastern flank. If any such there were, his present visible activity might well coax them out into the open after him—and very good, too. When, indeed, about halfway down that stone-studded slope, he paused in his hurrying to glance back and down, he saw three tiny figures far below and behind him, hastening in his direction, and he grinned to himself cheerfully. Let them all come. So far so good.

The next stage would not be quite so simple, though. Some-where between his present position and where the shoulder of the hill tailed away into the big wood to the north-west, he must cross over the dwindling ridge and show himself to those watchers he had seen waiting. The right spot at which to do this was important. To do so too soon would be to add to his difficulties and to the risks he ran—and he would run plenty, before the day was out—by giving them more scope to head him off. To leave it late was to risk the possibility of them not catching sight of him at all; he scarcely could be lingering on the ridge there, dancing a schottische maybe, to draw attention to himself, with those boys coming up at his back. And there might well be more right ahead of him—most likely was. He selected a place where a group of outcrops were prominent, roughly equidistant between where he was and the edge of the wood, and directed his pounding footfalls thitherward. There he would put his theories to the test.

He was still some distance from this limited objective when his plan was changed for him. Over to his right, perhaps a quarter of a mile off, and downhill, a man rose out of the heather, and even as he reconsidered the situation another got to his feet almost directly ahead, and nearer too. Reacting immediately, he swerved left-handed and was up and on to and over that crest in a few leaping paces, and running hard, really hard. Things were warming up.

Thudding down the bare open brae-face he trended away at an angle from that ridge of the hill that had been his cover—but not at too much of an angle—and he used his eyes for more than picking his way. Indeed, his feet seemed to choose the route of their own accord, and do it well too, for the going was treacherous, sliding scree and scattered stone, quaking bog and clutching heather. And still he sped light-foot, seeming to skim the pitfalls, avoiding danger with a split-second prescience that was almost uncanny. Alastair MacIver had not been brought up a tinker for nothing. And soon his busy eyes saw what they were looking for. Down where the pitch of the hill levelled out, deep in the pit of the valley and over on the farther slopes beyond the stream, men were appearing, getting up out of their hiding-places, their faces towards him. He did not count them, but there would be half a dozen this side of the burn alone. He made no grumble at that. The more the merrier.

Out of the corner of his eye he caught a glimpse of the fellow that he had swerved to avoid some moments back. He was outlined now on the crest of the ridge, and despite his cutting of the angle he had made no ground meantime, an elderly man and no match for the gipsy on the hill. His presence was no trouble to Alastair at all, but he was shouting and gesticulating, and the direction in which he was looking might indicate trouble, nevertheless. It did. Following the line of his gaze, MacIver saw an answering arm wave from a clump of rushes, right in front of him and no more than a couple of hundreds of yards off. Mother o' God, the place was thick with them—the gentry were doing things in style, whatever! His decision had to be speedy, but while still he reflected, swiftly, the head and shoulders lifted up after the arm, and he recognized Bert Clarke, barring his way. And the decision was taken, immediately, inevitably. Straight for the keeper he raced, and his teeth under the wicked crescent of moustache grinned whitely.

For a moment Clarke knelt irresolute, then he jumped to his feet and stood wide-legged, one shoulder hunched forward, his intention plain and aggressive. But he did not stay that way. Perhaps it was the expression on MacIver's features that changed his mind, perhaps the very obvious resolution of his headlong charge. Anyway, he stooped suddenly and picked up a shotgun and threw it to his shoulder, menacingly. "Stop, damn you!" he roared.

The gipsy came on, unfaltering.

And swearing, quick-breathed, the keeper fired, both barrels.

Black Alastair, no more than thirty yards off, sensed the decision behind the man's face, in his whole attitude, even as he pressed the triggers. In the instant of certainty he hurled himself forward and down, felt the blast and whistle of shot above him and a searing sting in his left shoulder. No doubt Clarke had fired high to frighten rather than to hit him, anyway to stop him, but twelve-bore shot at thirty yards makes a wide pattern. And it did not stop him. Seeming hardly to touch the ground in his fall, the dark man was up again, and if he had been charging before he was bounding now. The other had reached into his pocket for more cartridges and was fumblingly putting them into the open breach, when he saw that he would not have time. He would have been wiser to have grabbed his gun by the barrels and used it as a club, or even to have thrown it away and left his hands free, but he hesitated and was still holding it uncertainly before him when the gipsy thundered upon him. He had no chance, of course, from the first. MacIver's temper, that could be cold or hot or sheerly blistering, had been roused to white-heat by that single pellet in his shoulder. Like a battering-ram he drove down on the luckless keeper, in the impetus of his rush, and, big man as he was, Clarke reeled backwards and over under the furious hail of blows, falling heavily, with the wind knocked out of him, and his assailant on top. In a moment MacIver was on his feet again, and, crouching over the other, had jerked him up by the front of his jacket, and with a savage underarm swing his fist crashed beneath the keeper's jaw. "That," he hissed, "is for the shooting!" and hitching the lolling head forward again unmercifully, he drove in once more at the point of the chin, terribly. "And that's . . . for the lies . . . you told the Sheriff." And as he let the sagging body drop back he struck for the last time, an open-handed swipe across the face. "And that's the interest . . . on the debt . . . you told the lady . . . !" Stepping across, he picked up the shotgun where it lay, breach open, and whirling it round his head he brought it down with all his force upon a rock of moss-grown granite, round which the slender steel barrels bent like lead-piping. Then tossing the ruined weapon on top of the recumbent Clarke, he looked round him, fierce-eyed. The people from the low ground were coming up at speed, but the nearest were still a fair distance off. The elderly man from the ridge at his back was quite close now, not more than a hundred yards, but not hurrying too hard. "And to hell with *him*!" MacIver snorted, gasping, and raised a threatening fist in his direction. The other, wise man, faltered and stopped. The tinker laughed, mocking, and turned and set off at a steady trot. The black edge of the long wood was in front of him, not a quarter of a mile off.

Alastair made the wood without any difficulty or further incident. Apparently he had broken through the screen of would-be interceptors, and the Laodicean behind him was keeping his distance. Indeed, the dark man took his time to that last stretch of open ground; he was anxious that as many as possible of his pursuers should see where he entered the trees, and should follow him therein, and at no great distance. He was being his own decoy this day.

Though no forest, or extensive wilderness like Am Fasach, the wood of Rymore was a fair-sized place, of spruce and larch and birch and juniper, and its thickets and shaws were important for MacIver's purpose. In and out and amongst them now he made his way, and he who could move through woodland softly as any of the wood's silent indwellers, today trampled and blundered. The pigeons flapped away from his noisy progress in protest and alarm, and other quieter things withdrew affronted. And every now and then the man paused and listened; when, from behind him and to either flank, he heard halloos and a widespread cracklings of twigs, he smiled, and plunged onward.

A long dance he led them, those hirelings of the prideful Southron, always keeping within earshot, for he did not want them to lose him—yet. And he laughed as he led them on, did Alastair Dubh MacIver. Some of them were not over-anxious to catch him, no doubt, and he laughed at that too. But what was in his mind, what he meant to achieve before the day was out, he did not laugh at. So he pressed on, leaving his trail of sound and signs, and whatever his pursuers thought, it was his own game that he was playing, and on his own pitch that he played it, and the heather that had bred him played his game with him.

There was a place, roughly half a mile from where he had entered the trees, where an open ride had been cut clean through the thickness of the wood, in the interests of the sportsman, a lane perhaps twenty yards wide wherein only grasses and berries and heather grew. Alastair approached this with care. If whoever was running this chase had any sense in him—John Robertson, likely—he would have sent a lad quickly round each edge of the wood to watch the ends of this ride, and see if he passed over. And it would be a pity to disappoint them. So when, presently, the trees thinned in front of him, MacIver stumbled imprudently out into the open, paused in the middle to glance right and left furtively, and then hurried on into the farther cover—but not before a hail from up on his right confirmed his judgment. And once well within the screen of the trees again, he turned sharply to the right to run swiftly up, parallel with that ride, and no longer did rustlings and crackings advertise his passage. Silently he flitted, and soon through the tree-trunks he saw and passed the fellow who had shouted at sight of him, now dashing hotfoot down the centre of the open ground to mark where the fugitive had disappeared. A little way behind him came another man, in less haste—Ian Dunbar, and no enthusiast,

120

puffing a pipe. Alastair slipped on, through the rust-tipped junipers, a shadow amongst shadows.

Up near the top margin of the wood he paused and turned back towards the edge of the ride once more. Gliding from tree to tree he came to the place he wanted, and, after a comprehensive survey, got down on his knees, on his stomach, and began cautiously to worm his way out into the open. It was not difficult, with high old heather and tall grasses and broken branches to give him cover. Out in the middle, where no one would look for him—he hoped—he stopped and lay still, and was glad to. It was his first breather in quite a spell of activity.

If MacIver was quiet and still, he seemed to be the only one who was so. The wood before him echoed and re-echoed to the shouts and bangings and flounderings. Down near the middle of the ride the vociferous individual who had most recently spied the quarry was clamant in drawing attention to the fact, and his cries were being answered from right and left. Though he was a great help indeed, Alastair decided that he was a poor creature. Folk were now breaking out of the trees throughout the length of that avenue, with a knot of them collecting down beside the man with the lungs. The gipsy counted eleven of them, a good proportion carrying shotguns—they should have had the military out, too, so they should! A man, Peter Rennie the underkeeper, emerged quite close to him, no more than five or six yards away, but his gaze was on the concourse farther down, and he passed by the hidden tinker without a glance. In a matter of a minute they all had disappeared into the lowermost belt of trees, lost to the eye if not to the ear, and the ride was clear. It was all dead easy. Crawling forward, Alastair slipped into the wood from which he had so lately come, and through its gold and russet glades, hushed now and empty, he took his silent way. But he hurried, nevertheless, for now time could work against him.

As the last trees of the wood of Rymore thinned before him to reveal all the wide sun-soaked slopes of Beinn Druim again, Alastair MacIver reached for his telescope just a little anxiously.

Here was where he would get the answer to some of his questionings of a while back. First of all, had he drawn away all the opposition that had encircled the hill? It was important that he had. But more important still—was the deer-stalking still going on? Had Telfer and Shaw, seeing the general hurried convergence of their men into the wood, seeing even his own headlong rush, as well they might have done, continued with their stalking, or had they promptly given it up, their part in the game finished? In fact, was the stalking episode merely a pretence, a bait to the trap, or was it the real thing, with the trap conveniently arranged round it? The Major, it was said, was a keen stalker—indeed, he was supposed to have stayed on thus late in the season expressly to have a go at Marsden's stags, a programme that the weather so far had balked. And Donald Shaw, a man with pride in his craft, working up to the deer, would not look kindly on the idea of getting up in the middle of a stalk, under the very noses of the beasts, and walking sheepishly off—that could be assumed. The chances were, then, that the two of them would be up there still. That the deer themselves might have been disturbed by the ongoings at the foot of the hill, was not very probable. There was a good mile and a half between the corries and the scene of the activity below, as well as nearly a couple of thousand feet of difference in altitude, and the beasts' eyes were not on the same par as were their noses and ears. They were fine and snug up there in their corrie, and the cantrips of foolish men so far beneath not likely to alarm them. That shot of Clarke's might have scared them, of course, though the wind was the other way. Damn the creature! Thus the dark man reasoned. He crept forward to investigate.

Lying on a hummock amongst outcrops he made his survey and learned his answers. Farther down, where the wood dwindled to the valley-floor, the ponies still waited, presumably with their gillie. Then his glass swept up towards the hilltop. Yes, the beasts were still there, feeding contentedly, Glory Be! It took him a while to find the stalkers, though; eventually he discovered them, creeping up a burn-channel much farther over to the south than seemed advisable—in fact, they were now farther away from the deer than when first he had spied them. There could be only one explanation to that; those stags were not the quarry. There must be other deer in the last, the most southerly, of the corries, unseen from here. So much the better; it would give him more time for what he had to do.

And so MacIver was on his way again. It would be wearisome to chronicle his cautious slantwise progress up the long side of Beinn Druim, how, utilizing the folds and fissures of the hill, the watercourses and hollows, and all the outcrops and the broken ground—and more humble cover than these where the going was bare—sensitive to observation from below as well as from above, he worked his way up in the wake of the stalkers, and at a speed that taxed even his fitness for the task. It was a long stalk, done mainly bent double, and lower, and it was all uphill. Only those who have attempted the like will appreciate just what strain is involved to lungs and heart and muscles—and the gipsy was far from fresh to start with. But that man did not know what it was to spare himself, and speed was essential. Suffice it to say, then, that in little more than half an hour, his breathing heavy and his complexion darker even than was its wont, he was up in the vicinity in which he last had discerned the stalkers. And he was grateful to be there, undiscovered presumably, and grateful also that the shot for which he had listened all the way up had not yet sounded. They were not rushing things, anyway.

He had not caught a glimpse of the others recently, nor had he yet seen their quarry. A long spine of naked basalt, actually the tail-end of one of the high buttresses above, while providing excellent cover had obstructed his view for some time now. Until he gave up the protection of its flank for the prominence of its crest, he would remain hidden but uninformed. So, choosing a spot where the edge was torn and serrated with broken stone, Alastair pulled himself up warily, and peered over.

What happened then happened quickly. A single comprehensive glance revealed the situation . . . and the need for action. In the green skirts of that last corrie, not more than a hundred yards from where he crouched, the two men lay, very low, and in front of them, perhaps seventy yards farther, three deer stood and one lay, three long-eared hinds standing at gaze and one great stag—the same big ten-pointer that he had caught a glimpse of yesterday—sitting at ease. Or, more accurately, had been sitting, for now the big beast was in the act of getting to its feet, and the sunlight gleamed redly on its massive shoulder and heavy mane and on the wide-spreading, white-tipped antlers. This, then, was the attraction that had led the stalkers on, bypassing the other stags, taken them patiently in a wide semicircle, and then, after drawing them slowly and painfully over a great stretch of bare featureless moss and gravel till they dare go no nearer, had kept them waiting while it lay half-hidden and unshootable, chewing the comfortable cud in the smile of the sun. But the time for waiting was over—for all of them. The fact that the stag was getting to its feet, and the direction of the three hinds' wide-eyed gaze, told its own story. Some wandering wind-current, some sound, some instinct, had roused the deer's suspicions; though not yet alarmed they were uneasy—and the difference between unease and alarm in red deer may be as the twinkling of an eye or the drawing of a breath, and alarm means but one thing, flight, immediate, swift and final. Already Donald Shaw was passing over to the Major the rifle that he had carried all this way, and the other, receiving it, was edging forward into a comfortable firing position. It was seconds now. For a moment Alastair MacIver hesitated, loath to do the thing that he had come so arduously to do; that stag had been well stalked, good work and much patience had fetched its stalkers thus far, and it was an eminently shootable beast, ripe for the rifle. His instinct was to hold his peace. What was it that man Telfer had said about sportsmanship . . . ? And yet—hadn't they tried to trap him with this same game, even used their firearms on him, like vermin to be exterminated, who'd heard tell of sporting vermin? Moreover, for his purpose he wanted Telfer angry, violent; with his fine stag dead before him, he might be too well satisfied with himself to be bothering with a blackguard tinker, and that would not do at all—he was not finished with Jeffrey Telfer yet. And a picture of his prison cell rose before his eyes, stone and concrete and iron bars, and he nodded, twice. So let it be.

Frowning, Alastair MacIver scrambled to his feet on the crest of that basalt ridge, and his hands went up to frame his mouth. "Eirich, Iverach!" he cried, his clan's war-cry. "Rise, Iverach!"

That cry had set these hills afire many a time, and briskly, but never, surely, more swiftly than it did that day in the corries of Beinn Druim. Without pause or interval, as though sped from a bow, the deer were away, in great springing bounds, and after them a despairing furious shot cracked viciously if harmlessly. Before the echoes of his cry had died away they were reinforced by those of another, a shout, high-pitched and prolonged and angry enough for any man, as Jeffrey Telfer springing up, turned and raised his fist and his rifle as well as his voice. What he said was neither intelligible nor material; his face and gesture and attitude was eloquent enough. At his side Donald Shaw, less demonstrative but more practical, was already on the move, and watching him coming Alastair saw that his look was grim. Raising his arm again the dark man waved insolently, derisively, and his voice rose in skirling mockery, challenge in every line of him. He waited only until he saw Telfer following hotfoot on the heels of the head-stalker and then he turned and jumped down from his ridge of rock. His strategic withdrawal had begun.

XII

IT is to be feared that, as averred by certain considerable folk from the South, Alastair Dubh MacIver had some elemental insolence of character in his make-up. Certainly, what he now set out to achieve could only have been conceived in sublime insolence, in wicked disdain, and in sheerest arrogance. For not only was his plan based on the assumption that he was more than a match for these other two men in wits as in limb, weary as he was from his earlier strenuous efforts, but his concern was, not that they might, indeed, possibly gain the mastery, but that they might instead be too apt to give up the unequal struggle and retire from the fight. So they must be coaxed and tempted and led on. That he did not know either of them particularly well only added to the indictment. Awkward folk, the MacIvers.

Almost from the beginning of that chase he started his play-acting. With the pursuit over the basalt spine, they found him not much more than fifty yards ahead of them, and going unsteadily, heading due north along the line of the corries, a stumbling unsurefooted figure who ran with his head over his shoulder and wasted much precious time and breath on shouted defiance and fist-shakings. The Major now led the chase, in righteous wrath, a few paces ahead and apart from Donald Shaw, who now, it was to be noted, was once again the custodian of the rifle. Telfer was the younger man, in his mid-forties, and fairly fit as became one who sought conclusions with the red deer; moreover, he was an affronted man. His stalker was nearer sixty than fifty, a grizzled, lean, typical Highlandman out of Moray, long-legged and deep-winded, who ran with a steady, unhurried lope, selecting his route with a careful eye, in contrast to his companion's precipitate straightforward rushing. But either method, they both ran a lot more effectively than did the wavering jaded figure in front—which, nevertheless, it might be noted, just managed to keep its fifty-yard distance.

So they ran, the three of them, along the high side of Beinn Druim, between the rocky ramparts of the summit and the long screes of the brae-face, leaping green slippery aprons of surface-water, skirting sweating slides of naked rock, and clambering over the tumbled treachery of great stone-falls, risking their ankles at every second step—three urgent discordant figures in a wide, empty desolation wherein only the quiet procession of the cloud shadows made any movement.

By the time that they had reached the north-west shoulder of the hill, where Alastair first had started this running business an hour and a half before, he noted that Telfer, now well in advance of his companion, was puffing a bit, not running so strongly. This would not do; he would need encouraging, the man, until he got his second wind. So, after a yard or two, MacIver's foot slipped on a rounded stone and he pitched forward on his shoulder to roll over and over twice, before picking himself up wearily and running a hand up and down his leg. When he set off again, more unsteadily than ever, he had developed a decided limp. The Major, now less than thirty yards off, seemed to recover his wind at approximately the same moment, for he had sufficient to shout something very authoritative and threatening, and he came on in good style.

They were going downhill now, north-easterly, into the area from which Alastair had drawn his first three pursuers, the first that he had noticed, anyway—he hoped that he had flushed them all, indeed, and that no odd stragglers still waited for him down here. The hill fell away before him in a slow slope, short heather and blaeberries, then levelled out and gradually lifted again to a low ridge. It might take some nursing to get Telfer up over that ridge . . . though the same man was doing fine and well at the moment, for sure. MacIver increased his pace just a fraction and the length of his uneven stride by an inch or so. He was finding his limp almost as much trouble as it looked.

Down that long brae they plunged and thudded, and gradually Shaw crept up on Telfer, and Alastair noting it, frowned. He did not want that long man in the lead yet—this business took a bit of controlling. There was something he could try, though, if the stalker would keep to the rear for just a little longer. Down at the foot, before the farther slope rose towards the low ridge, a burn ran; if he was to turn and follow that for a bit . . . ? Painfully slowly it seemed, he neared that stream. Heavier going it was here, in the lower ground, with water lying amongst the tussocks. His limp noticeably improved, and one or two of his stumbles were not premeditated. At last he reached the stream, and leaping it, he turned sharply right-handed to run down its soggy, reed-lined bank. Out of the corner of his eye he saw Telfer, lumbering on heavily, roughly the same distance off, with Shaw still, fortunately, ten or fifteen yards behind him. Would he turn, would he do it? If he didn't, the trouble would be worse than before. But yes, Praise Be, he would, he did! From his rearmost position, the stalker had started to do the sensible, the obvious thing. He had half-turned to his right likewise and was now heading across to cut off the fugitive in his course. Alastair let him get well established on his new line—across a fine boggy stretch, too—and then turned abruptly, almost right-about, and headed back and uphill, away from the burn and towards the ridge. This brought him very close to Telfer, but without overmuch concern. That man was fully occupied in setting one foot down before another, and turned to follow him up only mechanically. Cursing, Donald Shaw swung back also, now left well behind. The slope up to that swelling crown of heather was neither long nor steep, but it was a trial and an ordeal to all three of them. Most notably so to Jeffrey Telfer, no doubt, not bred to the hills and of softer fibre than the other two, and he toiled up the hill slowly, leaden-footed, his breath coming in great gulps, his normally colourless face crimson and puffed. MacIver, looking back, and only a score or so of paces ahead, watched him anxiously, and feigned a still greater fatigue than he felt; he must get that man up and over the crest before his heart or his spirit gave out on him—the downward easy slope beyond must look after itself. Donald Shaw, too, though much less spent, was feeling the weight of his years and the stiffness of ageing joints, also the rifle and the bumping telescope that he carried on a strap at his back were no help; moreover, he had ground to make up.

As for Alastair himself, he was glad enough to go slow for the encouragement of the Major, the lame-duck business suiting his weary limbs very well. He had had just about enough running for one day.

But he had more to do yet, even when, at last, he stood panting at the summit. Before him the land swept gently downwards, in brown heather waves, smoothly swelling at first but pitted with the black of peat-hags lower down, till, nearly a mile off, it faded into the vast spreading expanse of Am Fasach, formless, boundless, under the midday sun. He looked back anxiously. Could he entice these two that far? It seemed a long way. Telfer was making no pretence at running now, plodding upward bent nearly double with his hands bearing on his knees, his distress apparent. And Shaw, though in better shape, obviously was tiring rapidly. The dark man knitted his brows. He had been afraid of Telfer packing up before this, and so had striven to keep him in the front, determined that he should not despair, or, trailing along behind his stalker, call off the latter in disgust. Having got him thus far, he must not fail on the last lap, for reach Am Fasach they must. So, deciding swiftly, he limped on over the brow and, as soon as he was out of their line of sight, cast hurriedly about for a hiding-place, and choosing a slight hollow amongst the heather, flung himself down and pulled the stuff around him. He would give them the breather that they needed.

In a little while the two men were on the skyline, panting, and there stopped, at a loss. Presently, out of their gasping came words, singly and in little groups, regulated by available breath. "Lying low ... hiding ... can't be far. All-in, probably ... curse him! God, I'm foundered. Sit ye down, sir ... take a rest while you've a chance. That's it ... put head 'tween knees. Where the hell are the others? Lord, let me get ... my hands on him."

Alastair lay and listened, well content so to do. They were in no hurry, up there, to start searching for him, and he did not blame them. Soon they fell silent, and peering through the heather he made out the hobnailed soles of Shaw's boots as he lay flat on his back, and Telfer still crouching relaxed, heaving

129

shoulders bent to his knees. As well that they were in the same state as himself, or the steam-hammer thudding of his heart would have shouted aloud his whereabouts.

It was the stalker that stirred first, sitting up and reaching to his hip. "Have a bit swig at this, sir," he suggested, passing over a metal flask, no doubt filled with Sim Campbell's amber whisky. The other accepted it without comment and, raising his head, drank deeply. Shaw had a mouthful himself, and then got to his feet, scanning the terrain. Not much would escape those eagle-eyes, and Alastair prepared to move. When, consequent to some muttered question of the Major's, his companion stooped to listen, MacIver seized his chance. Springing up, he was off again, not too fast and not too slow, his limp much in evidence. Shouts behind him proclaimed that the chase was resumed, this time with Shaw in the lead. Surely Telfer was safe as far as the wood-edge, at any rate, with that outsize gill inside of him.

That last stretch was a trial and a weariness, the gipsy's wing-trailing business being more of a tax to his strength than he had imagined. Especially amongst the mosses and peat-pools of the last stages. And here, with the pursuit flagging likewise, he was constrained to a more intensified demonstration of exhaustion, staggering and falling with increasing frequency, and allowing Shaw to approach closer sometimes than was comfortable. But the trees ahead urged him on, scattered outriders of all the open ranks of Am Fasach. Only a hundred or two of yards now lay between him and the end of the second stage of his plan for this day. So far he had been successful. He did not think that himself and Am Fasach would fail in the rest. Rounding the first gnarled and ancient pine on its heather knoll, he nodded to it grimly. It was not one man against a crowd any more; he had allies now, hundreds of them, thousands of them. Let Jeffrey Telfer watch his step.

He entered the still glades of Am Fasach with Shaw about thirty yards behind him and the Major fully a hundred yards farther back. Half a dozen of those rounded identical hillocks he skirted in a scallop-like progress, not in any consistent direction, but keeping scrupulously just within sight of the older man, and once or twice he heard Shaw shout a guiding halloo for Telfer following. And the gipsy grinned as he heard it, albeit wide-mouthed and breathless—wasn't he the clever one and them playing his game for him just as if he'd taught them it! Then, suddenly, while he was hidden momentarily, he spurted into an agonizing all-out dash, darting a little way ahead and then plunging full-length into the knee-high heather that dotted that place. Deftly, swiftly, he pulled and arranged the twisting stems to shield and cover him, and then lay still, as still as his pounding heart would let him.

In a few moments the head-stalker's heavy dragging footfalls were approaching, and the sound of his breathing was a pain to listen to. He was up with him, he was passing, he was past. But only by a yard, when MacIver leapt up and sprang. Out of the corner of his eye the other saw him coming, and half-turned. But it was too late. Like a panther, the gipsy was on him, right arm around his shoulder and neck, knee in the small of his back; and the older man, staggering already in his sudden attempt to turn in his stride, and struck by this thunderbolt from behind, crashed forward on his face, his assailant on top of him. Swiftly his arms were jerked and pinioned behind his back, in a grip related to a half-nelson, and Alastair's knee was digging into his spine. "Shout, and I'll break you in two halves!" he growled.

But Donald Shaw was not shouting. His fall, and the weight on top of him, had knocked out of him what little breath his sorely-tried lungs had been retaining, and he was winded quite. His open mouth and frantic gulping proclaimed his state, and Alastair took advantage of it. Reaching into his pocket for a length of cord, tied in a slipknot just for this purpose, he got it over one wrist of his feebly-struggling victim, and then the other, pulled it tight, twisted it round and round till he had the man's arms secure. Then, crouching down beside the other, he took his knife and, raising the stalker's jacket, heartlessly cut off all the braces-buttons of his trousers.

Major Telfer came in sight, but not for long. Having got too far behind, he had failed to follow the twists and turns of the gipsy's progress, and now was struggling on, vaguely in a straight line beyond the point where last he had seen his stalker and guide. And who would blame him, in that welter of featureless brown hillocks? Presently they heard him call, a questioning plaintive call, and Alastair gripped Shaw's shoulder threateningly as he lay. "Answer that, and you'll be sorry!" he warned.

They listened to one or two more of the Major's calls, gradually fading, before Shaw, his wind in some measure recovered, made to sit up. The dark man assisted him. "I'm sorry to be after doing this to a man like yourself, Mr. Shaw," he mentioned, "but you've asked for it, whatever. You're keeping bad company, you know."

The other looked at him keenly. "What are you going to do now, MacIver?" he asked quietly.

"I am going to deal with the man Telfer, who was the start of all this trouble," Alastair Dubh said simply.

"Have you not done enough?" the older man suggested.

"I have not then, my God!"

Shaw was silent. He was not a talkative man.

MacIver eyed his companion fixedly. "I am going after him now . . . and you are going back out of here, by your own self."

"I am not." That was definite.

"I was afraid of that," Alastair nodded. "I'll need to be tying you to a tree, then . . . and it may be hours before I'm back to untie you again—dark it could be."

"What are you going to do to him MacIver?" the other questioned, narrow-eyed.

"Och, nothing very much at all—you need not worry, man. I'll not kill him or hurt him either, very much—unless I have to. And I will not lose him. You can't help him at all, Mr. Shaw, you see—you might as well be on your way back."

The stalker shook his head, unspeaking.

"Right, then—come on." Getting up, the tinker assisted his prisoner. On his feet, Shaw took a step, and promptly his pinioned hands at his back made a grab at his slipping trousers, and he frowned, biting his lip, but held his peace.

The dark man forbore to smile. He took no pleasure in

heaping indignities on this sound man, old enough to be his father, able man on the hill, and no man's enemy. But his purpose was strong upon him, and Shaw must be kept out of the way. So he led him, not foolishly resisting, to a tree on a neighbouring hillock, that he selected with some care—for the shape and outline of their trees was the principal means of recognition of these featureless mounds—and he was not wanting the man to leave his bones there, undiscovered. So, to a tall bare-trunked flat-topped pine he tied Donald Shaw, after only the token resistance of a wise man, securely yet not too uncomfortably. "Bide you there, then," Alastair told him. "If you lean against the tree, there, your breeks won't be coming down on you." He stood back to survey his handiwork. "You wouldn't be going to shout at all, by any chance?"

"Why not?"

"Because I'd have to be gagging you. Uncomfortable, if it's to be in a whilie. You'll have some sort of handkerchief for it, maybe?"

The other considered the matter briefly. "I'll not shout," he decided soberly.

"Good, then—that'll be best, whatever. There will be plenty shouting in it, without you, maybe!" MacIver, in the act of moving away, gave his victim a sidelong glance to the region of the hip. "Would there be anything left in yon fine flask of yours, Mr. Shaw?" he wondered. "A sip might be doing a power of good to both the two of us!"

The stalker did not smile, but there might have been just the merest gleam in the washed-out blue of his eyes. "Maybe," he admitted cautiously, "—but I canna get at it, with my hands this way."

"Och, but it's no trouble at all," the gipsy assured, and he had the flask out in a trice. He lifted it to his ear and shook it. "Man, there's just a mouthful left . . . or maybe two," he reported, and held it out to the other's lips.

Donald Shaw shook his grizzled head gravely. "After yourself, *Mister* MacIver," he said.

Alastair bowed, and took a drink. Then he shook the flask

133

again, listening. "Slainte mhor!" he gave him, and had another sip. "Just the top-half, exactly," he assured.

"Aye," the other nodded, with the mouthpiece held to his lips. "Slainte!" and he finished it in a gulp.

And that was that. Now for Major Telfer.

In any man's character there are many sides, and especially in so complex an individual as Alastair Dubh MacIver, with his peculiar ancestry and upbringing. That he was proud was apparent, hot-tempered indubitable, unforgiving seems to be indicated, and insolent has been suggested; whether cruelty also must be numbered amongst his vices is a moot point. Certainly, what he now planned to do might well be construed as such. On the other hand, it could be argued that he merely was being wholehearted; that having taken on a task, he was going to do it well and thoroughly. No one was likely ever to accuse that man of dealing in half-measures.

He had not much difficulty in locating the Major. Telfer was putting up a regular succession of shouts, ranging from the querulous to the urgent, demanding guidance, attention and company. Alastair Dubh was prepared to give him the first two, at any rate.

Heading in the direction of the calling, he slipped round two or three of the knolls, till presently, throwing himself down into the heather, he crawled over the round flank of one of them, to discover the Major wandering vaguely in the hollow before him—a harassed, weary-seeming, lonely figure in that strange still wilderness. Nodding to himself, the gipsy drew back out of sight, got to his feet and doubled around his hummock and across and into the mounds beyond the other's small valley. And there, after a moment for breath, he raised his voice, or better, a voice, since he sought to make it deeper than his own, throatier altogether. "Over here I am, Major Telfer," he cried into the quiet. "This way, sir."

An answering hail came immediately, relief in the ring of it, and, grinning, the dark man slipped away round the hillock behind him to wait and watch. Soon Telfer came in sight, at a

134

half-trot, and, satisfied, Black Alastair moved away swiftly, farther on, to presently halt and shout again. "Are you there?" he called. "This way—we've near got him now!"

And again he got his reply.

So commenced a grim and heartless game of hide-and-seek amongst that brown tree-dotted sameness, a strange unnatural chase that led on and on, ever farther into the empty trackless wastes of Am Fasach. And the gaps between the gipsy's decoy-calls grew longer, and in due course the calls themselves changed in their character through encouragement and urgency to a final mockery. The answers, too, altered, irritation succeeding relief, and apprehension irritation. When, in time, a quality almost of hysteria sounded in the crying, Alastair was satisfied. They were deep buried in the unchancy heart of the place now. He had done his share; Am Fasach could do the rest . . . with maybe just a little assistance.

Am Fasach was well able to, unaided. Even for those who were unprimed in its name and reputation, its influence was apparent, undeniable. Here, in its deepest fastnesses, no man could ignore it. There are woods that speak of peace and quiet, tall ancient woods solemn as any stone cathedral, dark forests hushed deep in contemplation of their own dark secrets, and open woods that smile and enfold and shelter. But this was no wood at all, though it was open and hushed and ancient; it was a far-flung desolation, a land, a territory of its own, detached and distinct from the rolling uplands and the soaring peaks that surrounded it, spiritually as it was physically. It was silent, not with the dead silence of inertia but with a brooding quiet that was aware, sombre, malevolent, and somehow vigilant. There was no escaping it.

Jeffrey Telfer did not escape it. And the frame of mind imposed on him through Alastair MacIver's agency did not help. It was an anxious man, an exhausted man, and a dejected man, that, hearing his cries for guidance unanswered, came to a halt beside a crooked leaning pine, frowning and gnawing his lip. Twice, three times, he shouted then, his voice rising to a high quivering note that told its own story, shaking and unstable, and not even an echo came back to him out of the still bleak aisles of that place. For a while he stood irresolute, gulping his breath, his hand on an aching side, while he fought with himself, his body and his spirit. Then slowly, unwillingly almost, he began to move on, dragging leaden feet, in the direction from which that last hail had seemed to come. And as he went his eyes darted and flickered from side to side and frequently he looked round and backwards; he did not know what he was looking for, but look back he must, for he knew that he was being watched, with hostility in the watching. The whole damned empty place was watching him. He knew it. And where was Shaw? Why had the man not heeded his calls to stop? Why had he led him on, and now stopped, deserted him? Why had he stopped calling? Where was he? Perhaps he was struck down—that devilish gipsy would do anything! Perhaps, perhaps he was dead? God . . . ! Telfer stopped in his tracks abruptly. "Shaw!" he yelled. "Shaw. . . . Sha-a-a-aw!" and that last was a scream. And, not waiting for answer or result, he turned and started back whence he had come, hurrying.

For how long Jeffrey Telfer plunged on through the pathless featureless maze of Am Fasach he could not have told. Time was not relative. But it was not so very long before he feared that he was lost, nor so very much later that he knew it. And it was not a good thing to know. There was no means of judging by which of all the series of identical valleys he had come. Every one was the same, every knoll a replica of its neighbour. And there was no vista, no field of view; no hill stood higher than another, and though he climbed many, he saw only the round tree-dotted shapes of their immediate fellows. And some time in that stumbling anxious progress he began to run again.

It was when, startled for the third time by a bounding silent roe-deer that leapt up from the heather before him, he glanced up at a hillock whither it fled, and gasped and stopped. Near the summit of that mound two trees stood, one uprooted and alean against the other—and he had passed those trees some time before, a long time before, he thought. They were unmistakable. . . . Wearily, despairingly, he drew a hand across his brow. And from somewhere near the silence was broken, and a voice laughed, mockingly. Wild-eyed, Telfer stared round and about. There was no misunderstanding the malevolence of that laugh. But there was nothing to see, nothing moved. Hurrying, desperate, he scrambled up the nearest hummock and started, not very expertly, to climb the tree that crowned it. A view he must get.

It was not hard to climb, the broken stumps of former branches making a stepladder all the way up it. For all that, the man all but fell twice in his haste, and tore his hand grasping a jagged broken spike of wood. But, at the top, there was no view, no prospect, only the tops of a myriad other trees like his own and the rounded breasts of more hillocks than even he had dreaded. Reluctantly, wild-eyed, he commenced to climb down again, clumsily fumbling his way, till, two-thirds of the way down, his foot slipped as a dead stump broke under him, and down he fell. He picked himself up and stood for a moment, swaying dazedly, then, staggering a little, he set off downhill once more. And as he went, that laugh rang out again, taunting him.

Telfer plunged on, whither he knew not. He had to keep moving, however sluggish his legs' reaction and uncertain his footwork. He dare not halt. That laugh . . . that devil . . . this damnable place! Desperately he sought for a direction. The sun could have helped, shown him the south-west at least, but there was no sun now, clouds covered the sky and the autumn afternoon was drawing towards the early night. Lord, if he was to be left here in the dark . . . ! So he dragged out his own travail, beating up and down those dreary corridors of heather, tripping, stumbling, falling, and often when he fell that horrible laugh rang out, now behind him, now to the side, now in front. But he no longer attempted to seek out the laugher. Slowly, but surely, apprehension was mounting towards terror.

It was the bats, unwholesome creatures of the night, that turned the screw to breaking point. With the onset of the dusk they began to appear, singly to start with but presently in groups and then in flocks, bevies of flickering, darting, soundless things, swooping and circling and twisting. At first the man did not notice them, his mind and senses preoccupied. Then, suddenly, in front of him, he saw a drove of them fluttering, and next moment they were all about him and the cold draught of beating wings enveloped him. As something chill brushed his cheek and ear, and something dark beat over his eyes, a cord seemed to snap within his brain and he knew that he could not go on, that he was finished. Gasping, choking, he tottered forward, arms across his face, to hurl himself down beneath the nearest tree. And there he crouched, his head in his hands, and shivered to the fleering laughter. He was a weary, brittle man, exhausted and out of his element, and he had eaten nothing since breakfast, and he had drunk more whisky on an empty stomach than had been wise. Sick in body and in spirit, he waited.

The silence was intense. Straining his ears, he listened. There were pulses throbbing at his temples, his heart was like a hammer, but through and over these the silence weighed down like an evil curtain. He pressed palms against his ears to shut it out. He could not stand it, he could not stand it! And then through it he heard a sound, a rustling and the crack of a twig. Starting up, he stared, but there was nothing to be seen, save heather and trees and shadow and the damned bats. Then he heard it again, farther over, the brush of movement, the snap of trodden wood. The silence succeeded, and then again, more rustling, working round. Presently it was behind him, somewhere near at hand but invisible, moving, moving. Getting to his feet slowly, Telfer glared, his staring eyes following the deliberate progress of that sound around him. And abruptly he raised a pointing arm. "Stop . . . come out," he cried chokingly. "Will you come out! Come out . . . !" and ending in a convulsive sob, he threw himself down again beneath the tree.

The silence returned.

When next the man lifted his head out of his hands, Alastair MacIver stood before him, still, waiting. Telfer shrank back and swallowed, and he shook his head wordlessly.

The gipsy made no move and said nothing.

The other's lips moved as though seeking to form words that would not come. But when MacIver stepped a pace forward, his arm stretched out wide-fingered as though to halt him, to ward off a blow, and words came quickly, jerkily. "Don't . . . don't come any nearer. Keep away. . . . What do you want?"

Alastair came another two steps closer, to tower over the shrinking figure. "What I want I take," he said briefly.

That got no answer.

He took his time before he went on, slowly, deliberately, and his voice, though quiet, had a steely quality. "You are a poor creature, Major Telfer, and not much of a soldier, I'm thinking, and I could break you this minute in my two hands!" He stooped, and the other flung away from him. But the dark man only picked up a stick fallen from the tree above, and holding it up, he snapped it in two, "Like that!"—and he threw the broken ends on to the hunched figure at his feet in a gesture that was supremely contemptuous.

Telfer found no words, but his eyes were busy.

"You would have broken me, if you could," the tinker resumed evenly, carefully. "You showed me no mercy. You drove me off your ground, and me doing it and you no harm. You got the police on to me, and had me locked in a little small cell for thirty days and nights, and said I was not to come back to Strathalish—me, Alastair MacIver. And this day, one of your men used his gun on me, like vermin to be shot." He nodded. "You've taken on a lot, Telfer man," he said softly. "You have asked for your trouble, a lot of trouble." MacIver paused and looked down at this man that he had lured on to retribution, and regretfully he shook his head. "But you are not worth it, not worth it at all," he sighed.

A bat zig-zagged between them on soundless flight and, somewhere near or far, an owl hooted. Telfer shivered.

The gipsy took a pace or two back and forth, his head down, as though debating with himself and he did not bother to look at the other man, who watched him so fearfully. "There's the one thing I can be doing, anyway," he decided at length. "A small thing, but fair enough." He rummaged in his inside pocket and produced some crumpled sheets of notepaper, from which he selected the cleanest. He also found a pencil. "You're going to do a bit of writing, Major Telfer," he announced. "You still can write, man, can you? Is that a pen you have there?" and stooping, he extracted a fountain-pen clipped into the other's breast-pocket. "That'll look better than my bit pencil," he declared, and thrust the pen into the Major's nerveless fingers. "Here's the paper, then. Write you on that just what I'm telling you, or. . . !" He left the rest unsaid.

The other stared at the blank paper, the pen held loosely, uselessly, in his hand. A heavy lethargy seemed to have come over him, the surrender of his limp and weary body overcoming even the fear and agitation of his mind.

Alastair frowned. "Write, damn you," he barked, "—if you want ever to be getting out of this place!"

Whether it was the sudden violence of the first phrase that penetrated, or the faint hope implied in the second, Telfer looked up, with more of the old concern than of the new lassitude. "What—what do you want?" he muttered.

The dark man shrugged. "You'll find out. Write what I'm telling you, and I'll get you out of here. Write now—'I hereby certify . . .' "

The pen hovered uncertainly over the paper while the man hesitated. But a grim "—or would you rather bide here?" seemed to decide him, and he began to write in an unsteady hand, with the paper supported on a none-too-steady knee. "I hereby certify . . ."

Slowly Alastair dictated his terms, and after a single upward glance that had more resignation than protest in it, Telfer wrote on as required. His writing even improved a little. "Now sign it," he was directed curtly.

The gipsy took the paper from him and read it through.

"I hereby certify that Alastair MacIver, and any in his company, has permission to proceed or camp upon my lands of Farinish, to come and go as he pleases, to cut wands and withies for baskets, and to take a reasonable quantity of fish and game for his own use. Moreover, I agree to take no further proceedings against him in respect of previous disagreements, and to use such influence as I possess with Sir Charles Marsden to do likewise, recognizing that an injustice has been done to the said Alastair MacIver.

I make this declaration voluntarily, agreeing that MacIver has neither threatened nor offered me violence at any time.
(Signed) JEFFREY TELFER."

"That'll do fine," he nodded. "Clear and straightforward and no taradiddles. The writing could be better, but as long as folk can read it. . . ." Folding it up, he put it in his pocket. "Now to get you out of this. You're fit for some walking? Right, then—follow me . . . and you can be saying a bit prayer that we are where I think we are, whatever."

If Alastair was not too sure of his whereabouts, he knew his direction, and he followed it confidently. Even so, it was dark before they won out of that hushed domain of the bats. And fast as MacIver walked, he had no trouble with Telfer lagging behind: he clung closer than a brother. At last they were out in the open and the wide shadowy moors rolled before them, and the murmurous Allt Luinn welcomed them quietly. Leaving the Major at the waterside, not without protest, the dark man turned back into Am Fasach once more to find and loose Donald Shaw—no easy matter in the dark. But at length it was done, and the cramped and silent stalker led back to the lip of the valley, and shown his gentleman hunched and dejected below. "There he is, then," Alastair pointed out. "Fine and well, if a wee thing tired and his spirit run out of him. He'll get back on his own feet right enough, and no harm done. He knows his own place, that man . . . now!"

"What have you done to him MacIver?" Shaw asked shrewdly.

"Nothing, man—just nothing at all," the gipsy assured. "He'll tell you the same himself. Goodnight to you, Mr. Shaw," and raising his hand, Alastair Dubh turned away, back to his own place. And he was tired, tired.

Two days later, Major Telfer was on his way south.

XIII

SIR CHARLES MARSDEN found himself in a somewhat unsatisfactory position apropos this confounded tinker. That their elaborately organized field-day against him had been a complete failure was rather distressingly obvious, the more so in that the large number of local people they had enlisted in the attempt were, by the same token, now the witnesses and advertisers of that failure—an annoying thought. Then his colleague, Telfer, had deserted him suddenly and rather mysteriously, without even calling to explain, leaving only a note advising that he give up the whole business as unprofitable, which was ridiculous but provoking. Moreover, that fool Clarke, his new underkeeper, had apparently fired his gun at the fugitive, and though he swore that he had fired over his head, the damned gipsy seemingly had been spreading the tale that he had been hit in the shoulder. Though Clarke, by all accounts, had taken a good hiding for his pains, it was the sort of thing the tinker-fellow conceivably might make trouble over—he had nerve enough for anything. Also, his niece Angela was taking rather a difficult line over the whole affair. She never had been enthusiastic, but of late had become positively hostile—and Angela, hostile, was not a comfortable person to have about the house. Not that he would have her away—far from it; he found her company stimulating and a little flattering, minus the hostility—though, for that matter, she seemed in no hurry to deprive him of her presence, hostile or not. It was strange that she should want to stay on up here so long after the season was over, but there was no accounting for the ways of women. She would stay just as long as she liked, even if he had to keep the Lodge open for her—but in the matter of this MacIver fellow she was no help. And even Shaw, his head-stalker, had become surprisingly tepid all of a sudden about bringing the scoundrel to book. A man might think that he could rely on his head-stalker against a notorious poacher. It was all very disappointing. Sir Charles was a man of some determination and not apt to give up a struggle in the midst of it, but continued failure, with general apathy and a strain of disapproval, can sap the urgency out of many a man's ire. Marsden was no foolish Gaelic fanatic.

So when, on a forenoon some days after the stalking episode, Sir Charles, driving with his niece along the sandy shore-road after a visit to Sim Campbell's store, perceived the strolling figure of the gipsy, dog at heel, at the roadside, his foot lifted only momentarily from the accelerator, and then pressed down again, and the great car swept on and past and down the white empty road with a barely perceptible pause. And the dark man, stopping to look back, following it with his eyes, smiled a quiet, satisfied and just slightly malicious smile. Two things that he had wanted to know he had learned in that brief moment, as the Rolls passed him. Firstly, Marsden, no longer so finely sure of himself, was going to hold his hand, meantime at any rate, sensible man; and secondly, his niece apparently was not going to let even a well-spanked bottom deflect her from whatever wilful woman's course she was on—or maybe, on reflection, she had liked it. Angela Denholm, passing him, had lifted a single slender finger and a slim sickle of eyebrow, in a brief gesture, restrained, casual, but eloquent. It implied an intimacy, an understanding, that he scarcely had expected after that last parting. And yet, and yet . . . ! So he smiled, and resumed his walking.

That night his small tent was pitched again in its old site in the green haugh of the Allt Buie, below Balnacraig.

So commenced a period of surface calm and seeming quiet in Strathalish, a calm that deceived no one and a quiet that was brittle and rooted in caution rather than in peace. Here was no truce, no agreement nor compromise: only an apparent interval, a strategic pause. But as such, it was acceptable to all concerned.

Not that Alastair MacIver became suddenly a trusting innocent. Though his tent stood once more in its old place and the blue smoke-column of his little fire lifted slenderly from amongst the junipers, no creeping searcher would have found him sleeping there by night nor caught him unprepared and unawares by day. Though the chop of his axe amongst the hazels, the tap of his hammer on metal, or even the thin song of his fiddle, proclaimed his presence and his busy-ness, no man was likely to approach him without himself first being observed. The gipsy's eyes and ears were rather better than most; like so many of his kind he had a strongly developed sense of danger acquired through generations of uneasy relationship with the Law; also Rob the collie was an excellent watch, with an unquiet conscience to assist him; moreover, the haugh of Balnacraig was a good place from which to escape, selected not entirely by chance. So, if MacIver was brazen, as Sir Charles averred—while doing nothing about it meanwhile—he was not actually foolhardy.

But, anyway, friend or foe, he had not so many visitors to his green meadow beneath the towering birch-clad craig that gave the croft its name. Hughie Bell he saw, of course, about his own place, and David Kennedy, the Farinish keeper, paid a duty-call, grimly civil, to show that he was keeping an eye on him, whatever queer-like caper he might have had with the Major. To him Alastair showed his paper, famous already, and was rewarded by the other's patent though dissembled mystification. But these were Telfer's men, and Telfer was gone. By far the greater part of the folk of Strathalish were either employees or tenants of Sir Charles Marsden, and Sir Charles was not gone and his attitude a little uncertain. It behoved his people to walk warily. Willie Maclay came early on, to be sure, but Willie was something of a law unto himself and a little soft in the head. It was not until the laird's niece, Miss Denholm, peculiar woman, was known to be visiting the tinker's encampment, that humbler folk reckoned that they could follow her example. It was all rather ambiguous.

Strange or otherwise, Martha Forbes was not amongst his early callers. The day after his return to the haunts of men, Alastair Dubh had paid a brief visit to Lagganlia, where he had some word with Alan Forbes and collected certain chattels of his that good man had been keeping for him, his fiddle included, and betaken himself off again without waiting to greet the girl who had been out bringing in the cows to milk. For so doing he had had his reasons, no doubt—but Martha was not aware of them, and woman-like, she conceived reasons of her own, and, as woman-like, found them unpalatable. So she refrained from visiting the haugh of Balnacraig, and achieved both virtue and prudence in the doing of it, but only limited satisfaction.

Not so Angela Denholm. The same day in which she heard of Alastair's whereabouts she came to see him, in the grey of late afternoon, walking this time, and clad in long maroon slacks with her canary jumper, and a light jacket slung about her shoulders, for the autumn air was searching. As she approached down the tree-lined bank from Hughie Bell's croft-house track, the dog Rob, that had been growling in his throat for the previous three minutes, let out a furious yelp and flashed off to do battle with the two elegant Irish setters that accompanied her. In the subsequent uproar it was Alastair MacIver, hastening, that, adding a judicious boot-toe to his peremptory commands, managed to restore the whirling, snarling maelstrom of caninity into three ruffled but individual dogs once more, two apprehensive and one scornful, while the girl, typically perhaps, stood aside and laughed immoderately.

"It would be a pity," he observed a little grimly, "for a small bit of a sheep-collie to be damaging two beautiful fine beasts the like of those, Miss Denholm."

She glanced at him sideways. "I suppose it would—but rather amusing, don't you think? They are my uncle's—very decorative but entirely useless."

"Many there are such, dogs and others," the man said obscurely. "The pity that we cannot keep our hands off them— 'tis just our tinker's manners."

"And just what do you mean by that?" the girl wondered slowly.

" 'Twas just me apologizing . . . for the dog." He turned and led the way back towards his tent. "It is not a bad day at all for the time of the year that's in it," he observed speciously.

Her glance, at his back, was a curious one, and hardly the

reflection of any one simple emotion, as was her suitable habit. As well that he did not see it, complacent man. At his little fire she tipped a smouldering birch-log with the toe of her shoe, and eyed the spurt of yellow flame that she produced thoughtfully. "So you are back," she said. "Back from where you started. All your battles won. The Tinker Triumphant—Alastair MacIver, the man they couldn't lick!"

He was watching her heedfully. "Winning—not won," he corrected mildly.

"You are not finished yet, then?"

"Is your uncle?" he countered. "He's of different stuff, that one, from the man Telfer."

"Perhaps. But maybe he'll find it simpler just to call a halt to this silly business, now."

"I believe you. But any halt that's called, my own self it'll be that calls it."

She shook her head over his aggressive masculinity.

"You think you're the hell of a fellow, Alastair MacIver, don't you!" she said.

From his stance over by his tent-door he answered her seriously. "No—but I have a job to finish, see you. Why should I be leaving it half-done?"

"You are an unforgiving type, I'm afraid," she deplored. "Is this the result of your famous prison cell, or were you always like that, I wonder? Always, probably, from what I've heard of your father. A ruthless lot, the MacIvers."

"Like yourself, ma'am."

"Me! I'm not ruthless. It's just a pose I adopt to shield my supersensitive heart." And she laughed her old laugh. "And for Heaven's sake don't call me ma'am. After what you did to me last time we foregathered, it's just dam' ridiculous."

Alastair rubbed a hand over his chin. "What happened then was unfortunate—but necessary, whatever," he averred carefully. "There's times when a man—even a tinker—must show his self-respect. . . ."

"Lord, is that what you were showing!" she cried. "Just as well that I had my breeches on! But it's all right—I'm not complaining. I deserved all I got, no doubt." She raised a wicked eyebrow at him. "Maybe more," she added significantly.

The gipsy found the dogs in need of attention. "Thank you, anyway," he said presently, "for not going back and giving me away, telling your folk where I was. You might well have done it then, and you angry. Thank you, too, for warning me about yon ploy on the hill—the trap they set for me. You went to a lot of trouble to help me there, and you with no need."

The girl nodded derisively. "Yes, you owe me a lot of thanks, don't you? Perhaps one of these days I'll see about cashing in on it."

"In that day the good Lord deliver me!" the man cried fervently, and they both laughed.

She inspected his camp, admired his tent, compared his bracken couch unfavourably with the heather one she had sampled up in Am Fasach, and presently discovered his violin in its old tartan bag. "Ah, the famous fiddle. Play me a tune, Alastair," she commanded.

He shook his head.

"Oh, go on. Don't pretend to be bashful—*you!*"

"I am not in the mood, at all."

"Churl!" she accused. "What about all your thanks now?"

"You wouldn't have me play it with me not in the mood, woman?" he cried.

Angela Denholm glanced up, a little startled at the heat behind his words. But she smiled. "The authentic artistic temperament, too," she murmured, while he glowered at her.

She was sitting on a log beside his fire, and now she patted it invitingly. "Come and tell me what I really came to hear," she said. "I want to know what you did to Major Telfer?"

He came over beside her but he did not sit down. Tossing a few twigs of kindling on to the smouldering embers, he stirred them with his boot. The newborn flames leaping up eagerly illumined his face redly as he towered above her in the half-dark, etching even more strongly in flickering light and shadow the strong features of brow and nose, mouth and jaw. When he seemed in no hurry to answer her, the girl went on: "You needn't

147

tell me that you did nothing to him, nothing at all, as you told Donald Shaw. I had a word with Mr. Shaw, and though he wasn't very communicative, I could see he was impressed. What happened?"

Alastair shrugged. "In a way it's right enough that I did nothing to the man at all. All that he did, he did his own self. I was just by way of encouraging him."

Her upturned gaze, even in that half-light, was eloquent in its scepticism. "Go on—I believe you," she assured him sarcastically.

"You have no choice," the man said. "I never laid hands on him or threatened him . . . but myself and yon wood of Am Fasach were after putting the fear of death on him, just the same." His voice quickened a little, as he warmed to his theme. "First I decoyed away his folk from him, that was to be trapping me, then I crept up on him and Shaw at the stalking and scared his stag away just as he was after shooting it. That made him mad, and I got them on to chasing me, leading them on, till I had them into Am Fasach, where I took Shaw from him. And then I wandered him, and the man still thinking he was chasing me, and I let that place have its way with him. And when he was exhausted and all his spirit had died on him, I gave the wood a bit of a hand, till he was frightened to the through-other soul of him, and he was ready to talk the way I wanted. And, God, when I came up to him at the last, I reckon he was even glad to see me! To get out of that place and the trouble he was in, he wrote what I told him. And that's it all, whatever."

Angela stared into the fire. "And you planned all that out beforehand?" she asked presently.

"That is so."

Almost she shivered, though, since she was Angela Denholm, possibly it was only the night air that caused it. "Poor Jeffrey Telfer—I'm almost sorry for him," she murmured. "He did not know what he was taking on. He was hardly worth it all, I think—just a commonplace creature."

"He asked for it—he tried to turn me, a MacIver, out of Strathalish. A challenge it was."

148

"Poor rash little man! And have you some such programme laid up for my uncle, may I ask?"

"He'll find out, in time."

She was looking up at him intently, and with a new interest, a new conjecture. "You are a dangerous man, I think, Alastair MacIver."

The gipsy shook his head. "I am a peaceable, quiet man—but I have my pride." He did not like that look that she was giving him, calculating, pregnant, it might well be, with trouble. He cleared his throat. "I would not like to have you think me uncivil," he mentioned, "but it's time I was away after giving Hughie Bell a hand with his beasts."

"So I'm to be got rid of again . . . and not escorted home either, it seems! I've known more attentive cavaliers, Alastair."

Grimly he smiled. "You have so, I'll swear—lots of them. You should stick to the idle rich—they've more time for manners."

"You think it's manners I want?"

"No." That was bald if truthful, and he bent to draw three turfs over his little fire, a gesture that was telling and final, like snuffing a candle. He dived into his tent and brought out a bundle, and fetched out Rob with a word. The girl was on her feet, with her dogs beside her. "Coming?" he called, and without a word she followed him.

He went with her as far as the road, gleaming palely before the dark uncertainty of the loch. "There you are, then. Come again some time, will you?" he said half-quizzically.

"I will—if you will play your fiddle for me."

"I might, then, and the mood on me."

"I will hold you to that."

"You will try to, anyway. Goodnight, lady."

"I prefer it when you call me woman, I think," she said sombrely. "Goodnight, tinker-man."

Leaning on the Balnacraig gate he watched her on her road. A lonely road she made for herself, that one, and always would. When he turned up the track for the croft, the man's face was sombre also.

A busy evening MacIver spent with Hughie Bell, first in the byre, with his hands, and then in the kitchen, with his tongue. Hughie was a youngish man, high-complexioned and thickset for a Highlandman, and, being a bachelor, was as glad of a hand about his untidy steading as he was of a good crack, with maybe a glass to go with it, in front of his own well-doing but ill-cleaned fireside. A good listener was Hughie, with a nice turn in encouragement—he would have been snapped up long ago had there been more young women in the district.

After he had talked and sat and drunk enough, Alastair took a hunk of cheese and bread and his departure, and found the night air grateful. Down the cart-track went man and dog, not to the tent in the haugh, but passing on, down to the road and along the shore to where, amid a clump of alders, the Farinish boat lay moored just above the water-level. Unhitching the cable and tossing his bundle into the small craft, he balanced it on an even keel and pushed it down over the rounded pebbles with ease and little sound above the lap-lap of the wavelets. The tide was highish and he had not far to push, and in no more than a minute he was afloat and in and the collie with him, and sculling out quietly over the darkling waters, all with a deftness and lack of fuss that seemed to indicate familiar custom. A careful scrutiny would have revealed those rowlocks to be greased with butter. So he headed towards the small tree-clad island of Eilean Beg, invisible now in the gloom, and lying about quarter of a mile out from the shore, a silent purposeful shadow that faded quickly into the night's embrace. And he did not come back, not that night at least. Alastair MacIver was not going to be caught napping.

XIV

ANGELA DENHOLM did not lag behind her promise, or her threat, whichever it was. Only three afternoons after her first visit to the riverside encampment she arrived again, in some style and circumstance this time, driving up to the Balnacraig gate in the great Rolls, where perforce she must leave it, half-blocking the modest road, to pick her careful way along the mud of the cart-track and down through the dripping birches and junipers—careful, because high-heeled suede shoes and sheerest silk stockings go but ill with common mud, and an elegant Glenurquhart suiting is no match for clawing bushes. But if her approach was therefore lacking in any of the fine poise that she might have wished, it did not matter. For Alastair MacIver was out on business of his own, not unconnected with the modest stocking of his larder, and his first indication of a visitor was a sight of the big black car, seen from high ground, parked at the road-end. And since that lordly equipage, placed there, might mean more than just the one thing, he and Rob approached his camp circumspectly. Far from reassured by what he discovered, save in the matter of his mere physical safety, he emerged from cover, his little rifle over his arm and two rabbits and a wild pheasant about his person, to find the girl, with the turfs removed from off his banked-up fire, flapping her scarf above it in an effort to fan up a flame.

"What are you after doing to my fire?" he called loudly to introduce his presence, for he had some of the instincts of a gentleman. "You'll have it all blown away on me, and me with trouties to bake for my tea!"

"So there you are." She straightened up, and shook the heavy flaxen locks of her hair back off her forehead in a single assured toss. "I was getting cold waiting for you—but I didn't get much help from your miserable fire."

"Treated rightly it would have roasted you." He threw down

151

his trophies, and shook a head over her efforts. "My, oh my, you've ruined it, whatever."

"Nonsense—you had it suffocated under all those divots. And what's the meaning of this?" She touched the fur and feathers with a suede toe. "Poaching, theft, and illegal practices, naked and unashamed."

"Far from it," he averred stoutly. "That's the reward of skill. Have you ever shot a rising pheasant—a wild pheasant, not one of your hand-reared barn-door fowls—with a twenty-two rifle? Well, then. And, forbye, it's only a reasonable small quantity of game such as even the man Telfer admits is necessary and proper. He says so himself—I have it in his own hand of write!"

"Hypocrite!" she accused. "Anyway, I'll be damned if you've got a Game Licence?"

"Save us," he complained, "who'd have thought you'd have backed up the thieves of the Inland Revenue, the plague of all decent folk! Stand aside, woman, and let me get at my own fire."

He got down on his knees, and replaced two of the girl's discarded turfs and withdrew another, and all of her added fuel, till he had what remained of his fire in a narrow trench between turf walls with its axis approximating to that of the wind. Soon the blackened embers began to glow red, and raking away some of the clogging ash and adding a judicious twig here and a crumble of peat there, he nodded approvingly. "Another ten minutes' blaze and my stones will be cooked."

"Stones?" she obliged him.

"Just that. I've got stones baking in there, for my trouties, like I told you. You'll see." He got up and went off to stow away rifle and game, and he whistled as he went.

Angela Denholm looked after him speculatively. "You are very pleased with yourself today, Alastair MacIver," she observed.

Inside his tent the man shook his head at himself. He mustn't overplay his part. "Satisfaction it is, at being a useful well-doing man again," he suggested devoutly, emerging. "I'm as good as an extra keeper, unpaid, to Major Telfer, I tell you. The fine order I'll keep the place in—keeping his cock-pheasants down, the cheeky brutes, and the wicked destructive rabbits, besides. David Kennedy can be after retiring, whatever. Yon pheasant was fair asking to be shot . . . and it no' bad shooting, either," he added modestly.

"You are a complete scoundrel, and all that my uncle says you are," the young woman commented. "I always knew you were, of course. But"—she smiled provocatively—"at least, since you're so satisfied with yourself, you'll be just in the mood for playing me a selection on that fiddle of yours?"

"Mother o' Mercy, what have I done?" he cried. "Can a man not look cheerful for a minute without having to sing and dance and play the fiddle? Blackmail, it is." But he went and got his old violin out of its bag, just the same. "A bad day it is when I must play before I can smile!"

He plucked a string or two gloomily. "A lament's the thing, a lament you shall have, woman, or nothing."

And standing beside his eager, sizzling little fire, he tucked the ancient blackened instrument beneath his chin and began to play, and, playing, became a different man.

Martha Forbes, cycling along the loch-road *en route* for Inveralish, saw the Rolls at the Balnacraig gate—she hardly could do otherwise, with it taking up two-thirds of the road-way—and pondered. It was not the place to expect to find that car or any car—and neither of its two possible occupants was likely to have started visiting Hughie Bell. Her pondering had brought her off her cycle, a trim, businesslike figure in her dark homespun tweeds, and then, as she stood, brows furrowed, the thin high note of a fiddle, improbable but unmistakable, sounded across the haugh. Wondering still, but no longer hesitant, Martha turned back, and leaving her bicycle within the gate-way, she took her way up the track. And she, too, picked her route carefully, though not through fear of mud or dripping branches, and she frowned as she went.

Martha Forbes was not a suspicious person, and, as has been said, her nature was frank. Yet she approached the tinker's encampment by the chuckling Allt Buie heedfully, almost stealthily, as, indeed, Alastair MacIver also had done but fifteen minutes earlier—and had he been frank and unsuspicious? In the cover of the last of the trees she paused to watch, not a dozen yards from where the man stood and the woman crouched by the fire, to watch and listen and bite her lip. She could not do other than listen, and listening to that music did not help her to marshal her thoughts as she ought.

Alastair was playing the Lament for Duncan Mor, and wringing tears and an ecstasy of sorrow out of its exquisite pathos. He played with a verve and sureness, a perceptive touch, that owed little to tuition and much to intuition. It was unorthodox playing, in style and stance and fingerwork, partly typical of the gipsy-folk, who made music like they understood horses and judged whisky, as a congenial means of adding to their livelihood, partly inherited from his father, but mainly developed by the instinct of his own clamant needs and urges and interpretations. For music moved that man, wrought upon him, with an intensity, an importunity that he knew and dreaded while yet he revelled in it, labelling it a flaw, a weakness in his character, whereas it was rather the revelation and explanation of it to those who could but see. But not many saw, or were permitted to see. Alastair's reluctance to play for Angela Denholm was more than just a pose; always since he had discovered what the fiddle could do to him, he had hidden away his talent for it, to be exercised, indulged, when he was alone and private and need fear no exposure. Few knew that he loved the fiddle and fewer still had heard him play it. All this Martha knew or guessed, and her listening now was the less easeful for the knowledge.

The last of Duncan Mor sobbed and shivered to its sorrowing close in a searching aching chord that was the very essence and refinement of all beauty and all pain, ultimate, inevitable, and clear, starkly clear. The girl at the fire lifted her head, and her voice was low and husky and somehow strained. "That was terrible . . . and wonderful, Alastair. I have never heard anything like it. You played it—how shall I say?—as though your whole heart and soul were in it . . ."

Martha was making to step out from under her tree, but the man was too quick for her. "Nonsense!" he barked roughly, almost angrily, and jerking up the fiddle to his chin again, flung headlong into a wild, ranting, tripping reel, that skirled and jigged and set the feet atwitching, the antithesis of beauty and emotion. Yet it was well played, with a dash and deftness that neither skipped nor slurred any of the scrambling rushes, bitter though it sounded after what had gone before. When, in a final precipitate cascade of notes the thing was finished, the girl sitting by the fire, looking at him strangely, did not speak. It was Martha Forbes who spoke, issuing from her cover somewhat dramatically.

"Aren't you gay today, down here!" she said. "Is it a *ceilidh*, or what? I'm not intruding, I hope?" She stooped to pat the collie that came forward to welcome her, head down, body swinging lithely with its tail, having been watching her with bright-eyed interest from the tent door these last few minutes.

Alastair, turning, raised his brows at her, smiling. "*Failt' is furain ort*," he greeted. His mind busy, he shook his head at her, decidedly. "Intruding—could you be, ever, Moireach *a ghraidh*?"

"I might—who knows."

Angela Denholm did not rise from her log. "Welcome, Miss Forbes," she smiled coolly. "You're just in time for the recital. We've had Tragedy and Farce so far; perhaps we'll get something Romantic now!"

"You will not." That was the man, emphatically. He turned to the Highland girl. "Nothing would do but she must hear the fiddle—but Duncan Mor should have cured her. Her own fault it is, entirely. I was fair badgered into it. I'm glad you came, Moireach." And he bent for the tartan bag to cover his violin.

"But I want to hear more," Angela objected. "Don't be an idiot—you've only just started!"

"Don't stop for me, then," Martha protested. "It's seldom enough he'll play at all, and more than I can do to get him started at it. You must have been very persuasive, Miss Denholm!"

They both glanced at her, the man doubtfully, the woman keenly. "Was I, Alastair?" the latter asked brazenly.

The other girl flushed just a little. Perhaps it was the casual use of the Christian name Alastair that did it. But she was apt to flush, was Martha, on occasion, and knew and hated it, though it did her beauty no injury.

The man, looking, cursed beneath his breath. These two women did not love each other, most apparently—but they were not going to make his little camp their women's battlefield if he could help it. " 'Twas just to be filling in ten minutes while my stones were heating," he put in quickly. "I have trout to bake to my tea, you see. You will have them with me, the two of you? You will so, I say!" Suddenly he was fierce, commanding. "You are at my fire, and you will eat my food, both of you. Moireach, get you some brackens, the greenest you can—you know what I'm wanting."

As the girl went, unquestioning, Alastair nodded quick approval, and leaving Angela Denholm lounging where she was, he strode over to the river-bank, where, bending down, he lifted out some half-dozen or so cleaned and beheaded fish from a little stone water-larder dug out under the bank. They were bright, gleaming, neat little fish—and one or two not so little, either—the speckled, pink-fleshed Brown Trout of the peat-stained Highland waters, and fresh-caught that morning, with patience and cunning, if without rod or line or hook. He brought them over to the fire and laid them out on a large slab of basalt that he kept there. "The bonniest, sweetest fish in the world, whatever," he assured the watching girl, and went on to scoop out the loose soil from a circular patch of bare earth nearby, uncovering, in the process, a little basin-like pit, perhaps eighteen inches across and nearly a foot deep, roughly lined with cracked and blackened clay and gravel. Returning to his fire, he carefully raked aside the red cinders and ashes, disclosing beneath them a number of round, flattish stones, white-hot and brilliant with tiny racing sparks. These he lifted out expertly with a couple of forked sticks, and deposited in the floor of the pit. One he dropped *en route*, and set up sufficient fuss and clamour over it as to set Martha, back now with her bracken, laughing, despite herself—which was all as it should be.

Covering the hot stones with a layer of the still-green bracken fronds, he placed the fish lovingly thereon, head to tail like sardines in a tin, and covered them over with his blessing and another layer of fern, thicker this time. And on top of the already-steaming greenery he pushed back the loose earth. "Cook you there, little ones," he charged them, "with two fair ladies to feed, not to mention a full-grown man and him starving—fit to make up for the rest of the five thousand, indeed. All we're after needing now is the five barley loaves!"

Angela he admonished for sitting still and letting the fire die under her nose, and Martha he sent to his woodpile for little sticks to resuscitate it. Himself, he picked up the smoke-blackened can that he used as a kettle and went off to fill it at a piece of piping set into a little stream that ran into the Allt Buie nearby. And his whistle was sustained and determined.

When he got back Martha was down on her knees blowing at the fire in a succession of little puffs, like a human bellows. "God bless the work," he rumbled. "The grand pair of lungs you have on you, lassie. Well seen that your father's a smith," and, as she looked up, pink and bright-eyed, with her hair a tumbling glory about her, "—and that your mother was a beauty, forbye!"

She looked at him strangely, for this was not very like Alastair MacIver in company. Angela was looking, too, at both of them, and considering. She sat back, her hands clasped round one silk-clad knee, the other shapely long leg stretched in front of her, her whole aspect negligently provocative. And she was very good to look at—and was aware of it. She was elegant indolence itself—save for her eyes, searching, calculating, lovely eyes that belied her indolence, but not her elegance. Martha, very aware of those eyes candidly, thoroughly scanning her, her features and her figure, felt herself to be unclothed, naked, and her chin tilting, she was the more active as a result. The man, too, felt her regard, her assessment, and accepted it, man-like, reacting as men always have done to such. But something within him stirred to the challenge—which was not extraordinary either. "You are very busy, both of you," she said. "Industry personified, and too good to be true . . . or natural!" She had a tongue to match her looks. "I'm grateful that there doesn't seem to be anything you want me to do, in this rather hectic performance."

"That is so," the man gave back swiftly. "Your kind's not made to be useful, only ornamental, whatever."

"That's a lie, and you know it," she answered him, but without heat. "I can work—on occasion. For that matter, you're no worker yourself, my brave MacIver, except to create an impression. Am I wrong?" She laughed at his expression. "With Miss Forbes, now, it's different—she's one of the world's workers, God bless their hearts!"

"I do what needs doing," that young woman said simply. And with a cocked eyebrow, "and when you're not born rich, there's little choice."

"Rich! You don't think *I* was born rich, do you? I haven't a cent of my own to my name. But I have rich friends—who are willing to pay for what I can give. And an uncle who's another of your workers, thank the Lord!"

Alastair straightened his back from settling the kettle on the fire, and whatever else there was in his glance, there was a gleam of admiration also. Some sides of her he understood pretty well, he thought. "The black heart you've got!" he mocked.

Martha was patting her hair, so very unprofitably. "Expensive it will be, Alastair, being a friend of Miss Denholm's, don't you think?" she said shrewdly.

"He hasn't found it so, I think—as yet." That was not said casually at all.

The man, while considering all the implications of that, eyed the two of them narrowly. This would have to stop, in self-preservation itself he'd have to stop it. The menace of two women—the good God be thanked that Anna wasn't in it! "Was ever any woman's friendship inexpensive for a man?" he demanded, purposely truculent. "Lord preserve me from all such!" He sighed. This tea-party was hard work. "Martha," he said with some authority, "there's some of Mary Campbell's scones in the tent there. Stale they'll be, but they'll toast. The butter you'll be finding there, too. See you to it. The milk will be hanging in its pitcher up on what Hughie Bell names a fence, by the track—if the same man hasn't deserted on me. The lord's daughter will go and fetch it, too, fine shoes or none—if she wants any tea at all."

"And you?" that young woman demanded, getting up to go, nevertheless, with considerable show and display.

"Me—I will go and pray over my trouts," he said stoutly. "Also I will cut a green stick, two green sticks, for you and the girl there to use as toasting-forks."

"Only two?"

"Only two." MacIver nodded emphatically. "Myself, I will watch the two of you to see you toast the scones and not each other, and in between I'll play my fiddle to make the kettle sing."

And that programme he saw to it they carried out.

On their logs at either side of the well-doing fire, then, the girls sat, and toasted their scones on the forked sticks, and their faces, and Angela Denholm's knees. For she sat in such a way as to make this inevitable, despite rubbings and complaints, compared with which the other's sideways seat, half-kneeling, was as much more convenient as it was discreet. Martha could have wished that the creature was still in her outlandish breeches—at least they would have been better than this uncalled-for display of silk stocking, whose smooth extravagance made her own bare legs feel brawny in the extreme. Not that Alastair appeared to be interested, meantime. At the head of the fire, to windward, he sat, his eyes closed, or half-closed—it was hard to tell which—one foot tapping to the rhythm of his fiddling. He had given them "The Reaper's Song" and "The Berneray Love Song", and now he was playing "The Milking Song", ancient, lilting, Gaelic airs, distilled out of all the haunting beauty and colour and proud hopelessness of the West. At the last, most lovely to her of them all, Martha had discovered herself crooning its coaxing tender melody, as generations of her folk had done before her to the warm flanks of their beasts, at the same time as she discovered the other girl watching her curiously; and that had been the end of her singing. But Alastair played on, gently,

159

reflectively, as in a dream, and the pile of browned scones grew and was finished, and the toasters sat still, enthralled. He gave them "The Skye Boat Song" and then, as the water bubbled and steamed in the can, he flourished to a close with "The Piper's Wedding."

"That's it, then," he cried. "There's the tea, Moireach—put in plenty." Wrapping his fiddle up carefully, he strode over to his oven. He lifted out the covering soil, now caked and hardened with the heat, and at the hot savoury aroma that rose up through the top layer of bracken he sniffed ecstatically. "Yon dish, Moireach," he shouted, but she was already at his side, anticipating his need, with an old enamel plate in her hand. Removing the cover of fronds, now brown and shrivelled, he almost reverently exposed the row of golden, steaming trout. "The darlings!" he exclaimed, "That one with the curled-up tail is mine. Will you hold the dish still now, girl!" With Martha laughing happily at his schoolboy excitement, and shaking the plate in the process, he got a hand under each end of the ferny tray of fish, yelping when he burned his fingers on the still-hot stones, and in a single swift lifting movement deposited the lot on the enamel platter intact. "Off with you, now, to the fire," he commanded, ". . . and stop waggling the dish, I tell you." Getting to his feet he promptly tripped over the much-interested Rob. "Devil sweep you, dog!" he roared. "Out of my way." A couple of paces, and he stopped. "The salt," he cried, "I've forgot the salt!" and dashing over to the tent he was to be heard rummaging about and declaring piteously that the damned stuff was lost on him, and the wee fish cold and ruined whatever. But in a half a minute he was back by the fire, and with a large gesture proclaiming his feast ready. "Here you are then. Let us sit down and eat, with God's blessing—and the one with the curly tail is mine, see you!"

So in that spirit they ate, with the firelight reddening their faces, for the dusk was already upon them. They ate from the one plate, dipping into the communal pile of salt on a handy stone, and, since there were no forks provided, they used their fingers like sensible folk. Angela Denholm, after brief initial hesitation, being nowise backward. And why not? Those fish smelt delicious, superb, and tasted even better, worthy of all MacIver's heroics. Sweet as a nut, yet savoury as any fish can be, firm of flesh yet melting in the mouth, their cooking had retained all their natural juices to produce a delicate flavour, piquant as it was appetizing, to which the bracken in which they had been bedded undoubtedly had contributed. Eaten with the crisped scones, dripping with Hughie Bell's butter, and washed down with scalding strong tea, they made a tasty meal, an adequate, even sumptuous meal, and a memorable meal. If the latter attribute was enhanced by the fact that there was only one cup to drink out of, and that an old enamel mug, it appeared to arouse no qualms; at least, no one refused their tea on that account, or any other, and Alastair's offer to sup from the still-simmering sooty can itself was cried down by both the ladies. There were protests, too, when the man claimed eloquently that the odd fish left over should be his, for hadn't he caught them, that ended in it being divided up into three portions, with some sidelong glances and calculations. That is the sort of meal it was, and about all the talk that went with it, too.

Thereafter, they sat idly for a time over the glowing embers, while the gipsy expiated knowledgeably on fish—brown trout and common trout, grey or bull trout, sea and salmon trout, and the lordly salmon himself in all his stages, catching and cooking, times and seasons, while the dark settled down around them and the things of the night announced themselves in their own quiet way, hooting softly or calling mournfully or quacking sleepily. And presently Angela Denholm remembered that her car was standing in the road with no lights showing, and Martha that her dad would be looking for her and his supper. And the man admitted affairs of his own to see to, but did not specify what, and detained them not. So he smoored the fire with peat and turfs and the Gaelic incantation to the Holy Trinity that goes with them, Martha assisting at both. And with a brief finger-dipping visit to the rushing river, laughing at them all, as well it might, he escorted them down to the gate and the road.

There, after switching on her lights, Angela produced a coat out from the car interior and threw it about her shoulders, in tribute to the warmth of the fire they had left. There was a significant pause as she came back to them, awkward for such as allowed it to be. "Can I give anyone a lift anywhere, I wonder?" she asked blandly, and it was an invitation, even a challenge, and not a question as she asked it.

Martha drew a breath quickly. "I have my bike," she said shortly, and went over to the fence to pick it up and wheel it back.

"And you?" she put to the man, her eyes busy.

Looking at her, he shook his head. "Not tonight," he said slowly. "You could not be taking me where I want to go, tonight."

"Could I not—I wonder? I can go most places . . . in a car!" At his head-shake she laughed. "The bold MacIver!" she jibed, and opening the door, backed into the deep seat. "Goodnight, then," she said, through the open window. "Thanks for the tea, at any rate—and for the music—a surprise, both of them."

"To me, too," he told her, grimly truthful. "I surprised myself, forbye."

"Goodnight, Miss Forbes. I don't think I ever thanked you sufficiently for telling me where to find this ruffian, the other day. So helpful of you, wasn't it? I was able to do all that I wanted—or nearly all—thanks to you." Smiling wickedly, she pressed the self-starter and released the handbrake. "Oh, and by the way, Alastair, I came to tell you that my uncle has decided to go South tomorrow. Isn't it a pity, with your vengeance still unsatisfied! Bye-bye," and with a throaty purr, the big car slid forward and away.

In silence they watched till the gleaming red tail-lamp disappeared round a bend in the road. "Aye, then . . . ihm'mm," the man said. "It's a cold wind that. Winter's not that far behind it."

"Yes."

"Better be moving, then. I'll see you home."

"No need—I have my bike."

"You're after going home, aren't you?"

"I was going to Inveralish when, when, I heard your fiddle.

162

It's too late to be going there now."

"It is so. I'll push your bike for you."

"You needn't bother. I wouldn't be taking you out of your way . . . and I'd be quicker cycling anyhow."

"All right, then—cycle, woman!" he cried. "But I can come and be having a word with your father, can't I, if I want!"

"To be sure," she said, and turned into the road. But she did not mount her bicycle for all that.

The man walked a foot behind her, speechless.

They had approximately a mile and a half to go, and the first third of it they covered in silence. On their right hand the water lapped and splashed on the shingle of the loch-shore, driven by the breeze in fussy little waves. On the left the land lifted away, dark and mysterious, towards the brooding hills, and out of it came no sound but the sough of wind over far-flung spaces. It was the man who tired first of the crunch of their feet on the gravel of the road, and the tick-tick of the bicycle's free-wheel. "It's an awful rush you're in," he complained loudly. "If there's such a hurry in it, you should have taken the lift you were offered, in the car."

"You could have done the same yourself, if it was just my father you wanted to see."

"I could," he agreed, and then rather puerilely, "but I didn't."

At this piece of juvenility the girl smiled, but to herself. "I'm thinking you were wise, maybe," she said.

"Wise? There was no wisdom in it, at all," he declared. " 'Twas just the way I was feeling."

Silence for a little farther. "You seem to be getting very friendly with her," Martha resumed presently.

"Friendly is not just the word, perhaps."

"Oh?" That was frigid.

He did not rise to the challenge implied. "I am getting to know her, yes," he said heedfully, "and to understand her a small bittie, I think."

"And that would not be so hard, either!"

"I don't know. There's more to her, maybe, than she'd have

163

you think, at all."

"I shouldn't wonder—all the more reason to watch your step, Alastair MacIver." Her tone had changed suddenly, to an urgency and sincerity that it had lacked before. "She's a dangerous woman, Stair. Be careful."

At her change of tone he glanced at her quickly, out of the corner of his eye, and his own changed likewise, for his own defence. "Aren't you all?" he answered lightly.

She drew a breath, and when she spoke her voice had altered again, noticeably. "But you don't play the fiddle to the rest of us!" she flashed at him. And that might not have been Martha Forbes at all.

Surprised, he stared at her, across the bicycle. So there they had it! He opened his mouth to speak, and then shut it again, almost with a click. When he did answer her his words were carefully chosen, heavy. "I had my reasons for that."

Behind that there was a finality which the girl knew and recognized. She made the smallest sigh, but no other comment, and the wind and the wavelets came into their own again.

They were nearing the Lagganlia road-end and might well have completed the journey in this silence had not the bicycle pedal in one of its uncalled-for semi-revolutions caught against the girl's leg, causing her to trip, and exclaim with the small pain of it. Swiftly the man jettisoned his sternness, and, taking the bicycle from her, pushed it in front of him and around so that he walked between her and it. "You're not hurt? Your ankle, Moireach—it would be sore?"

She shook her head. "No, it was nothing—just a scrape. My own fault it was for walking by it instead of riding."

"My fault it was, then," he claimed, all contrition. "Me it was made you walk. I'm sorry, Moireach."

"Wheesht, I'm fine, silly," she said, but not severely. And the atmosphere was transformed therewith. Of such is the weave of life.

The transference of the cycle from one to another had caused contact, perhaps inevitably, between arms and hands. And now, as they walked side by side, occasionally shoulders touched, and the man was reminded of that last time they had walked thus together, last time that they had seen each other, indeed. The thought half-turned him towards her. "Remember the capper, yon time?" he asked her.

Perhaps her own thoughts had not been so very different, for her response was prompt. "The horrid noisy brute!" she said, with a little laugh that negatived her indictment of the clumsy bird. And her hand slipped lightly within his arm again, at the memory.

He pressed gently but firmly with his own arm. "There's worse beasts than cappers, whatever," he observed charitably.

The lights of the house of Lagganlia gleamed before them, and they were in no hurry at all, any more.

XV

IF Strathalish and district looked for a period of peace and
tranquillity with the departure for the South of Sir Charles
Marsden, it was to be disappointed. For one thing, astonishingly, his niece had not gone with him. Whatever the reason for
this—and there were a number propounded, not all complimen-
tary—it was a disturbing factor, unsuitable as it was unnatural.
Always the gentry went southward with the shortening days and
the autumn winds, leaving them in peace from October till July,
which was desirable and as it should be. Folk could relax, hats
needn't be touched and 'sir' and 'ma'am' could drop out of the
vocabulary, gamekeepers could become human again, and the
Game Laws and suchlike sink back into decent desuetude. But
this ill-advised and autocratic young woman lingered on in the
half-shut-up Lodge, a source of perplexity and vague discomfort
to all around. She did not shoot or stalk, and though she seemed
to be taking a small interest in the fishing these days, she was no
enthusiast, obviously. She was not seen so often on her horse in
this colder weather, and being no climber or much of a walker
either, apparently, it was anybody's guess what kept the woman.
And anybody's guess is apt to be catholic.

The other development militating against a general serenity
was the return of Anna with her husband. Anna, to be sure, was
quiet and peaceable enough for anybody, but the same hardly
could be said, in all circumstances, for Ewan MacIver. He was
a boy, was Ewan, and few were the dull moments when he was
around. Born of Colin Bán's second wife, a half-Irish quean
from the Isle of Mull, he bore a distinct resemblance to his half-
brother, and not only in features. But he made a very different
man out of the same material, nevertheless. It was as if, driving
the same horse, one used the whip where the other used the
bearing-rein. Alastair was passionate, dramatic, hot-tempered,
and proud, but all these under a curb as fierce as any of them.

Ewan was all these likewise, and revelled in them. And they did not make the easiest of bedfellows.

Ewan's arrival was this way. A few evenings after Marsden's going, with Sim Campbell's bar just settling down to the comfortable steamy business of a wet night, the swing doors suddenly were flung violently open and the damp but anything but dejected figure of the gipsy strode in. Four great paces he took, with two lip-curling dogs slinking at his heels, to reach the counter and there turn around. "God save all here!" he cried, deep-voiced, to add with a flash of ivory teeth, ". . . if He can!" He laughed at the startled glances and raised eyebrows around him, and his dogs snarled wickedly at the chorus of growls from under the seats and tables. "Save us, but you're snug in here, snug as bugs in a bloody rug!" With a fine swirl of the ancient tattered kilt he wore, he swung round to the bar again. "Aye, Sim, you fat old skinflint, it's happy I am to see you—you've as good whisky as any I know between Kyle and Tongue."

The other did not deny it. "Well now, Ewan, it's the stranger you are," he said mildly. "A dirty wet night it is, indeed."

"A stranger, is it! My God, yes, I'm a stranger, whatever," the newcomer shouted. "Three months they had me shut up, three months in a jail, three months without a drink in it, damn and blast their souls! And all over a perishing polisman, a pot-bellied wall-eyed runt, and a bastard Englishman at that!" A grin chased the fury off his dark features, astonishingly. "But, b'dam, it was worth it. Man, you should have heard him squeal—just like a pig he squealed. It was a treat to hear him, whatever." And throwing his head back, he burst out into a yell, high and shrill and blood-curdling, and, by its suddenness, more than somewhat alarming to the other occupants of that low-ceilinged room.

In this abrupt gesture the gipsy had stepped backward a little and his arm, accidentally, had come in contact with that of another customer standing at the bar, a mug of beer in his upraised hand, who stood and stared in undisguised wonder at the latest arrival. Instantly Ewan MacIver was a changed man again. Moving a step away from the counter he stooped low in

167

a sweeping bow, graceful as it was extravagant and unlikely in that place. "I beg your pardon, sir, and myself a clumsy borach," he said impressively. "If you will be finishing what I've left in your glass, now, it'll by my pleasure to be filling it up again, whatever."

The other, one Rutherford, a shepherd and newcomer from the green Borderland, stared embarrassed. "Ye needna' bother—it wis naethin'. But," and the embarrassment changed to suspicion, ". . . if ye're trying tae be funny . . . ?"

The tinker drew himself up, as Sim Campbell's hand went out towards the shepherd instinctively, before faltering and returning to the counter. "Sir, I haff not the honour off your name, at all," he said, with a changed exact enunciation, "but my own iss Ewan Ranald MacIver, and I do not try to be funny, see you—efen to such ass your own self . . . !"

"Aye—okay, then." The shepherd was no fool, and not a large man either. "Nae offence meant or taken—an' ye didna' spill mair than a drap."

Campbell coughed and smiled nervously and rubbed his hands. "Eh, but you're looking wet, Ewan man," he exclaimed. "Terrible wet. Just soaked. . . ."

"Wet, is it!" The gipsy was all smiles again. "Wet on my back, maybe, but not here, for sure," and he tapped his throat. "*Dia*, I'm as dry as a board. Since fifteen miles I've been needing a drink, from Achnagarve where I had the last one—and you know the like of John Cameron's liquor. The creature's after making it himself in yon shed at the back with the paraffin oil! Let's have a right stiff one, Sim. And fill up this gentleman's glass, see you—fill up everybody's glass, whatever. Drinks all round! A celebration, and me new out of jail."

Campbell looked his doubts. "There's a lot in it, Ewan," he cautioned.

"Damn the lot! Here you are, man." And tossing a crumpled pound note on to the counter he turned about, and the sweep of his arm included all there. "The gentlemen will all be drinking with me, for sure?"

"For sure, Ewan," Archie McKillop acceded heartily, his eye

on the pound note. "Why wouldn't we, then?" and a polite chorus of agreement supported him.

"Fine, then," the gipsy cried. "Fill them up, Sim, and . . ."

From a corner of the smoke-filled room a voice came clearly. "You can count me out, Campbell," it said gruffly. "I'm drinking no tinker's beer. I can buy my own."

For a long moment there was silence in that place. Then Simon Campbell began: "Och, just as you like, Mr. Clarke . . ." when he was interrupted. Ewan MacIver had not looked round nor moved. "Wass I hearing anything, at all?" he asked slowly, but very distinctly.

For answer there was only a muttering from the corner. Peter Rennie, sitting with the other keeper, was leaning over and whispering urgently. "That's MacIver's brother, and madder than the ither. Just out of jail for knifing a polisman. Watch your step, man!"

The big man, in the act of speaking up, evidently had a second thought, and only an incoherent syllable or two materialized.

But it was enough for the gipsy. Swinging round he stared straight at Clarke. "You were saying, I think, that you would be fery pleased to drink with me . . . ?"

More than one of the onlookers shifted a little on their seats. When Ewan MacIver started to change his *v*'s into *f*'s and double his sibilants, onlookers were justified in so doing.

The big man glanced around him and found every eye on him. His great jaw was out-thrust, but he cleared his throat nevertheless. "I've got plenty here," he said. "I don't want any more."

The other's smile was dazzling. "Och, but a man can nefer haff plenty, at all. Unnatural it is. You would not be an unnatural man—what iss the word for it?—you would not be one of them, would you, Mr . . . ? I haff not the chentleman's name, I'm afraid."

"Mr. Clarke, it is Ewan," Archie McKillop obliged solemnly, but there might have been a gleam behind his eye. "Mr. Clarke is a new keeper on Inveralish."

Ewan, moving forward, stopped abruptly. "A keeper, is it, my God!" he cried. "Fancy that, now—a keeper, and me loving keepers." He was over at Clarke's table in a stride, grinning widely, his right hand rather obviously hidden in the pocket of his stained and steaming jacket. "Keepers are meat and drink to me, Mr. Clarke—keepers and polismen! You'll not be refusing to haff a drink with me, and me loving keepers?" and his hand shot out of his pocket.

Clarke jerked back, his chair scraping, but the hand was open and it only gripped the handle of the keeper's mug, now within an inch of being empty. Swiftly the gipsy turned about, strode to the bar, threw out the beer that was left on to the floor, and handed the mug to Campbell. "Fill that up for Mr. Clarke," he commanded. "Thirsty work, the keepering!" His eye fell on a full glass on the counter. "This will be my own, whateffer?" and picking it up he tossed it off at a single gulp. "Another off those, Sim man."

Wary-eyed, Campbell did as he was bid, a man whose responsibilities interfered with his proper enjoyment of many a situation. Grabbing the filled mug Ewan took it to the keeper's corner, turning as he did so, to cry: "The others, too—fill them up, Simon Campbell." He set the beer down, without a word, in front of Bert Clarke, now on his feet, and back he swung to the counter to take up his recharged whisky glass. He waited, smiling, while Campbell finished his task, but his glittering eyes, roving from face to face around him, always returned to the big keeper, standing flushed, angry, but uncertain.

Presently all tankards were replenished, and a silence fell. But for three, Clarke, Rennie, and the shepherd Rutherford, these men were Highlanders all, and actors inborn, and this scene was made for them—and didn't the maker know it! He was in no hurry, was that tinker, with every man watching him. Casual-seeming he lifted his glass to the light, to squint through its pale amber, and nod, satisfied with what he saw. Then, with a flourish, he raised it aloft. "Friends," he cried, "here's to us . . . and," he laughed, "to hell with the lairds and the Sassenachs, the polis . . . and the keepers!" His glass to his lips and the hush deathly, he turned towards the table in the corner, and gestured elaborately. "With the exception off our friend Mr. Clarke, off

170

course!" And he drank half of his whisky down.

With something like a sigh the room drank with him—all but the two gamekeepers. Rennie, a small mean man, eyes darting, hesitated, with his drink halfway to his mouth. Clarke, shoulders hunched, gazed in front of him, his mug untouched on the table. Glowering he stood, till, as though drawn by a magnet, his eyes came round until at last they met the gipsy's, black, glittering, metallic. So they stared, while the room waited. Ewan MacIver never stopped smiling, but his foot began to tap-tap on the floor significantly, and gradually the lowered tumbler in his hand began to rise again. The keeper's gaze, compelled, transferred itself to the slowly-lifting hand and glass. Seeming fascinated he watched, and the tinker's eyes did not leave his face. Inch by inch that finger of whisky rose, and with it Clarke's breathing appeared to quicken. Up, up, it came, level with the breast, the throat, the chin. And there, at the lips, it paused, and in that tense moment the big man's hand reached out and down, gripped his mug and lifted it, slopping, to his mouth. A single gulp he took, and Rennie drank with him, and he set the mug back on the table with a clatter. Then, stooping down, he picked up his cap, clapped it on his head, and almost upsetting the little table as he went, strode to the door, Rennie hurrying after him. And as he passed him Ewan MacIver bowed low, unspeaking. The doors slammed viciously, and the tinker laughed, loud-mouthed, and swaggered back to the counter amidst the murmur of his audience. "A last one for the road, Sim," he ordered, banging his glass down. "Touchy folk you're getting these days in Strathalish!"

"Yon was the man your own brother was locked up for putting in the river, Ewan," Archie McKillop volunteered. "An awkward sort of a man, indeed—but an Englishman, of course."

"D'you say that, now!" The gipsy's eyes narrowed. "Was that the one the fine Alastair was going to the jail for—him . . . and my wife! Damn, that's good. He's been coming on, has Alastair. Now I'm here to be giving him a hand, we'll see the sparks flying, my God!" He swallowed his third double whisky with practised speed, refusing the shilling or so of change with

171

a grand gesture, and made for the door, his dogs following. And he spared no further word nor glance for the watching throng.

Outside in the dripping gusty dark the shadows of two horses loomed, and a woman with them, still, patient, waiting. "You're there, then, woman," he threw at her casually. "I was guessing you might be off to my fine brother that you think so much of, and him so near! Come on, then."

Such was Ewan MacIver.

The two brothers did not greet each other till the next morning. Returning to Balnacraig late, after an evening spent in Alan Forbes's cheerful kitchen, Alastair had found his relatives already installed in his tent in the haugh, Ewan, indeed, bedded and snoring loudly. A few quiet words with Anna, brief but not ineloquent, and he had made a quick decision, said goodnight, and made his way down to the loch shore to row out across the slapping, splashing, inhospitable waters to his alternative bed on Eilean Beg—which he had abandoned only a few nights previously as a precaution no longer necessary. And he frowned thoughtfully as he went. He foresaw complications.

Nor was he disappointed. His first meeting with the bold Ewan—not quite so gay this morning, but bold still—substantiated his forebodings quite definitely. Ewan was effusive, presumptuous, and reproachful, in one. He was glad to see his brother, whatever—hadn't he been looking forward to it this long while back—they'd found the eggs and Anna would have the breakfast ready in no time . . . but what way was it to welcome a brother after months in the jail, to come creeping into the camp at night and creep out again, with never a word to him lying there, not so much as a handshake, and him come all this way just to give him a leg-up in this war he was having with the powers that be . . . ? Alastair's grim reply that he was drunk and unwakable anyway, or the hellish din that his ill-conditioned dogs had set up, nearly killing him at his entry to his own camp, would have roused him, also, that though his brother's family was welcome he needed no assistance in his affair with the authorities, was in the nature of a caution and a warning. Ewan

172

took it as a challenge. His eyes flashed and his colour darkened. Drunk—he had not been drunk. How could he be drunk and him with hardly a drop to moisten his throat in all the long weary miles he'd come? A fine thing for a brother to say, and him tired after the long road he'd come, all on his account. Was it the woman had been telling him lies—the fine talk the pair of them had been having; maybe they'd not wanted to wake him! And so on, until Alastair left him standing, to go and fetch the morning milk from the croft.

They had been wont to go their own way, these two, for some years now—even before their father had died. They failed to see the best in each other, most obviously. Perhaps because, deep down, their basic character was so similar, they grated on each other. They looked one at the other, and saw themselves as they so well might be, and were offended. They never had lived together nor even shared an encampment, save at a fair or a Highland Games meeting, when all the gipsies congregated—such as the occasion those few months back, at Torrachan, when Ewan had made his ill-starred attack on the constabulary, and Alastair, in an unguarded moment, had taken charge of the forlorn wife and infant, as seemed to be expected of him. And now, it appeared, arising out of that impulsive act, that either he must put up with his brother's embarrassing proximity or hurt the girl Anna, whom he had learned to appreciate. He was not going to hurt Anna if he could help it.

He arrived at a compromise—not noticeably satisfactory to anyone, like so many compromises. He allowed Ewan to pitch his tent alongside his own, sharing such amenities as the haugh provided; but he himself continued to sleep on the island in the loch—on the plea of security—and frequented his camp just as little as he might—to his own inconvenience, his brother's resentment, and Anna's unspoken distress.

And Anna, strange woman, complicated the situation in more ways than this one. From the first it was only too apparent that, with reason or none, out of honest conviction or otherwise, Ewan was hinting at an affection between the girl and his brother more intense than was proper—and moreover, was prepared to use the suggestion if he thought that its use would prove fruitful. Alastair did not know what Anna might or might not have said, or what her reaction to such suggestions might be—she kept her emotions, like her conversation, very largely to herself, did Anna. But his own attitude was strong, even violent, and he did not keep it to himself.

As a consequence of all this, it might be, Alastair spent more and more of his time along at Lagganlia, aiding Alan Forbes at his smiddy and his farming and his talking, and was welcome. Much good work was done, much wisdom was spoken, and controversial issues were avoided. His brother also, of course, soon found his way thither, and was received civilly, but in that house Ewan seldom lingered. Though an audacious man he was far from being thick-skinned.

And it was not long, needless to say, before the diligent Ewan heard something about Angela Denholm, discovered more, and imagined the rest. And being Ewan, that was not the end of it. To introduce himself to the girl was not difficult, any more than it was to interest her thereafter, and on that interest he played, in a fashion both blatant and subtle. Though, indeed, Angela met him halfway—perhaps more than halfway if the truth were to be known. She was no ingenue to be beguiled by Ewan MacIver, or any other man. Very quickly she saw through Ewan, perceived his attitude towards his brother and thought that she recognized something of the source from which it derived, that deep-seated bias of the subconscious so glibly labelled by all the world an inferiority complex. Very likely she was right. At all events, her strategy with Ewan produced results; she smiled on him and flattered him, she permitted, encouraged, familiarities while remaining very much the arbiter as to how far they might go, she even sought him out, seeming as though, on occasion, she selected his company in preference to his brother's—and whatever else she achieved thereby, she learned much about Alastair Dubh, indirectly, for whatever woman's game she was playing.

But if, thus, in personal matters, his brother's presence was apt to be an annoyance, an irritation, to be deplored, but borne

174

as patiently as was possible, in more general affairs it was something worse than that. For Ewan, with or without Alastair's approval, was determined to make good his promise to set the sparks flying in Strathalish. As far as he could see, his brother's defiance of law and order and entrenched privilege had been reasonably successful; it only required his own rather more spectacular methods to bring the campaign to a notable and triumphant conclusion. So, in this admirable cause he gave himself a free hand, deciding that all the signs showed that the keepers and other minions of authority had had enough trouble, and the course for a man of spirit obvious. He poached fish, game and deer, not merely for the pot or discreetly as a modest sideline, but wholesale, as it were, in the grand manner, even openly retailing the results at giveaway prices to such as would buy. He took every opportunity of provoking all connected with the management of the estates, singling out the keepers, of course, for special attention. Nor did he look upon property as sacrosanct in his offensive; of a morning, fences and dykes would be discovered to be collapsed just where their collapse would do most harm, cattle discovered in gardens and sheep in young plantations, keepers' ferrets turned loose and their traps and snares emptied, and even bothies and hutments used as accommodation for extra gillies and beaters at grouse drives and so on, entered and ransacked. Which was bad, but not so bad as Ewan's open boasting of the same on evenings following. For every night, while he had funds, he kept the vicinity of Campbell's hotel in a ferment of drama and excitement, consequent on drink consumed, and when funds were out, almost equally so for lack of it. The effect of all this on his brother was considerable, the more so as it was all only an unsolicited extension of his own efforts. What was suitable and proper for him to do was not automatically suitable for other folk—especially a heavy-handed, impious, dam'-fool half-brother, with the judgment of a stock-bull and the diffidence of a cock on its midden! So considered Alastair MacIver, and said so, too, though with little effect, save high words, eloquence indeed, and, if anything, intenser spark-flying. An oblique effect, however, was to quench in Alastair himself any further ardour for his own campaign of resistance, already largely damped for lack of opposition. Only in the one respect did he still envisage revenge against Sir Charles Marsden, and even that was a failing flame . . . though perhaps more influences were at work here than can be blamed on Ewan.

It must not be supposed that only Alastair reacted unfavourably to his brother's ongoings, or that the objects of this provocation took it, as it were, lying down. One and all involved objected strongly, vocally, and practically, but not very efficaciously, lacking the coherence of a central authority. For, like so many other areas of that hardly-used land, unnaturally deprived of both indigenous leaders and a large proportion of its population, there was no central authority for ten months out of twelve. As well as being owned by absentee landlords, both of the estates, being primarily sporting properties, were without resident factors or agents, and their head-keepers were only that, with no jurisdiction outwith their jobs; there was no local magistrate nearer than the doctor eight miles away, nor, as has been seen, a police-constable closer than Corriemore. In the absence of the proprietors it was nobody's business to organize concerted action—such as was required in dealing with an offender of the calibre of Ewan MacIver—or to stand forward as the representative of the law and authority, that was, indeed, only an alien imposition from the South. Miss Denholm might have taken the lead, or at least have acted as a rallying-point, but, strangely enough, she seemed to be unconcerned, uninterested almost, even slightly amused, giving the Marsden *ménage* less than no encouragement. The long-suffering Constable Grant did, indeed, make two warning journeys from Corriemore, embarrassing to himself as they were ineffectual with Ewan. Perhaps John Grant was hardly to be blamed for the seeming feebleness of his attitude. For one thing, he was not used to having to be aggressive; he lived amongst a mannerly community, which, when it had to break laws did so discreetly and in a fashion to which no one could take exception. Like so many of his kind he was a comfortable, wise man, leaving well alone on principle, singing a notable bass at a *ceilidh*, and tending a garden that was the admiration of the entire neighbourhood. A more suitable representative of the law would have been hard to find, or a better example to those around him—even if he was not just of the pattern for the C.I.D. or other such extravagant folk. Also, it is only fair to point out that he could consider, and with reason, that where the people concerned, themselves bigwigs and magistrates and all, had failed to make any impression on these tinkers, he was hardly likely to do so on his own— if it was his place even to attempt it. Anyway, John Grant had dealt with gipsies all his days, and it was his opinion that there was no harm in them—a little wild, maybe, but no real harm, at all.

And so Ewan MacIver ran his course.

Things had to come to a head some time, of course, human nature being what it is, and MacIvers being MacIvers. And Angela Denholm, not very surprisingly, was by way of being the cause of it.

XVI

THEY faced each other across the Balnacraig gate, the level-eyed woman and the bold-eyed gipsy, and assessed each other, in a way that came naturally to both of them, without embarrassment or disguise.

"Quite," Angela was saying. "But it's Alastair I want to see this time, as it happens."

"The great lack of judgment some folk do be having," Ewan MacIver declared, elaborately impudent. "Now, if it was . . ."

"Where is he?" she interrupted, unruffled.

"Where is he!" the man repeated theatrically. "Am I my brother's keeper, think you? That one would not be confiding in the likes of me where he might be off to—not him. He is the great one, Alastair Dubh, whatever. Himself he is! I'm just by way of being his brother. . . ."

"Poor Ewan," the girl commiserated tauntingly, "ill-used and misunderstood . . . but not by everybody! Anyway, I seem to have heard something like this before. He'll be back, I suppose—it's getting dark already. I might come up to your camp and wait awhile."

"You might indeed, ma'am." He was very lofty. "And you might stop all night, too, waiting on him . . . unless this was to be one of the evenings he would be coming to keep my wife from being lonely, at all!"

"And might it be?"

"You could be asking Anna that, maybe—it's not myself would be knowing."

"Anna is apt to be lonely of an evening, perhaps?"

The tinker shrugged. "A man cannot be tied to a woman's skirts day and night."

"Of course not—or where would Mr. Campbell get his profits?"

Ewan drew himself up to his full height, with some dignity.

178

"A message," he suggested distantly, "I could be giving him a message . . . ?"

"No. I'd better see Master Alastair himself, I think. I wonder if you'd ask him to come over to the Lodge tonight, when he gets back?"

The man's expression altered. "Oh-ho," he said. "To the Lodge, eh?"

She nodded casually. "When will he be back, d'you think, at the latest?"

The other smiled slightingly. "Sorry I am to disappoint a lady, and her anxious," he told her, "but I doubt whatever it is you're after wanting him for will have to wait. He doesn't be honouring us at night, does Alastair. He wouldn't be sleeping easy along-side his brother, at all—though he managed fine when it was just his brother's wife, so I hear! Where he's after spending his nights is his own affair—but it's not in his own camp, whatever."

"You mean Alastair does not sleep here?" She was surprised.

"Just that . . . and I didn't think I'd have to be telling that to *yourself*, lady."

If Angela Denholm perceived the significance of that phrase she gave no indication of it. She was frowning thoughtfully, as though looking back. "So that was it," she murmured. "I wonder . . . ?" She turned to him. "Where *is* he sleeping, then— along at the Forbeses'?"

Ewan shook his head.

"Where, then?"

"You'd better be asking himself!"

"But you *know* . . . or maybe you don't? Perhaps you haven't discovered that, either?"

"Och, I know fine. . . ."

"Then tell me." She was imperious. "The information will be safe with me. You know very well I've helped him before, and I'll help him again, if need be."

Still he looked at her, narrow-eyed, silent.

"Then you don't know . . . or you're just frightened to tell!" she charged him.

"Frightened! Who would Ewan MacIver be frightened for,

my God?"

"Alastair! You're scared stiff of him."

"That is a lie, woman—a damned bloody lie, I tell you!" he shouted in sudden fury. "I am frightened of no man on God's earth. Ask any man, at all . . ."

"Then you don't know." She was smiling at him calmly, provokingly. "I'll go up and ask your wife—she'll know, won't she?" And she laid her hand on the top-bar of the gate as though to push it open.

"You will not," he cried. "I'll tell you where he goes—and you promising you won't tell another soul?"

"What d'you think?" she gave back coldly. "What d'you take me for?"

He had swallowed his choler. "One or two things, maybe, but not just a clype, I think." He shrugged. "He says it's in case some of your keepers or the polis was to be paying him a visit at night—he's sleeping out on yon little small island in the loch, Eilean Beg. Has been since weeks."

"Is that all!" Her disappointment was obvious. "I thought it was something interesting. You needn't have been so ridiculously careful. . . ." And then, suddenly, a gleam came into her eye, as a new idea was born, and a half-smile proclaimed its development. "Which island is that?" she asked slowly.

"Eilean Beg—the little one with the trees on it, and the red junipers. See—you can see just the corner of it from here. . . ."

"I see." Her fingers beat a quick tattoo on the bar of the gate. Then she turned to him, her mind made up. "You could row me out there in a boat?"

The gipsy stared, frowning. "On Eilean Beg—you! What for would I do that?"

"Because I want to see Alastair—tonight. You can row me out—it'll take you no time—and he can bring me back."

"You mean me leave you there, on the island?"

"Yes."

"Mother o' God, woman, you must be keen to see him, right enough. What's your game at all, I'm wondering?"

Her brows came down. "Mind your own business, my

180

friend—or I'll maybe start minding *yours* for you . . . and after some of your games lately, that might not work out so well for you."

"Well, now—fancy that!" he said, but he was grinning his old tooth-flashing grin again. "All right—why not, then?" he declared. "I'll put you over, yes, and leave the rest to my bold brother." And he laughed abruptly at some private joke of his own. He was suddenly very much the cheerful Ewan again. "When would you be after going?"

Angela considered. "Now, I think," she decided. "I won't keep you from your evening's . . . entertainment!"

"Och, it'll be an entertainment in itself, maybe," he suggested hopefully.

"Perhaps—but not for you!" she retorted swiftly. "Shall we go, then?"

Together they followed the road into the freshening westerly wind, along the loch shore, and at the girl's initial comment that the Inveralish boat-house lay eastward, not westward, the gipsy laughed and asked if she took him for a fool—the Farinish boat lay infinitely nearer to Eilean Beg than did her ladyship's, and the man certainly was a fool who rowed farther than he must. She did not argue. They rounded a little headland, and in the bay beyond found Major Telfer's boat tied to its tree just above high-water mark, with the oars and rowlocks lying inboard, ready.

"He is not out there yet, anyway," the girl said.

"Why should he be, yet awhile? You're too early, altogether." Ewan put his shoulder to the prow, and the craft ran down the yard or two to the water without any trouble. Over-gallantly he handed her in, and got a flick of the wrist, and of the chin too, for his pains. Expertly enough, if with something of a flourish, he rowed out, the light boat dancing like a live thing on the jabbly, breeze-troubled waters, and the creak of the oars in the rowlocks, the sigh of the man's strong breathing, and the splash and gurgle of water under the bows, did for conversation.

Eilean Beg was no more than a couple of rocky acres in extent, with half a dozen windswept pines and a clump of juniper bushes to hide its nakedness. Ewan had to make a good half-circuit of it before he could find a tiny corner of beach to land on. There, he leapt ashore, and turning to offer his passenger a hand, found her already beside him. He was starting to pull the boat up on to the shingle, for the tide was barely full, when the girl stopped him. "No need," she said. "Thank you for bringing me over. I won't detain you."

He smiled at her knowingly. "I'll keep you company for a wee whilie, now I'm here."

"No, thank you," she said briefly.

"Och, don't be daft, lassie," he remonstrated. "Hours it'll be, maybe, before Alastair's out—you'll be lonesome and cold, too, with the wind that's in it!" He laughed. "I'll keep you from both the two of them. I'm good at that—ask anyone, at all."

"If you feel that way, go and keep your wife from being lonesome. She might appreciate it—and I wouldn't."

The man flushed. "So that's the way of it!" he cried, his voice rising on the words. "I'm not good enough for you, eh? When it's something you want done, it iss Ewan this and Ewan that, but now . . . ! 'No, thank you, kindly'—'I won't be detaining you,' my God!"

"Stop play-acting," Angela told him coldly. "You're not in a public-house here."

"I know that ferry well, indeed," he shouted. "I know chust where I am, and where you are, too, my fine lady. I am on a little small island in the middle of a loch, with a young woman that iss no better than she ought to be, whateffer. . . ."

"Ewan MacIver, will you get to hell out of here!"

He came a step closer. "Why should I, at all?" he demanded.

She did not move. "Because you are not such a fool as to stay where you're not wanted," she told him. "Also," she spoke significantly, "Alastair wouldn't like it, I think!"

"Alastair?" he exclaimed. "What has Alastair to do with it, then?"

"Plenty," she said, and looked him straight in the eye. She was as good an actor as he was, that girl.

The tinker drew a deep breath, and let it out slowly, silent for the moment, and his eyes, narrowing, reflected the new current of his thoughts. "That's it, then, is it?" he sneered at last. "The fine Alastair and his fine lady—the bonny pair of them . . . behind a dyke! Well enough I might have known it."

"Will you go now?" the young woman asked him quietly.

"*Dia*—yes, I'll go. You're right—it's not Ewan MacIver staying where he's not wanted." He turned with as much of a swagger as his circumstances permitted, to push off the boat and to jump after it. Standing on the floorboards he bowed to her, ironically and rather ridiculously. "I'm obliged for what you have told me, ma'am" he called. "Very obliged indeed. Others would be, too, maybe!" And, laughing, he sat down and took up the oars.

Thoughtfully the girl watched him pull for the mainland, and then, shrugging, she turned and moved up into the trees.

Alastair Dubh, leaning on his oars, frowned into the darkness, and did not bless his brother. It was about time that he gave up this island business. The wind off the sea was cold, distinctly, and with the tide now ebbing strongly, was, in conjunction, throwing up short, angry little waves that broke into spray against his oar-blades and the sides of the boat. Winter was almost upon them, and after the warmth of Hughie Bell's kitchen it seemed absurd and unsuitable to be rowing out to sleep on that wretched, exposed little rock. Twice he had to turn the boat's head up-loch to keep Eilean Beg, only a dim shadow in the gloom, in front of him against the pull of the water. He had had about enough of this, whatever.

At the island he tied the boat's painter to an upturned tree's roots, and thankfully sought the shelter of the junipers. He had his couch located with care and judgment; in a niche amongst rocks, with a fallen pine giving its aid and all the bushes to act as screens, he had cover from rain and storm and most of the winds that blew. There, on a mattress made out of the tips of spruce branches, dry and resilient, he kept a blanket and an old plaid or two for bedclothes, and beneath the tree-roots a little store of odds and ends, in case of need. And there, under the sighing, creaking trees, that night he came on Angela Denholm

183

and his own dumbfounding.

"Good evening, Alastair," she greeted him. "You've been a long time coming." She was sitting on his bed, with one of his plaids around her shoulders, smoking a cigarette. "The second time I've had to wait for you . . . and not even a half-dead fire to warm me this time."

The man stared, nonplussed. Twice he started to speak, and twice he stopped himself—which was where he differed from his brother. Then a black frown came down on his brow. "How did you get here?" he demanded, with rather evident restraint.

"The same as you did—in a boat," she replied carelessly. "How d'you think?"

"And where is the boat now?"

She shrugged. "Ewan rowed back with it."

"Ewan! *Diobhal! Tha mi sgith deth!*" Angela did not understand his Gaelic, but the expression behind his words was eloquent enough.

"I made him bring me," she told him. "He didn't want to, but . . ." she smiled, ". . . he's easier to handle than you are, you know, Alastair." A small pause. "*And* I sent him back!"

He looked down at her, sprawling there on his couch, nonchalant, at ease apparently, unpredictable, and his mind was busy. "What do you want, then?" he asked slowly, levelly.

"How very blunt you are," she reproved him lightly. "You get worse instead of better. Ewan is a great baby, but at least he's infinitely more gallant than you are."

He waited, saying nothing.

"I think you repress yourself too much, you know, Alastair, my friend," she went on judiciously, since he made no answer. "A little self-discipline is all very good, but too much is bad, so very middle-class, don't you think—unsuitable for such as yourself. You've got plenty of the right spirit in you—I've seen it often enough. . . ."

"I'm wanting to know what it was you came here for?" he interrupted her curtly.

She leaned back. "You are ill-mannered but I must admit you're modest, you know, Alastair, modest about your masculine magnetism, I believe the phrase is. Most men, I've found, are . . . well, less modest. But modesty is such a humdrum virtue, isn't it?—so unexciting!" In the darkness she could not see the expression in his eyes, but his immobility made her shrug her shoulders beneath his plaid. "Actually, I came because I wanted to see you at once. I have news for you that I thought you might be interested to hear."

"Well?"

"I had a phone message from my uncle this afternoon. He has had word from his agents about brother Ewan's activities here—only I don't think he quite understands that it's not yourself that's the trouble—and he is coming north by car tomorrow, and calling at the Sheriff's office at Ardwall on the way! This time he looks like business. I thought you ought to know."

"Tomorrow?" The man's whole attitude had changed swiftly and noticeably even in the gloom. "And the Sheriff's office— that means there'll be the Chief Constable and all in it, now. . . ."

"Ewan could scarcely hope to get away with it indefinitely," she pointed out reasonably. "I've made no complaint, but apparently others have."

"Yes, devil sweep him!" Alastair moved a pace or so to and fro.

"I didn't tell Ewan," she went on. "He wouldn't have kept his mouth shut, I imagine . . . and I've no desire for my uncle to hear that I've been giving away his plans to the enemy," and she laughed shortly.

The gipsy nodded, unspeaking.

Angela frowned. "Aren't you going to say thank you, then, Alastair MacIver?"

He stopped in front of her. "Yes, I'm grateful," he said. "The second time, that is, you've warned me. Why do you do it, I wonder?"

"Well, we are friends now, after a fashion, aren't we?" she suggested. "Come and sit down, and have a cigarette."

He shook his head. "I am fine here," he said, and waited.

There was silence for a little beneath the swaying pines, and

185

all around them the splash of the waves on the little rock-bound shore was the incessant accompaniment of the gusty sighing of the wind. The girl's cigarette glowed bright and dull, bright and dull, as she drew at it steadily.

"A dirty night," she commented. "Though it would be nice and snug here with a fire lit."

He looked up. "Time you were away back," he said. "That wind is rising."

"But I've no boat to take me back," she pointed out innocently.

"I'll take you back. Late, it is."

"I've nobody waiting for me in that big empty Lodge," the girl said slowly. "I think I'll just stay here . . . with you."

"You will not!" That was forceful.

"Why not—I'm sure we'd be perfectly comfortable!"

"Maybe, but you're going home now just the same, my lady."

"I needn't if I don't want to," she pointed out coolly. "I'm on my own property, not yours. I'll stay here if I like."

"But *I* don't like, see you," he said harshly.

Angela tossed her head. "Are you a man at all?" she demanded bitingly. "I said you were modest—I think I should have said frightened, just plain scared."

"Maybe I am," he agreed grimly.

"You're scared, and you're frightened of what people would get to know—you, Alastair MacIver! Martha Forbes, for instance, and that quaint sister-in-law of yours."

The man said nothing.

"Coward!" she mocked him. "Afraid of women's tongues . . . though at heart they'd admire you all the more, if you only knew," and she laughed. "Anyway, no one need be any the wiser—if you can keep Ewan quiet. And I think you can do that."

"I am waiting," he said with heavy patience. "I'm taking you home."

"And if I refuse to go?"

"I'll make you, then."

"Make me!" Her voice rose in strange fury, the stranger in

186

that woman. "If you so much as lay a finger on me, I'll make you pay for it, dearly."

It was the man's turn to laugh, angrily, surprised. "In the one breath it's yourself you offer me," he cried, "and in the next I mustn't touch you . . . !"

"Leave me alone," she charged him again, tensely, warning.

"All right, then," he shrugged. "I'll go my own self, and you can stay here."

"You wouldn't . . . !" Immediately she was on her feet, her eyes blazing.

"Would I not! You watch me—I'm on my way now."

"You beast!" she said quietly, but with a venom that made him blink, and abruptly she turned about and set off quickly towards the water's edge.

She was in the boat, waiting, when he got to it, her hair blowing in the wind. She did not speak as he clambered in and got the oars out. But as he pushed off she made a last comment, even-voiced. "And once you said you'd be at my service . . . for the asking!"

"And amn't I doing that same now?" the man said, with something almost like regret in his voice. "I'm taking you home, lassie," and pulling strongly on one oar, he swung the boat's head round against the tide.

Alastair had to put his back into that rowing, digging his oars in deeply, while the boat bucked and rocked. They had only moved a few yards from the island before he noticed that the woman, sitting in the stern, was bending over, tapping with her foot at something on the dark bottom of the boat. But he had more to do than just to sit idly watching her. When next he looked she was stooping down, handling something, apparently, and her whole attitude seemed different, somehow, more tense. In her crouching position she appeared to be tugging at the floorboards.

"What's that you're doing?" he demanded. The stretcher for a footrest was thereabouts—she wouldn't be after attacking him with the like of that, surely!

187

The girl gave him no reply, but went on with whatever she was doing.

"What is it? What have you got down there, woman?"

With no response but a grunt betokening the effort behind her heaving, the man leant forward on his oars, peering. And then he realized what she was trying to do. It was one of those boats provided with a plug-hole and stopper in the well near the stern-sheets, for draining out bilge-water when the craft was beached. The plug itself was secured by a length of twine, and it was at this that the girl was tugging violently.

"Stop it, you little fool!" he shouted. "You'll have us foundered."

"You can turn back to the island, then," she gave back breathlessly.

He only rowed the more strongly.

"All right, then—on your own head be it!" she gasped, and there was no doubting the fury and resolution behind her words. She even got to her feet, unsteadily, to obtain more purchase on the string of the plug.

"Sit down—is it mad you are?" the man cried. With the boat tossing, she looked remarkably insecure in that position. "Sit down, will you!"

She went on tugging. Fortunately, or otherwise—as indeed was only to be expected—the plug was well wedged in, and, moreover, silted up with sand and dirt. But how long it would withstand her frenzied pulling he did not know. With an imprecation he drew in and shipped his oars, and got half to his feet, crouching forward, gripping the heaving gunwales. He knew what to do. Reaching into his pocket, he drew out his clasp-knife, and, balancing himself on his knees, opened the blade, and crept forward.

What she thought he was going to do, he did not know— perhaps, with memories of Ewan, she had visions of herself being knifed. His plan was only to cut the twine attached to the plug, without which she would never pull out that stopper. Anyway, she would not have him near her. "Keep back!" she cried, and he was amazed at the blaze of her fury.

But still he came on, his hand stretched out, gripping the knife to cut the cord. And straightening, Angela Denholm stood upright, swaying perilously on that heaving platform, and kicked with all her strength at that hand and knife. He jerked back with the pain of it, the boat lurched to his movement, and one of the angry waves did the rest. With a choking cry, the girl lost her balance. Alastair grabbed at her as she fell, but it was no use. With a splash she was in, the boat heeling over with her. The man hurled himself to the other side just in time to save the craft from filling, though the oars were gone.

Kneeling in the stern, he stared over. He saw her, already a few yards away, struggling, and even so, there was method in her struggles as she started to swim. She had turned back towards the boat, and was trying to reach it. He shouted encouragement, and only stopped himself from jumping in to aid her with an effort; he was of much more use to her where he was, if she could reach the boat. Urgently he cast about for something to throw to her, and found nothing. There was only the painter, and it was not long enough. And watching anxiously, crouching with the slopping water halfway up his thighs, he saw that she would not make it. The tide was too strong and already the distance between her and the boat had lengthened. He could hardly see her in the dark; only her splashings in the black water. Desperately he strained his eyes, and cursed his inability to turn the boat, now drifting fast, without oars. In a moment or so she would be out of sight. Almost relievedly he made his decision. Staggering, he got to his feet, and half-plunged, half-fell, overboard.

Gasping at the shock of the icy water, he struck out strongly, his clothes like a balloon about him. From this low level he could not see the girl, or anything but the wave in front, but his sense of direction was good, and he had no doubts. After a few impulsive overarm strokes he found it tiring, his clothes grievously hampering his movements, and he returned to the more sober breaststroke. He must conserve his strength at all costs, he knew. It seemed a long time—he was beginning to have to batten down a growing panic that he had missed her in the dark, or that she had sunk—before he spied her. He shouted, but it was a poor effort, his mouth filling with salt water in the act. He swam on, and was surprised at his slowness in reaching her till he realized that she also, evidently perceiving the hopelessness of ever reaching the boat, had turned round and was now making for the island. He blessed her for that.

All the air had now escaped from his clothes, and instead of a balloon they were now like chain-mail about him, dragging him down. His boots, too, seemed leaden, enormous, and he wished he had taken the extra few moments to throw them off before plunging in. He was almost up with her now—she was not swimming so strongly as she had done at first—and he essayed another shout, and saw her turn her head and foolishly raise her arm in some sort of wave, and promptly sink under water for her temerity.

In a few strokes he was alongside her. "Good work!" he gasped. "Keep it up, lassie," and she nodded at him breathlessly.

Peering ahead, trying to raise himself as far as he could out of the water, he sought for the island. They could not be more than a hundred yards away, and yet. . . . At length he managed to make it out, and with some dismay. It was not where he looked for it at all, but well over to their left, up-loch. Obviously the tide was carrying them away past it, strongly. Urgently he gestured to the girl to change direction, and once again she nodded, but not so briskly.

The pull of the tide made itself felt immediately they turned. The girl's arm-work, getting heavier as it had been now flagged noticeably. "The tide!" he cried, warning her, and for answer she quickened her strokes gallantly, but they were abrupt, ragged thrusts, shallow and unproductive. The man, wearisome and dragging as he felt his own efforts to be, found himself drawing ahead of her, and had to hold back. Anxiously he watched her. Her breathing was short and painful to hear, and, very low in the water, her mouth open, was obviously swallowing a lot. She was not riding the waves as they came any more; each one went over her. Some went over him, too, for that matter, but he had no fear for himself in his anxiety for the woman. Every stroke her swimming became wilder, and soon the man knew that she would never make it, unaided.

He drew closer to her. "Hold my shoulder," he shouted in her ear, and when she shook her head, "Don't be a fool. Go on—and swim with one hand."

She obeyed, and immediately he went under, with the weight of her. But he was a strong swimmer, and soon he managed to adjust himself to the added burden, though it made an enormous difference to his headway; there was no more need for holding back. They made a little progress thus, but the girl kept rolling over on her side, and her hand slipping from his shoulder. He had stopped looking at the island, that seemed to come no nearer; all his efforts were concentrated on keeping his own and his companion's heads above water, forcing his leaden arms and legs to work, and overcoming each wave as it approached.

After a time that might have been long or short, but in which infinite effort was represented, and with Angela's hand slipping more and more frequently, he knew that he could not continue with it. "Over on your back," he gasped to her. "Kick with your feet."

She sobbed something unintelligible, and he turned over himself. When he looked for her he found that she had sunk. Fortunately, kicking out, his foot struck her, and, pushing himself down, he managed to grab hold of her, and pull her up. Somehow, he got her on to her back above him, and holding her under the armpits, sought to swim on his back using only his legs. It was painful, heartbreaking going, if going it could be called, at all. His feet, in those damnable great boots, would not stay up; he kept sinking from the feet, so that instead of being horizontal he was nearer vertical most of the time. The girl was like a dead-weight on his bursting chest—though every now and then she gave a spasmodic kick or two, as though through waves of unconsciousness she had glimpses of her urgent duty. The man had long since ceased to feel the cold; there was a roaring in his ears and he battled with a growing inertia more consciously than he battled with the endless waves. But he kept on struggling, almost automatically kicking, kicking, with those

191

leaden feet, while his mind fought one fight and his body another.

Perhaps his mind was not so efficient as his body. He must have blacked-out for a moment or two, for he came to with a jerk to find that his hands had slipped from the girl's shoulders, and she had slid away—probably her body bumping against his feebly-working legs had aroused him. Desperately he took hold of himself, struggled down to seize her again, and doing so turned round. At first he did not perceive the situation. Then, as he wrestled with her, something told his sluggish brain that things were easier, that the waves were not so high, that he was not having to fight so hard against the dragging water. And then he saw with his dulled eyes. Eilean Beg was not vaguely ahead of him any more; it was at the side, not thirty yards off—he was almost past it, in fact—and its bulk was acting as a breakwater for the swirling tide. Enheartened, revived in spirit if not in body, he made a last desperate effort, shouting encouragement to the semiconscious woman, and slowly, heavily, but surely they approached the island. Soon his feet were touching bottom, and plunging, stumbling, splashing forward, he reached the rocky shore, dragging his companion with him. And beside her feebly-stirring form he sank down on hands and knees, head hanging while his body was heaved and racked with the torment of his lungs. And after a little while, he raised himself and thrusting two fingers down his throat, was most thoroughly and satisfactorily sick.

XVII

ALASTAIR MACIVER shivered violently, and roused himself. This would not do at all. He looked at the girl by his side. She did not seem to be unconscious, but completely spent, rather, her breathing short and harsh and jerky, and every now and then a tearing sob shook her. He got up, tottering a little, light-headed, and then bent down and tried to raise her. At first she hung inert, a dead-weight, but after a little, at his urgent entreaties, she stirred herself, and with an obvious all-out effort sought to help him with her reluctant, drooping body. On her feet, her knees would not hold her up, but by putting an arm of hers round his shoulders and holding it there, and leaning forward so that she more or less lay over his back, he managed to keep her in some measure upright. He would have carried her, but in his own weakened condition knew that to be beyond him. Thus, eventually, he got her moving, half-supporting her, half-dragging her, stumbling, staggering, tripping, making for his little den amongst the junipers, that so long ago, it seemed, they had left. Fortunately, on that small island, they had not far to go, but it was over naked rock and through clutching, scratching bushes and amongst coiling roots. But somehow they got there, not without a couple of stops on the way, and he let the girl sink gratefully on to the pine-mattress of his couch, and stood back to lean against a tree-trunk, trembling.

He did not lean long. There was much to be done—and the doing of it might well be as good for him as the results would be for her. First of all, a fire—hadn't she been suggesting a fire already that night! Fortunately, he kept a spare box of matches in that little store of his under the tree roots, for those in his pocket now would light no more fires. Of tinder and kindling there was plenty under those pines, and in little more time than it takes to tell he had a spluttering, aggressive, small fire going, and in its cheerful radiance felt twice the man he was before—

which was just as well, with the programme that he had set himself.

His companion evidently felt the encouragement of it, too, for she struggled to sit up, and one shaking hand stretched out towards the darting flames. And then she shuddered twice, and swaying, began to cough and choke and retch in one.

In a moment he was down on his knees beside her, supporting her. " 'Tis the water in you," he explained, "the salt water you've swallowed. Could you bring it up, at all? You'll not be right till you're rid of it, Angela." It was the first time ever he'd called her that. She turned to him, wanly, but the faintest smile flickered for an instant at the blue corners of her mouth. "Must I?" she whispered.

He nodded. "Myself, I put a finger down my throat," he told her. "It came up just beautiful—no trouble at all!"

She showed no enthusiasm, but seeming to acquiesce, started to drag herself over, away from the fire; she was not going to be sick over his bed. But the effort of movement forestalled her fingers, and as she crawled she was suddenly and violently sick. It was no brief and complete eruption like his had been, but a prolonged, drawn-out agony, racking and straining her body in great spasms and convulsions. He knelt beside her helplessly, supporting her shoulders, and seeking to comfort her in scraps of murmured Gaelic. When at last there seemed to be no more to come, and the seizures had sunk to a succession of quaking sobs and shivers, she was quite limp within his arms, what was left of her strength quite consumed with the severity of the ordeal.

He got her back to the couch, where she lay relaxed, her eyes closed, a picture of exhaustion. But her breathing, though still unsteady, had lost that hoarse, snoring note. Alastair stood back, threw more fuel on the fire, and gathering his blankets, arranged them round the blaze, holding one up to the full warmth. He looked at the girl, and frowned. What was to be done next he did not want to do, but it had to be done if pneumonia and suchlike was not to be the outcome of this crazy night. Down beside her he spoke quietly. "Your things have got

194

to come off, Angela. Can you do it?"

She neither answered not stirred, and shrugging, he started to do it for her. He got her soaking jacket off easily enough, but her woollen jumper clung to her as though glued on. At his inexpert tugging she stirred herself and opened her eyes, and after a little dazed blinking, struggled into a sitting position and, swaying, began fumblingly to help him. Thankfully he left her to it. "They must come off," he warned, "all of them." He discovered that he was shouting at her, as though she had been deaf, and turned away to wring out the sodden jacket. Very thoroughly he screwed it till not another drop would come from it, and then he set it up on a stick to leeward of the fire, to dry. And taking up the warmed blanket he brought it back to her and put it round her shoulders, and her skin was cold, cold to his touch. Palely she smiled to him, and went on with her slow, trembling undressing.

The man was very brisk and efficient, taking her clothes from her and wringing the water from them, and handing her the plaids to wrap about her, so that presently she was happed up like an Indian squaw, while her things were steaming satisfactorily around the crackling, smoking, resinous fire. Eyeing them, the man grinned, for the first time that evening. "There's not much to them, at all, anyway," he commented. "They'll dry the quicker."

Then, building up the fire more closely to her couch, and gathering together a handy store of firewood, he took off his own wet boots and socks and jacket and trousers. His shirt he left on—it was nearly dry already, for he was not cold, with all his activities. And wrapping himself in the last plaid, he went and sat himself on the bed at her back, and held himself close to her so that the heat of his strong warm body should reach through to her. And thus they faced the night.

It was some time before Angela Denholm committed herself to speech—indeed, apart from the briefest word or two here and there, she had not spoken at all throughout their adventure and subsequently. For a while she had been sitting, crouching forward, staring at the fire, and whatever her thoughts she had

195

kept them to herself. The man, too, found little to say. And the hissing, spluttering fire and the windy noises of the night accompanied their thinking. But her shivers were less frequent now and less convulsive, and a faint reflection of his own warmth was coming back to him from her. Also, more than once, she raised a hand to touch and smooth the tangle of her hair. Alastair was satisfied with progress.

At length she did speak, slowly, quietly, as out of deep ruminations. "There is the fire, snug as I said . . . and here we are on your bed, alone, with me defenceless and *décolleté* enough for any man—though I daren't contemplate what I look like!" and her shoulders jerked with the shortest laugh. "But I am not very pleased with myself, Alastair." At her companion's silence, she glanced round at him. "You agree with me, I'm sure . . . but you needn't be too smug, just the same, you know. It is all your fault, Alastair Dubh MacIver!"

"Well, I'm damned!" he said.

"You are," she nodded, "—too damned noble and chivalrous altogether! And now you've turned yourself into a hero, too, you'll be quite insufferable."

At her back the man grinned. She was recovering quickly, whatever—she was so.

But her voice was low, pensive, without the fine hauteur that should have gone with her words. She was only making an effort to sound her old self, and but half-succeeding. "I don't think I'm even grateful to you for what you've done for me tonight. You see, you have shown me rather too clear a picture of what I really am, and I don't think I have anything to be grateful for in that!"

The gipsy tried to think of something light to say to that, and found nothing.

"I used to flatter myself that I looked things straight in the face, myself included," she went on, almost to herself it seemed. "But I was just kidding myself—it wasn't me I saw. And now I've seen myself at last—and don't like what I see. And you have to go and drag me back to look at it permanently. You would have done better to have let me go."

With some sort of a laugh he achieved the lightsome comment

this time. "And be up before yon Sheriff on a charge of murder, whatever, instead of the usual assault and battery!"

"Murder . . . ?" she repeated slowly. "You often must have felt like murdering me, Alastair?"

"Not just exactly murdering you, altogether," he rejoined judiciously. "A bit of a beating now and then, maybe—you'll mind the skelping I gave you one time, itself?"

"I remember," she said soberly. "Out of that came half the trouble."

For a while she was silent, broodingly, and the man, stretching over, threw some more wood on the fire and rearranged some of the drying clothes. As he leaned back she snuggled close in to him again, not coquettishly but naturally, gratefully. "How strong and warm you are," she murmured, and sought to borrow some of both from him.

"How does it feel to have won your battle so completely, so finally?" she asked him presently, out of the quiet. "Does it feel good, or have you got used to the flavour by now?"

He frowned perplexedly. "Won—what have I won, at all, now?"

"Everything you set out to win, haven't you?" she returned quietly. "You beat my uncle and Telfer at their own game. Then you humiliated and got rid of Telfer, and let the whole neighbourhood see who was on top. But you had never quite got your own back on my uncle, and you came to the conclusion that the only way you could do it was through me. And now you have done it—though not quite the way you meant to, perhaps. You have saved his favourite niece's life, and he is your debtor for ever after!"

Alastair was staring at her. "How did you know?" he wondered. "It was only a kind of vague notion I had . . . about you and your uncle." In the circumstances, reticence, prevarication, would have been absurd.

"I am not quite a fool, if I am a knave," she told him. "You and I are too much alike, Alastair, in some things—I'd take warning from that, if I were you! I can divine just how your mind works, nine cases out of ten, I think, because my own works the

197

same way. I have known for a while that you intended to use me against my uncle, somehow. You did, didn't you?"

He nodded. "Yes, then—in a sort of way. I'm not just very proud of the idea, either. Some notion I had, not very distinct at all, of getting you into a situation where I could be using our, our—what's the word? . . . association—yes, our association, to bargain with Sir Charles; he's an ill man to get at, Sir Charles." And he laughed without humour. "And when I got the chance, I just could not do it, at all!"

"No," she agreed, smiling a little, "you couldn't. And I was going to be so clever, too—cleverer than you, by half. I was going to outsmart you and my uncle and everyone else. I was going to show you what a woman could do . . . not just any woman, of course!" Staring into the leaping flames, Angela Denholm shook her head ironically. "I was going to master you, the wild gipsy that the others couldn't handle, by seeming to give you myself—or some of me, anyway—and catching you and holding you and taming you, the way that women have done to strong men since time began. At first it would be surrender for me . . . and I might not have hated that so much, either, perhaps! . . . but it would end with me calling the tune, and you, my proud Alastair, eating out of my hand . . . and I would not have hated that either! I would show them, my uncle and Telfer and the rest, that what they couldn't do with their schemes and their police and keepers and authority, I could do with just what I was made with. That's why I came out here tonight." And suddenly she was spirited, vehement, in a moment, for a moment, turning to face him. "And I could have done it, too," she exclaimed, ". . . but for one thing I couldn't get past—the same thing that stopped you from carrying out your scheme."

He eyed her warily.

"The fact that you were in love with that chit from Lagganlia— Martha Forbes!" she cried.

Staring, frowning, the man gulped. "But that's not right, at all . . ." he began, but she cut him short.

"Don't deny it, Alastair MacIver. You may not admit it, but you know it's true. I've known it almost from the first, but I thought I could ignore it, get round it, and . . . well, I couldn't. That's what wrecked our schemes—both of them!"

He did not answer her, and she fell silent, stirring the fire and drawing the blankets closer around her. The man was gazing into the night, his brow furrowed, seeming to debate within himself, and more than once he shook his head, dumbly. "I suppose you're right, then, in a way," he said at length, almost grudgingly. "I do love Martha—for a long time I have loved her, I think. But it is not a thing I could be telling her—or anyone, see you. For I am no good to her, altogether. I am a tinker, you see, a man of the roads and heather—it is in my blood—and I could not settle down in a house or a croft, whatever. And I could not be taking Martha on the roads with me, either."

"Why not?" That was even impatient.

"Och, it is not a thing I could do, at all. It is not the sort of life for a girl like Martha. My father did just that . . . and killed my mother. Martha has been used to a good home, and I'm not offering the daughter of Alan Forbes, that brought me up, the tail of a ditch to sleep in. If she was marrying a decent man, that would take over the farm and the smiddy when Alan was gone, with Willie Maclay to be helping them, she'd be well off for her life. . . ."

"A Heaven-sent opening for one Alastair MacIver, I should say!"

"No." He shook his head. "Not for me. I'd be frightened. . . . You said I was a coward, once. I'd be frightened, suffocated. . . . One day, I'd maybe run away. I've thought about it. . . ."

"I think you are foolish, selfish. Even if you went away, you would come back. . . ."

"No, it would not do at all—not for Martha."

"But you don't know . . ."

"Be quiet, woman, will you!" That was both anger and pleading. "It is not a thing for talking about, I tell you. You know nothing about it. . . ."

Shrugging, she held her peace. After a time she turned her head to look at him. He was still staring out beyond the swaying trees, and his face was set. "Poor Alastair!" she murmured.

"Poor us!" And she tucked in a loose corner of her draperies against the draught and huddled closer to him.

So they waited for time to pass.

Slowly the night went in. The fire died down and was replenished. One or other of them drifted into sleep, and wakened with a start, cramped or stiff or cold, drew their covers closer about them, sought gingerly a more comfortable position, and dozed off again. They dozed much more than they slept, both of them, their bodies in a combination of lassitude and discomfort, their minds weary and hazy with sleep, but restless. Some time in the small hours the wind dropped, and the man noted the fact with a vague satisfaction, without puzzling out why. And the girl was aware, off and on, of an owl that hooted, foolishly and untimeously, as at an old joke that everyone else had seen and laughed at and had done with, long ago.

The fire had settled and sunk and lain untended long enough to become only a circle of white over which wandering eddies of air drew little patterns of glowing red and tiny spirals of wood ash, when Alastair awakened painfully to the stark grey of early morning. Owlishly he stared at the smouldering embers and at the still black trees, and had no joy. The girl had slipped over, half on her side, and a bare shoulder projected from out of her plaid, startlingly white against the stained tartan. Gently he covered it up, and carefully stretched out one leg and then the other, and presently was on his feet, leaving her undisturbed. He stood for a minute or so, dully, and then he stooped to feel the laid-out clothes. They all were practically dry, and he disentangled his trousers and drew them on. He was picking up his jacket, likewise, when he paused, shook his head rather grimly, and laid it down again. Hardly worth while putting it on. Then he selected some small twigs and with these and his two lungs soon had the fire blazing again.

The crackle of it awakened Angela. She sat up stiffly, yawned, and was starting to stretch when she recollected the inadequacy of her coverings, and restraining herself, huddled more tightly into her blankets. Like him, she looked on the new day without enthusiasm. "It's cold," she said briefly.

"It is so," he agreed. "We've let the fire get down, but soon it'll be hot again. Your clothes are dry now. How do you feel, lassie?"

"Lousy!" she said frankly. "Like a second-hand tramp . . . and look it, I bet."

He shook his head. Admittedly she looked untidy, with her heavy flaxen hair awry and her face pallid and etched with shadows that were not normally there. But there was lustre to her hair yet, and a gleam in her eyes, and she still was eminently worth looking at.

"I'm hungry," she vouchsafed presently, and the man laughed.

"You're not so bad, then, and you hungry. You're not dead yet, altogether."

"What happens now?" she wondered then.

Alastair grinned wryly. "I go swimming again, that's what!"

"What! You mean swim to the shore? Oh, that's ridiculous. You'll go and drown yourself again . . . I mean—you know what I mean. It's a long way. You can't do that, Alastair."

"And how are we to be getting out of here, then?"

"Couldn't we signal, somehow? There must be some way of attracting attention . . . ?"

"And do we want attention attracted, at all?" He shook his head. "I'll manage fine, you'll see. The wind's dropped, and the tide will have turned. I'll roll up my clothes and boots and push them in front of me—it was the tide and the boots and clothes that were after worrying us before. I needn't have bothered to be drying my things . . ."

"It's a shame," she cried. "Surely there's some other way . . . ?"

"I don't see it, then. But I'll be all right. It's not that far. And there's no other boat on the loch, now that Telfer's is lost on us, barring your own up at your boathouse. I'll swim across, and dress, and be away up there and back with one of your boats in no time, no time at all."

"It's a long row back from there. . . ."

"Och, it'll keep me warm. And you keep warm, too, mind—keep the fire going. I'll be maybe an hour, or a bittie more. You'll

201

be all right?"

"Of course—once I see you safely landed across there. I don't like you doing this for me, Alastair—risking yourself for me again. I'd swim with you . . . if I thought I could make it, but . . ." She shook her head and left the rest unsaid.

"Nonsense, woman—I'm not risking anything, not a thing." He was very brisk. "I've swum farther than that often. I'm a grand swimmer—ask anyone at all!" That was so like Ewan that his companion smiled despite herself.

So while he sought out a lump of wood to tie his things about—for his boots were heavy and might sink the clothes—the girl got herself dressed in her crumpled garments, and was ready to come down to the little strand with him, to see him off.

The waves had sunk most satisfactorily with the falling wind, and the shore did not look too far away in the morning light. At the edge, the gipsy slipped off his trousers again and wrapped them round his bundle—he'd have to thole his shirt for foolish modesty's sake. "Well," he said, "here's me on my way."

She took his arm and pressed it hard. "Good luck, Alastair . . . and thank you."

He smiled, squeezed her in return encouragingly, and wading forward two or three uncomfortable steps, plunged in.

MacIver found it an easy swim, actually, after the first few rather painful strokes. The tide, running in fairly strongly, carried him with it, and there was no comparison in swimming thus in only a shirt, and swimming fully clad. And his bundle bobbed along in front of him without any trouble. Even, for the last hundred yards, he broke into his grand overarm crawl, and ended up in fine style and a prodigious splashing. Soon he was on the beach, waving back to the island, and presently, his clothes on, damp and clinging and uncomfortable, he moved up over the shingle, through the trees, to the road.

In less than an hour he was back, in the smallest Inveralish boat, no longer stiff or cold, to find his companion markedly changed in appearance—a comb and a pocket-mirror from her costume-jacket, and her own woman's genius for smartening herself, being responsible. Only her stockings were missing, and he forebore to ask the state they were in, being a wise man on occasion. They rowed back across the quarter-mile of water, sparkling now in the new-risen sun, silent and thinking their own thoughts, and they walked up quickly from the shore and across the road into the trees and cover of the higher ground, not furtively, but not displeased that there was nobody visible on that road to see them do it. Without prior consultation, but without question also, Alastair led the way by secluded paths of his own through morning woods still shadow-bound, and across quiet glades and shaws where veils of mist still lingered, and they saw no man and were seen by many eyes but none human. And they had little to say to each other now, either.

At the edge of the plantation by the Inveralish drive, with the Lodge a bare hundred yards farther, the man stopped, to leave her, and at her invitation to go in with her shook his head.

"No, not this way," he decided. "Better slip in by your own self. I have things to be doing, too—plenty. But I'll see you before, before . . . well, later, anyway. What time is it you're expecting your uncle to be?"

"Not till late evening, I imagine. It is a long journey for him, especially calling at Ardwall. He may well be held up there . . ."

"Good, then. That gives me plenty of time. I'll away down to Balnacraig now, and see whether Anna has left me a bite of breakfast . . . and the saints preserve her if she hasn't! Run now, and don't stand there getting cold again . . ."

She moved away, but after a step or two, paused and turned. "Alastair," she called, "I'm sorry—about last night. I feel . . . well, sorry."

"And it's sorrier still you'll feel if you don't go now, this moment!" he cried. "Run, girl!"

She ran.

XVIII

ALASTAIR MACIVER made his way back to Balnacraig thoughtfully, and for all his hunger he did not hurry. The furrows were deep between his brows, and, with the tight lines at the corners of his mouth, betokened no joy in his thinking. He had come to the parting of the ways, he knew, and the path that he had to take was plain to him now, starkly plain. Always, at the back of his mind, he had been aware that this should be his path, but cravenly, he had refused to acknowledge it, and it had taken this woman Angela to make him recognize it. It was a straight path, and long, long.

Approaching the haugh by the Allt Buie, he smelt no cooking-fire, and knew himself ready to be angry. A hungry man is an angry man, they say, and anyway, he had business to settle with brother Ewan this morning. He could be doing with the anger, perhaps. But when he reached his encampment, he forgot his anger in his surprise. For the place was empty—empty, comparatively speaking that is, for his garron still grazed there, and his dog, Rob, tied to a stake, was yelping at him foolishly. But his brother's tent had gone, and his pony with it, and all other signs of him as well. Staring, Alastair made for his tent. Inside, on his bed, lay only the newest of Anna's baskets, and in it a tiny sprig of bog-myrtle, and Hughie Bell's empty pitcher from last night's milk. He took the myrtle and inhaled its heart-catching fragrance, and nodded his head at that basket, understandingly. Then he picked up the pitcher, untied his dog, and set off through the trees towards the croft.

Hughie Bell was forking fresh reed-straw into the byre when Alastair found him, and very willingly, on perceiving his visitor, he laid by his fork and prepared to use his pipe instead. "Eh, but you're late, Alastair man," he cried. "Where have you been at all, all morning?" Obviously he was as full of news as an egg of meat.

"Here and there, Hughie," the gipsy returned noncommittally. "Has Anna been here?"

"Indeed she has—last night, it was. And Ewan, too—but that was this morning. And my, oh my, he was wild, was Ewan—I was glad to see the heels of him." Hughie, filling his pipe, chuckled. "Swear—man, you should have heard him swear . . . !"

"I've heard him," his brother answered sourly. "What's become of Anna . . . ?"

"She left a message for you last night." The crofter, lighting up, reached for his fork again, but only to lean on. Like the rest of his kind, he knew how a story should be told, and would do it no injustice. Recognizing the signs, Alastair summoned his patience. "It was the evening that she came, just as it was getting dark," he began. "She had the baby with her, and the pony, all packed up, and the dogs, all ready for the road, whatever. She was for off, she said, and when I asked her where was Ewan, she said she did not know, at Sim Campbell's likely, but he would follow. She said I was to tell you that it was time they left you, and them no more than a nuisance to you, and Ewan worse than that, whatever. She had been trying to get him to go for long enough, but he would not go. That is why she was going this way, at night, on her own. He would be drunk when he came back, but in the morning he would follow her, for she had taken everything he had. It was the only way she could do it, at all. She said I was to tell you that she was sorry for the trouble they had been to you, and that she would be all right, and that she'd see you again, one day." Hughie took a long pull at his pipe.

"She said you were her friend always, and that you did not need her now, but if ever you needed her, she would come from the end of Scotland for you." He coughed. "And then she went."

"Where?" The gipsy's voice came tightly.

"Away north, to Corriemore and beyond, she said."

For a little there was silence, while the crofter watched the coiling column of his tobacco smoke, and Alastair stared at the ground at his feet. "Well?" he demanded presently.

"Ewan arrived, about midnight it would be, and me just new into my bed. Difficult he was, whatever—he'd been after having a big night of it, I'm thinking. A right stramash he made, and me feared for my life! He has a great tongue on him, has that one." Another cough. "He seemed to be thinking Anna had gone away with yourself, at the start of it, and was fair laughing his head off one minute—something about an island—and just about crying the next. He slept the night in my hayloft, and was away off after Anna this morning early, with a face on him like thunder. And, losh, I was glad to see him go."

"And well you might," the other agreed, but absently, his mind elsewhere.

Hughie's strategic pause for further revelations or elucidations was more automatic than optimistic, for he knew his Alastair.

"North, she was going, beyond Corriemore?" that man mentioned pensively.

"That is what she said."

"Aye, then. Ihm'm'm. Thank you for giving me the message, Hughie. I'm sorry for all the trouble you had with Ewan—and you not the only one!" And in a different tone altogether: "Man, my stomach's fair flapping with hunger. . . ."

He made an adequate breakfast of cold porridge, milk, and bread and cheese, and with that to digest, as well as the news Hughie had given him, he returned to his camp. He had two less tasks to do, at least, that busy day.

Alastair rowed back the Inveralish boat to its boat-house, and made his way across Alan Forbes's rough pasture and water-meadows to the farmplace of Lagganlia. Though he caught sight of Martha, emptying a dish of kitchen scraps for the poultry, he did not go to her, but sought out her father first. It would be easier that way.

He found Alan cutting logs on a little petrol-driven circular saw he had, behind the steading, and his hand raised wordlessly in greeting was answered by a smile of welcome. Shouting would have been necessary above the high-pitched whine of the saw and the bark-like chugging of the petrol-engine, and both men were possessed of an inborn dignity that accepted such as unsuitable. The elder, finishing the branch in his hand, was stooping to switch off the motor, when the younger stopped him with a gesture, and picking up a bough of spruce from the pile, set it to the whizzing blade likewise. The other nodded, and together they worked at that satisfying task, while the heap of logs and branches dwindled and the pile of sawn billets grew higher. And the song of the saw and the aromatic tang of resinous wood were good things, like the companionship of labour shared.

The last of the wood cut Alan Forbes turned off the engine, and with a final spluttering gasp or two and a sighing whirr from the saw, a great silence fell, through which only gradually the other small sounds of that place percolated and prevailed: the quiet clucking of hens, the ring of hammer on anvil, the ever-present murmur of running water, and the soft tones of Martha's singing from the kitchen. The men surveyed their handiwork complacently. "That will keep the fires going for a whilie," the older man said. "A fine day it is after the wild night that was in it."

"That is so," Alastair agreed slowly. "A fine day for the road."

Something in the way that was said caused the other to glance at him quickly. "The road?" he repeated, "Not *your* road, though, Alastair?"

MacIver nodded. "My road, Alan." And he laughed rather forcedly. "Isn't it always the road for us tinkers?"

"It need not be—for you."

He ignored the offer therein implied, as it had been implied—and ignored—so often. "Aye, but it does," he asserted. "The man Marsden is to be here this night after me, and the police with him, from Ardwall."

"So-o-o!" His companion frowned. "That is not so good, at all." He picked up a piece of birch wood, turning it this way and that. "Are you sure . . . ?"

"Yes."

Alan Forbes leaned forward and carefully placed his birch log on the top of the pile. "And you are not waiting for them . . . this time?"

"That is so."

"Aye—well, then. You will know best." He sighed. "Martha will be sorry to see you go—I will be sorry my own self."

"She is kind, Martha—both of you are kind." The gipsy sounded stiff, formal. "But I must go, see you, just the same."

The frail man straightened up. "Aye," he said. "You'll have time for a bit dinner with us—your own roe-haunch it is, whatever? Come away in." Almost reluctantly Alastair followed him in—though, indeed, he had come for his dinner.

Martha, bustling about with up-rolled sleeves and an apron, amidst an appetizing aroma of roast venison, greeted them cheerfully, and waved them off into the front room till all should be ready. They obeyed without question, Alastair noting soberly as he went, that though she had her hair bound in some sort of a kerchief, most of it characteristically had escaped and was standing out in proud confusion. She had gallant, fine, untamable hair, that girl.

But when, presently, she came through minus her apron, to call them to the meal, the cheer faded from her eyes, as she looked from one to the other of them. "What for are the two of you standing there like a pair of dummies?" she demanded. "Is anything wrong, at all?"

MacIver was starting to speak when her father cut in. "Alastair is for the road again," he told her. "The laird is coming back tonight and the police with him. He'll have to go, Martha." He did his best for a friend.

She turned to the younger man, wide-eyed, protesting. "But why?" she demanded. "He was here for weeks, with you about, and did nothing. You've done no harm to him since." She stopped short, and her eyes blazed. "It's Ewan," she cried. "It's him that's done it—that great foolish baby! What did he have to come here for, at all, spoiling things? Nobody asked him to come. He is no good, that Ewan, to himself or his wife or anyone else. This is his fault. Wait you till I see him . . . !"

The men quailed before the sudden storm of her anger. Alastair cleared his throat, but said nothing.

"It's a shame, that's what it is." She frowned, her toe tapping.

"But it's not you Sir Charles will be after, Alastair—it's him, Ewan."

"He'll be after the MacIvers," the gipsy answered her. "He does not love me, the man."

"But you're not going to let him hound you out of here—you didn't before . . . ?"

The man smiled. "I seem to mind someone advising me to be leaving the district for a bit, not so long back, till things eased up a bittie . . . !"

"Och, that was different then, entirely." The suggestion was dismissed with a toss of her head. "And you didn't go then, anyway."

"There wasn't the police in it then."

"You weren't so—so respectful for the police at Corrie-more . . . !"

"That was just John Grant," he pointed out. "This'll be the Chief Constable and all his folk, from Ardwall."

Quickly she took him up. "And how is it you know all this, then? Was it her again . . . ?"

He nodded stiffly.

"It would be. And what for, I wonder? What does she want from you this time . . . ?"

"Maybe it's just that she doesn't think so ill of me," he gave back. "Couldn't she be seeing that her uncle was mistaken . . . ?"

"My, but you're a great softie, Alastair MacIver, to be letting that, that woman twist you around her pinkie . . . !" And as he smiled grimly at his own thoughts, she glared at him exasperatedly. "Och, come and get your dinners," she cried at them, and left them standing. Wordlessly they followed her in.

Despite the excellence of the fare—the broth a treat, the venison done to a turn and crumbly to the knife without being dry, the rice pudding rich and slaked with cream—the meal was not a great success; in fact, only Willie Maclay's shrewd inanities and loud laughter saved it from depression. Their host was automatically courteous, but his brow was puckered in thought, his daughter was frigidly polite, and the gipsy found practically nothing to say at all. He wished that he had not stayed now, had

209

not come at all—though to have gone without a last visit would have been unthinkable.

After it was over the men got themselves outside as quickly as they might, by mutual consent. They studied the hill-slopes and the cloud-shadows and all the spread of the land about them, and after a suitable lapse, Alan Forbes held out his hand. "Well then, Alastair, it's goodbye—but you will be back soon enough, maybe?"

"I think not, perhaps, Alan," MacIver said carefully. "This time, maybe, I'd better be staying away for a while. I've been thinking about it, and that is best, I reckon."

The other shook his head. "I'm sorry, lad—don't make it too long, whatever. I am an old man getting, and tired a wee thing. I could be doing fine with you about the place. . . . Always you were next to a son to me. I wish . . . Och, well, what's the difference. Forgive an old man's havers, lad . . . but do not be away overlong."

"I do not go because I want to go, Alan *mo charaid*," the gipsy told him, low-voiced.

"No, I know that, Alastair—I know that fine." His glance was keen for a moment in those tired eyes. "I was proud myself as a young man, I mind—and suffered for it, too. You will do as you must. Goodbye, then, and the good God go with you," and turning quickly he went away, round the corner of the steading, an ageing man and weary.

For a while Black Alastair stood, looking whence he had gone, unseeing, and then, with a sigh, he turned into the house again.

Martha stood by the kitchen fire, leaning against the mantel, her back to the door and him. "I'll be off, then Moireach," he said to her haltingly. "Thank you for the dinner, for all the dinners, for everything, indeed. You have been very good. . . ."

"Oh, be quiet, Alastair," she interrupted him, but she did not look round. "Talking like that, as though you were never coming back." But there was a catch in her voice that there was no hiding, and abruptly she turned to face him. "Must you go, Alai?" she asked him, and there was no anger and fire any more, but only a woman sorrowful.

"I'm sorry, *a graidh*, but I must," he nodded, tight-lipped.

"You are so stubborn, so hard." She came over to him. "Send Ewan away, Alastair. If the laird finds he's gone, maybe he'll leave you alone . . . ?"

"Ewan's gone already," he told her. "Anna took him away, to be helping me. Last night it was, not knowing about all this. But Marsden hasn't forgiven me, never think it."

"Couldn't . . ." She stopped, and started again, as though forcing herself, and her voice was strained and unnatural. "Couldn't . . . she . . . your friend, convince her uncle to leave you in peace . . . ?"

He looked at her, surprised. "And would *you* have me stay on those terms, Moireach?" he wondered.

"I don't know," she said, head ashake. "I do not know, at all. Oh, it's all wrong—everything's all wrong."

He did not answer her, indeed he looked away, to the window and beyond.

Noting it, the girl drew a deep breath and spoke calmly. "Where are you going then, Alastair?"

"Does it matter?" he shrugged.

"I'd like to know whereabouts you are. . . . It will be strange not to . . ."

"The land's wide. I thought I'd go south, this time."

"South!" A new note, almost of fear, undefined but real, was behind that word. Out of the south came all the hurt to that land, and into it its youth had drained for generations, and had not come back. And then, at a tangent, another thought: "What about . . . her? Does she know you're going?"

"I have not told her so."

Martha was silent, they both were silent. There seemed to be nothing more to say. It was almost with an effort that the man spoke. "I could send you a letter, maybe?" he suggested.

"A letter—what's a letter!" she cried, and then stopped herself, and changed her tune surprisingly. "Yes, then, Stair— send me a letter. I've never had a letter from you. . . ."

At the tremor in her voice the man glanced at her. She was

biting her lip, and suddenly he knew that he could not look at her any more. "Goodbye, Moireach," he said thickly, and swung about and was gone.

She stood where he had left her, and the square of the open doorway was blank, empty, and its slanting sunbeams a mockery.

With the need for action strong upon him, Alastair MacIver went straight back to his camp, packed up his few things and struck his tent, making the lot into two bundles and hoisting them on to the back of his garron. Then he went and said farewell to Hughie Bell, and set out, pony and dog complete, for Inveralish Lodge.

For the first time, and probably the last, he took the main drive to that pretentious house, tethered his shelt to a tree at the front of it, climbed the steps to the main door, and rang the bell. Mrs. Gregson, the housekeeper, opened to him, but did not ask him in, needless to say. Her surprise, when Miss Denholm, summoned, repaired her omission, was only equalled by her disapproval.

Angela led him into a bright room of cream paint and mirrors and chintzes, where a fire blazed and a couch was drawn up to the hearth-rug. "Forgive me if I'm almost as much of a sight as I was last night," she pleaded. "I was making up for some lost sleep, in front of the fire," and she yawned widely, to prove it.

"And you the wise one," he agreed. "But I won't be keeping you off your beauty sleep more than just a minute. I only came to say goodbye."

"Goodbye?" she echoed, staring. "Why goodbye? Where are you going?"

"Away," he said briefly.

"You mean you're leaving here—the district?"

"I am all packed, and on my way, now."

"Alone?"

"Alone," he nodded. "Ewan's gone already. Your uncle could have spared himself the journey."

"This is very sudden, surely?" she wondered.

"Maybe—but it is not before time, whatever. I should have

gone long since."

"Why? You needn't tell me it's because of my uncle coming that you're going. What I have to tell him will spike his guns pretty thoroughly. You're quite safe from Charles Marsden."

"You needn't be bothered telling him now, then."

"Of course I shall. I don't quite follow this, Alastair," she went on slowly. "Ewan's gone. And you're not frightened of me any more, I'm afraid . . . !"

"Was I ever?" he protested, but as a matter of course.

She ignored that. "Only one thing, one person, can be driving you away—Martha Forbes!" She pointed at him accusingly. "You are running away, Alastair MacIver!"

He did not answer her, but his look was first guarded, then stony.

The girl was eyeing him keenly, consideringly. "You are hard hit, aren't you?" she said. "You must be, or you wouldn't be clearing out like this. But why this sudden move—don't tell me you didn't really *know* you were in love with her till I told you?"

The man swallowed, and spoke with some formality. "Miss Denholm, I will be obliged if you will mind your own business, whatever."

She laughed at him. "Keep that sort of thing for somebody you've not had your arms around all night," she advised lightly, confounding him. "Have you really just got wise to yourself, Alastair?"

"Maybe I have—in a sort of way," he admitted shortly. "I have been thinking."

"A fatal habit," she mocked, ". . . unsuitable in a gipsy. And this is the result of your deliberations? You're taking the easy way out, and running away . . . !"

"Easy!" he barked, and then shut his mouth firmly. And after a moment: "Well, I'll be going, then."

She shook her head over him. "I believe you will," she said. "You are an obstinate, determined man, with the pride of the devil!"

MacIver frowned. He had had about enough of this. Hadn't Martha herself been calling him hard and stubborn back there,

213

and him just trying to do the right thing, the best thing for all of them. How long would his patience last him, he wondered.

Angela sighed. "Well, if go you must, you will, I suppose." Her attitude changed, and she was suddenly quiet-toned, sincere. "Is this goodbye then, Alastair? I had not thought of it this way, somehow. I saw me going away, not you . . . though I will be off soon now, too. It has been rather wonderful knowing you—for me, anyway. What picture of *me* you will take away with you, I don't know—not a very flattering one, I'm afraid." She looked away. "For some reason, I would like you to think a little well of me."

"I could not do other," he told her truthfully.

"Maybe, but you could think a lot else, besides. I know that I have offended all your ideas of what a woman should be—I have done it purposely, indeed, to shock you. I know you think I am a loose woman, and immoral, barely a step above any girl of the streets, self-centred and spoiled. It is true, too, I suppose . . . though sometimes I catch a glimpse of myself in another light. If you could see me that way, just for a moment. . . ."

"I have done, often, Angela," he assured her gently. "I do now, whatever."

"And what do you see, Alastair? I have never been sure, myself. I would like to know . . ."

He looked at her for a moment thoughtfully. "I see someone lonely and brave and—and defiant," he said. "A fighter, with a lot to be fighting against—herself most of all, I think. And kind, too . . . when she thinks nobody at all will be noticing her kindness."

"Yes . . . ?" she said strangely, almost breathlessly.

"I see someone that is strong, whatever else she is, and honest, too, behind the wicked tongue she has. The rest I see, too . . . but I am not casting any stones, now or any time, for I would rather have that one for my friend than my enemy, my God!"

"Thank you, Alastair MacIver," she answered him soberly. "That last wish you have, at all events, always. You almost make me think that perhaps I was worth your while saving from the loch, last night, after all . . . and that"—her voice wavered a little—"that is more than I expected to think." Abruptly, boyishly, she thrust out her hand to him. "Goodbye, tinker-man," she said.

He took her hand, held it for a moment firmly, and then, stooping, raised it to his lips.

"I will not forget that, ever," she whispered huskily, and followed him to the door.

XIX

AS his track issued out above the tree-level, Alastair Dubh turned from the pony's head to stare back and down whence he had come. Far below, over the wide, green-black cloak of the pine-woods, the loch gleamed like burnished gold in the last rays of the sinking sun, a long vivid weal amongst the blue shades of evening, and beyond it, across the sprawling woods of Inveralish, the hills lifted in fold and ridge and scarp, to the great peaks of Beinn Garve and Beinn Druim and others farther still, flushed in the glory of the sunset. It was not often that he looked on this view of the strath, for his usual comings and goings were northerly, into those same high hills towards which now he looked. Not that it was at the hills that the man was staring. It was into the well of shadows at the foot, near the glitter of the loch, that he peered, trying to make out the gleam of a little whitewashed house and the tiny patches of small stony fields. He thought that he had it—he knew just where to look, anyway—but he could not be sure in that blue haze, he could not be sure at all. And shaking his head at the uncertainty, at himself, at all the confusion of thought and emotion within him, he turned back to face the long lift of the rolling brown moors into which his slender track wound southwards.

He was conscious of a weariness as he went, a thing unusual in that man, and the long climb up out of the strath seemed never-ending. It was not surprising that he was tired, perhaps. Already he had covered many miles, though still he could see his starting place: Loch Alish, like all the sea-lochs, was only an invaded valley, long and narrow, and to travel south of it, with a led pony, he had had to go right to its head, many miles inland, and back down the south shore, since the little ferry at Kinlochalish was not for such as he. Halfway, perhaps, along that nether shore he had left the road, striking off due south, and started his climbing by a track that was the relic of an old drove road, cutting across the hills to reach the sea and the road again ten miles or so farther on, thereby saving as much again of the twists and bends of the coast-hugging highway. But the saving was at the price of a long, long climb. Moreover, the man had slept little last night, and had taxed his body to the full with that nightmarish swimming, and reaction was inevitable. And then, he had left something of himself, some vital part, back down in that valley, and he was feeling the lack of it sorely. How long would the hurt of it remain a gnawing, searing pain, he wondered, before it sank to a dull ache, ever-present but bearable? He did not know, at all—but he would find out.

He would not go so very much farther this night. He would cross the summit of this long-drawn-out ascent, and put the trough of Strathalish and all its affairs behind him, and he would camp in a hollow that he remembered on the high plateau where there were a few stunted birches and rowans to give him fuel for a fire and a stream for water. And there he would sleep, and pray that he might not dream. That would be three miles yet, maybe, and far enough.

Two of those long miles, then, they covered, man and horse and dog, while the sun dipped into the western sea and the chill breath of the night sent its heralds across the heather. The moors were levelling before him now, and soon the summit would be past and he would not have to climb any more that day. Sunk deep in the tangled forest of his own thoughts, the man was aware of it and was thankful. And then something, some consciousness, penetrated the thickets of his forest, via his ears. It was a tiny thing, but in that silent void of heather and sky it was notable—once noted. The soft pad of the dog's footfalls had changed their rhythm. At this moment they had stopped altogether, and some corner of the man's mind told him that it was not the first or second time that the beast had stopped and then hastened on after him, in these last minutes. He turned, and saw his dog, a few paces behind, gazing down the road, his feathery tail wagging slowly. Alastair looked likewise, and something inside him thudded and rose and nearly choked him.

She was not far off, a bare quarter of a mile, a climbing,

forward-stooping figure, slight in that wide expanse of rolling moorland, but sturdy, and determined, too. There was no mistaking her at all. The man, swallowing, sought to control the wild, disjointed, surging thoughts of him, and waited for her in a great uncertainty.

When she got near, he saw that she was tired and a little afraid, and her lower lip kept steady only with an effort. But the determination was evident, too, and he eyed her, wondering. She managed a smile for him, nevertheless, even if it was a strained one, and his heart turned in him, at it, and her. "Well, Alai," she said simply. "Here I am."

He shook his head a little, at a loss for words. His hand went out towards her, open, enquiring. "I see that, yes, Moireach . . . but why?" he wondered.

She looked away from him, down at her feet, tired feet in dust-covered, stout brogues. "I have come . . . to be with you," she said, her voice low. "If you will have me."

He stared. "But . . . but I'm going south, lassie—far away I'm going, for a long time. . . ."

She nodded, eyes still down. "I know," she agreed. "I will go with you . . . if you will take me."

"But . . ." The man took a deep breath. "I do not understand at all," he said helplessly.

"It is simple enough," she told him, and now she looked up to meet his eyes. "It means that I love you, Alastair—enough to go with you . . . always." And as she saw his eyes widen, and the light in them shine, she went on, before he could speak: "Do you love me, Alastair, like that—truthfully?"

His hands thrust out and gripped her shoulders hard, roughly almost. "Dear God, I do!" he whispered hoarsely. "I love you more than that, even, I think. I love you enough to leave you . . . for always, my dear."

Martha's own breath came out in a long sigh, that was part relief, part resignation, and she shook her head dumbly.

"I was climbing up here, with my heart breaking for you, Martha lass, just breaking. It was kind of you to come after me, and more than kind. But . . ."—he squared his shoulders, and his hands dropped to his sides again—"I am no man for you, *a graidh*, no husband at all, a tinker, a man of the roads. . . ."

The girl spoke, as though to herself. "She was right, then—Miss Denholm was right, in this, too." She touched his arm. "Miss Denholm came to me this afternoon," she told him in a hurry, as if to get it over. "She said that you loved me, and that you were not going away because of her uncle at all, but because . . . because of me. She said that you were too proud to marry me and settle down in my father's house, that you were afraid of being tied there, and you loving the heather, and, and, more besides." Martha stopped, flushed, and forced herself to go on again. "She said that I was a fool, and other things as well, and that if I loved you enough I'd come after you, anywhere—*she* would, she said, and think herself lucky." She laughed shortly, with a choke behind it. "I slapped her face for her, too—before I realized what she was saying, for I did not know that you loved me, you see, and it seemed wrong for her . . . Oh, I don't know . . . but I'm sorry I did it now. She said if I loved a tinker, a tinker I must be—and that is true, I see, now. So I packed my things," and she patted the bundle, strapped on her back like a pack, "and I rowed across the loch . . . and here I am!"

"But, Mother o' God, you can't do that, woman dear!" he cried. "You can't be giving up your home, your whole life, whatever. . . ."

"One of us had to," she retorted, and with some spirit. "One of us had to, and us loving each other. One of us had to swallow our pride . . . and you wouldn't. She said that—Miss Denholm—she said you couldn't swallow your pride, ever. So . . ."

"She said that, did she!" he interrupted, frowning blackly.

"So I swallowed mine," the girl went on, unheeding. "I've said goodbye to my father and Willie . . ."

"Yes, then—and what does Alan Forbes say?"

"He told me to go, with God's blessing."

"Alan said that!" The man stared, and then suddenly he turned away, right away, for he was a man of emotions, and proud in more ways than one.

At his back she spoke quietly. "So I am a tinker now, Alai,"

219

she said.

"My God, you're not!" In the twinkling of an eye he had swung round, a changed man—or perhaps his own man again, Alastair Dubh MacIver of the Ross MacIvers, and a man with his mind made up. "You are going back to Lagganlia this night, woman, and I am going with you. And tomorrow I will take you to Corriemore, to the priest, and we will do what is to be done, and Alan will have the son he wanted, and myself the grandest fine wife in the world. And I will be a good crofter, God helping me, and a good husband—and I'll be needing no help in that, for I love you, Moireach dear, I love you more than ever I can tell you, at all."

"Yes, Alastair," Martha Forbes said meekly.

"And sometimes, maybe, when the call comes on me, we will take to the heather, you and me, Moireach, for a whilie, till the fever's out of me and I will show the breadth of Scotland to you, and the islands, too. And that will be all the tinker I'll be, any more, and you too, my dear." And his arm slipped around her, and he drew her to him. "Saints of Mercy," he wondered, "what are we standing here for?"

"I do not know, Alai," she whispered.

But they stood there a little while longer, just the same.